W. Henry Rankine, William A. Scott

A Hero of the Dark Continent

Memoir of Rev. Wm. Affleck Scott

W. Henry Rankine, William A. Scott

A Hero of the Dark Continent
Memoir of Rev. Wm. Affleck Scott

ISBN/EAN: 9783337193638

Printed in Europe, USA, Canada, Australia, Japan

Cover: Foto ©Andreas Hilbeck / pixelio.de

More available books at **www.hansebooks.com**

A HERO OF THE DARK CONTINENT

Your affectionate friend

W. A. Scott

A HERO

OF

THE DARK CONTINENT

MEMOIR OF

REV. WM. AFFLECK SCOTT,

M.A., M.B., C.M.

CHURCH OF SCOTLAND MISSIONARY AT BLANTYRE
BRITISH CENTRAL AFRICA

BY

W. HENRY RANKINE, B.D.

MINISTER AT ST BOSWELLS

WILLIAM BLACKWOOD AND SONS
EDINBURGH AND LONDON
MDCCCXCVI

PREFACE.

THE names of Livingstone, Mackenzie, and Mackay are sufficient guarantee that Scotsmen will never forget the real founders of our empire in East Equatorial Africa. Beyond all dispute it had its genesis in the enterprise of Christian missionaries in their endeavour to bring to the African the benefits of Christianity. What has been accomplished others have told. It is sufficient for us to mention that, where Livingstone mourned over the devastations wrought by the slave - trader, the power of the traffic in human souls has been utterly broken. It is not only conceivable but highly probable that the African children of the next generation will hear the story of the capture of not remote ancestors, and of their disappearance in slavery, as the record of a stage of their country's history as completely past as is the struggle for Scottish Independence to our own children.

However our new territory in Africa may be *administered* by the officers of the Crown, no political officer can claim to have laid its foundations. These were laid before the days of "spheres of influence" in the Dark Continent,— laid, too, in blood and tears. When the history of British Central Africa comes to be written, it will begin with a glorious roll of heroes from Livingstone onwards, who laid down their lives for the salvation of Africa and the healing of its "open sore." Many of these — martyrs in the truest sense of the word — rest in lonely graves in the land of their labours, their patient sufferings, their deeds of heroism, unknown and unrecorded. The old spirit of Chivalry of the Knights of the Cross has not died out of Christendom. It has only transferred its operations to a nobler and a bloodless sphere, and this memoir is an attempt to keep alive the memory of one of the noblest of the sons whom Scotland has given to Africa.

The writer desires to record his thanks to many schoolfellows and friends of Dr Scott for their assistance and encouragement in the preparation of his life: to Mr James Reid, his colleague and friend; to Mrs W. Affleck Scott, without whose aid the task would have been impossible; and to Messrs Adam Rankine, F.E.I.S., and A. G. Thomson, F.S.S., for the trouble they have taken in seeing the work through the press.

W. HENRY RANKINE.

St Boswells Manse,
Nov. 1896.

CONTENTS.

ILLUSTRATIONS.

GLOSSARY OF NATIVE WORDS.

Asungu	Europeans.
Bembo .	councillors or village headmen.
Capitao	foreman.
Chikoti	whip.
Dambo . .	plain.
Donna .	white woman.
Kachasu	brandy.
Machila	hammock carried by bearers.
Maluzi	native string of bark.
Masasa	grass hut.
Mlandu .	case at law.
Mtanga .	basket.
Mvuka mlota	rice for sale.
Nkuni .	firewood.
Ochenjera	sharpers.
Ulendo	expedition.
Unyaya	an immoral native dance.

A

HERO OF THE DARK CONTINENT.

CHAPTER I.

EARLY DAYS AT HOME AND SCHOOL.

WILLIAM AFFLECK SCOTT was the sixth child and youngest son of Mr David Scott, C.A., and was born in Edinburgh on the 11th March, 1862. He was carefully trained by a mother whose influence on his character never waned. She is described by one who knew her well as "a thoroughly human woman," and her minister in the last years of her life declared her to be one of the most spiritual women it had ever been his good fortune to know. These combined qualities

A

of heart and mind account, doubtless, for the
singular power she wielded over her children, each
of whom regarded her as the ultimate authority
upon questions of life and conduct. She lived
till 1883—long enough to see her eldest son at
the head of the Church of Scotland Mission in
Blantyre, and her youngest—" Mother's boy," as
he was called—busily preparing for service in the
Dark Continent. She created about her a religious
atmosphere quite consistent with the clear, ringing
laugh and merriment which burst forth without
restraint at every excuse. She watched carefully
the mental training of her children, guiding them
in their reading, and excluding with scrupulous
care every form of prurient literature. When the
writer on one occasion mentioned to her youngest
son a novel of very considerable notoriety, Scott
remarked, " That must be a bad book—mother
would not allow her girls to read it."

In the religious life of Mrs Scott there was
nothing in any way repellent or gloomy, nothing
savouring of " cant," and in this respect her son's
religion was like her own. She was among her

children to her last days truly one of themselves, able to enter into their pleasures and to join in their youthful romping at any time. For "Willie" she had a particular fondness, following with loving interest all his work, rejoicing in his progress, and encouraging him in every development of his fertile mind. It was her delight to look over his sketch-book, which told the history of his holidays better than any letters could, and she imposed no restraint upon the fun which was part of his nature. His spiritual history is really only the story of what he owed to his mother.

Her love and affection were thoroughly reciprocated, and Willie lavished on her all the devotion of a very chivalrous nature. One day a future friend of his passed along Royal Crescent after Mrs Scott's last illness had begun, and was struck by the group at the door of Number 10. There sat in the bath-chair the sufferer with patient delicate face, looking at the crowd amusing itself in the Gymnasium opposite, and beside her, Willie and a sister entertaining and watching her. It formed to a complete stranger an almost ideal

picture of happiness and love. He must have
been a cheery companion. In writing to a friend,
he says about his duties :—

"My mother is not well, or rather is fairly an
invalid with a bath-chair. I am generally car-
driver, and one of us always is. At some parts of
the drive where the road is smooth she is pro-
pelled with such velocity that a gentleman we
know said he could not tell what kind of chair it
was. We almost ran off with a policeman one
day, and came very nigh upsetting a postman.
We have not caught a lamplighter yet, but we
expect to !"

In his early days he was sent to Mr Hunter's
school in York Place, and had, strangely enough,
in his class one of a family which afterwards
played a prominent part in the work to which he
devoted his life. This was Harriet Bowie, afterwards the wife of Henry Henderson the pioneer
of the Blantyre Mission, sister of Dr John Bowie,
who died in that mission in January 1891, and
of Mrs David Clement Scott, who succumbed to
the strain of African life only nine days after

her younger brother-in-law. This school he left in 1874 for the High School of Edinburgh, which succeeded in winning from Scott the affection and pride which its splendid traditions were sure to call forth from a lad of his nature. Its honour he upheld on every hand : its successes in the fields of literature, politics, or football were always a subject of rejoicing, and his disgust at anything dishonourable could find no greater expression than the conclusion—" And he was a High School fellow too."

In the first three classes of the school he was easily first, and he gained a Sibbald Bursary. He was naturally clever and sharp, and in these earlier classes took the first place without any difficulty. In his fourth year he was chosen captain of the football club, a position which not a merely honorary one. It took up so much of his time that in the first year of his captaincy he did not take such a prominent place, perhaps because steady work now had greater effect than natural cleverness in deciding positions in the prize-list. He was much chagrined by the loss of his place, and tried hard to retrieve his lost position when he reached the fifth class. There he was second; but the effort cost him his health, and a threatened attack of lung troubles caused an almost continuous absence from school in the year of the " sixth."

In his school - days there were foreshadowed many characteristics which marked his later years. He was a born athlete, and in football especially was the leader of his companions. From his earliest boyhood he had great powers of endurance, and was able in one year to declare that he had never missed a single day in walking down to the Chain Pier at Trinity before breakfast and taking his bath in the Firth. He seemed capable of any exertion, and in the football-field was a player whom it was no joke to tackle—one who, when he got hold of a man, kept his hold till the ball was down, and who could always be depended on to stop a rush by dropping on the ball.

Full of boisterous fun, he was the hero of the school. Younger boys were specially attracted to him, hanging about him with something like reverence, offering to him a hero-worship which would have ruined most boys by making prigs of them, only with awe daring to ask him to their homes for a holiday, and feeling themselves some inches taller if he condescended to accept their invitation.

A lady, whose acquaintance he made through visiting her nephew who was suffering from a fractured leg, sent him a message pretending to be offended at a piece of badinage in which he indulged in a letter to his companion. To him he sent the following instructions for an apology :—

"I've got a request to make of you. I wish you to stand before your auntie (if you hadn't a game leg I'd ask you to kneel—standing will do, however); then hang your head on one of your crutches, and put your eyes on the ground—very much *corvus*,—and mix your metaphors, and tell your auntie that I'm awful sorry, and that I'll never do it again : and give her my compliments (two of them), and three of my best respects, and one kindest regard and a half, and as many good wishes as you please (say half-a-dozen), and as much of my love as you can possibly carry on crutches, and ask her to think kindly of a 'puir body as maybe knew no better,' and say nae mair about it."

A trudge of twenty miles had on him the effect only of a tonic, and boys hesitated before they accepted his invitation to spend a Saturday in taking a walk. It was a favourite occupation for his Saturdays, and if any of the youngsters became fatigued, Scott immediately mounted him on his back and carried him for a mile or two. No boy could fail to be the better of his company —he was so honourable in all his ways. In a walk in Arran with some companions the company got some milk at a little cottage, ate their lunch and proceeded, forgetting to repay the old woman who supplied the milk with anything more substantial than thanks. They walked on two or three miles, when it occurred to him that they had neglected to pay. A discussion arose as to how the oversight could be remedied, and the general opinion was that the money might be forwarded in stamps. "She may be needing it," Scott said, and off he trudged alone, thus walking the distance thrice over to discharge what seemed a plain duty.

His holidays, wherever they were spent, gave him the opportunity of making the acquaintance of every place worth visiting, and his numerous sketch-books are veritable guides to his movements. In one place we find sketches of Strathspey, in another of the Ayrshire coast, in a third of the fair Stewartry he had cause to love so well.

He was a member of the Rifle team in the year that the trophy came to the High School. There was a suspicion in the school that the Rector might not give the holiday the occasion deserved, but it was granted on the ground that the boys who won it were "good boys, and that the holiday was given for their sakes, that the school might remember boys could be thoroughly good and yet excel in all manly exercises."

At a very early age he showed himself to be possessed of no ordinary mechanical gifts. As a child it was recognised that he had a set of very useful fingers. On a holiday in New Abbey he suggested to his friend Mr C. E. Wilson, now a distinguished Indian civilian, that they might make a theodolite. After ' Alice in Wonderland ' he designated himself the " Carpenter " and his friend the " Walrus." They went to work and soon had the instrument completed. Their next course was to proceed to the top of Criffel, a hill of 1863 feet. They calculated also its height with the instrument, and worked it out to within 18 feet of the Ordnance Survey result. Scott's next work was to design a case for the instrument, and this he completed at last to his satisfaction, after having ruthlessly pulled it to pieces several times when it did not satisfy his ideas of neatness.

He cultivated the habit of early rising, although, like most boys, he experienced some difficulty in resisting the charms of his bed. An alarum-clock sufficed for a little, but soon began only to make itself heard as in a dream, without the desired effect of arousing his brother and himself. To overcome this difficulty he first devised the plan of balancing over his own bed a stick with a weight attached to one end and a free string to the other. The free cord he fastened about his hair, and arranged that the weight should be set free by the escape of the alarum of the clock, and thus give his hair a pull sufficiently sharp to arouse him thoroughly. This was rather an uncomfortable plan, and besides he had himself the trouble of awaking for two, as his brother shared his room. To give the latter a fair share he changed the contrivance so that the clock overturned a small zinc trough full of water on his brother's bed. His success was for a time complete, as he said, "When Gerry's awake there's no fear of me going to sleep again."

He did not require to make friends. His companions were drawn to him by an irresistible power of attraction. His fun was never anything but *bon camaraderie*, and malice was in his nature an unknown quantity. He was a thoroughly manly boy—the leader of the school in athletics, the winner of the quarter-mile race at the sports, and withal such a good scholar that he was

without any question assigned the first place
among his fellows. The testimony of all the
schoolmen of his time agrees in declaring that
no one can overestimate the effect he had in
raising the tone not only of his class but of the
whole school. He never preached at or to his
companions, but they felt instinctively that everything mean or dishonourable was inconsistent with
his presence. It was remarked in the home of
one of his close companions, that when he came
from school for the summer holiday he had all
the mannerisms of " Bill Scott," to the extent even
of speaking like him. This got rubbed off in the
long vacation, but by Christmas-time it was again
quite evident.

During his university life the press of class-
work made him think of retiring from the first
football team of the former pupils of the school.
He was a player not to be lightly parted with. A
deputation was sent to ask him to continue to
play. One of them asked the writer to use his
influence to prevent the retiral. Thinking it was
a great pity he should give up what was positively

his only recreation, I consented, saying, " You will need a very strong reason, however, to induce him to change his mind." I was instructed to say that when he was in the team no one would utter a profane word. On being told this, Scott remarked, " Do you mean to say so ? Well, old man, that's a very good reason for changing my mind. It's a comfort to know one can be doing good whilst he thoroughly enjoys himself."

During his school-days, when he was a very hard, active, unsentimental lad of sixteen, the following entry was found in one of his note-books : " It is very pleasant when one is bothered with football and things to take a rest on one's knees and feel Christ put His hand on one's head."

With all his fun he had the kindliest of hearts. He would, with his brothers, relieve the old nurse at home by carrying for her the coal-scuttles up to the bedrooms. Indeed she came to look upon this as her right, for she left them latterly at the bottom of the staircase for them. If a school-fellow was sick, Scott made it part of his work to go and sit with him. One can well imagine the pleasure given to a boy on crutches by a schoolboy letter of this description :—

"I have been a long time in answering your letter, and there are many reasons which could be given for my delay. If my letter had reached you while you were in Edinburgh, you would not have had time to read it, owing to the hurry-skurry of getting ready to go away, but now it will reach you reposing gracefully upon your crutches under the shade of a drooping birch-tree upon the sides of Tummel, and the good wishes of your lengthy friend will make the crutches hop,

> And put a deeper blue in the sky
> And a twinkling tear in your eye.

And that's rhyme and rubbish. Likewise, my friend Fred—

> The sky here was blue, and the winds breezy,
> And the woods were green and I was lazy,
> And paints were pressing and colours bright,
> And the weather 'galoptious' from morn till night.

I must beg your pardon for talking rubbish, but

how can I do anything else, for there's nothing
but rubbish to talk? If I tell you about the
grand old abbey[1] which stands ruined and
solemnly indignant at the desecrating hands of
profane builders, who tore down its warm red
stones to make a village; if I make a poetic
complaint about the hard-heartedness of builders,
&c., the man of £ *s. d.* will call that rubbish. If
I speak about the height of the pillars of the
abbey and the length of the knave who pulled
it down, the poet would call that rubbish. All
is vanity and rubbish, and that's moralising and
rubbish.

" To speak sense, I was extraordinarily puzzled
over the beautiful drawing contained in your
letter; but after mature consideration of all its
beauties, I decided it was meant to be a cow,
drawn from memory, as you lay in bed. (That's
a *cram* of course, but everything's fair in love and
letter-writing.) I hope your closer acquaintance
with Highland cattle at Blair-Atholl will show
you their shape and making better."

----

[1] Sweetheart Abbey.

This was followed a few months later, when he himself was ill, by another letter to the same friend, then suffering from a serious attack of congestion of the lungs, which had been reported to Scott to be brain fever :—

"J—— T—— was down yesterday, and told me that the M——s had reported you had brain fever. I was not quite sure of their veracity, but still my poor fiddle could only drone 'O Logie o' Buchan' and such mournful airs all evening. This morning, however, I went down to auntie Maggie (cab part way) and found that your brains were all right—at least as right as they ever were; but you must have been working too hard, Fred, and when you come back again you must not work so hard, but you and I will watch the other fellows stewing themselves till they are all as white as boiled mutton with 'sarce' over it, while we are as cool as cucumbers. Your poor wits seem to have been wool-gathering terribly hard lately—but I hope they have all returned safe home through the crack by this time. You must not answer this, as I suppose your brains will not be quite compact again. I'll write again soon, and till that 'soon,' I am, your affec. friend, BILL SCOTT."

Schoolfellows who knew him saw, however, a deep undercurrent of religious thoughtfulness, and an earnest desire after a true and noble ideal of life and duty. Not many schoolboys would write of their prospects in this style:—

"I have been reading the life of Livingstone, and am beginning to kindle. I do not see why I should fight and struggle with twenty or thirty other young men—most likely my friends—to get an opportunity of preaching and a place to settle, when there is the whole of Africa and a few more continents to preach in—room certainly to settle in. I don't see how I could preach, knowing that my object was not the good of those who listened, but my own advantage, and the hope of obtaining the place. It seems to me a fearful abuse of the sacred office of the preacher, and I don't see how I could dare to do it. I may be wrong in the way I look at it, but it seems to me that the present way of choosing preachers cannot be right. My present position seems to be—I will not preach for a place: I cannot get a place without preaching for it: I shall go abroad. Not that that would be my reason for going abroad, but simply a block in the way of staying at home.   The need abroad is a hundredfold greater than the need at home—*in fact the need at home is the need abroad*, though some people shut their eyes to the fact—and surely we are sent into this world to fill some place where there is need for us, and not to jostle each other."

CHAPTER II.

HIGH SCHOOL LIFE.

WE have already endeavoured to give a picture of Scott as he was in the early days of school-life. A short notice may here be made of his tastes in the direction of study. Of Latin he was very fond, but he never quite forgave it for being the language of the Romans, whom he detested, as a people who, he thought, subordinated poetry and art to the idea of law and order. Indeed he submitted to control very impatiently; his propensity for fun made it difficult for him to regard his masters without an air of good-natured hostility, simply because they were in a position of authority. Greek was his delight, as the language of a people whose pre-eminence in art and poetry he could thoroughly appreciate. Dr Ross was then English master, and in his class Scott felt himself at home, and ever spoke of this teacher with more reverence and affection than he was wont to bestow on any other master as such. For him Scott wrote a poem on Edinburgh, for which his master seemed to fail to get words to express his admiration, and which he read to the whole class as a very good example of the work of a boy of great poetic talent.

In the school-life of the day the magazine played an important part. Its early numbers are motley bundles of well-thumbed manuscript, which it is now next to impossible to decipher. Later it was elevated to the dignity of passing through the printer's hands, and there is found in almost every number something from Scott's pen. It is easy to see in his contributions the keen sense of humour, the grotesque imagination, and also the deeper undercurrent of thought which characterised him. His productions show extraordinary promise, and lead one to suppose

that had he turned to literature he would have
made a name for himself in that pursuit. The
following is from a poem entitled "Death's
Despair," in which he describes Death's journey
through the earth and his visits to various victims. It was written at a time when the craze
for magnetic belts had resulted in the opening of
several shops in Edinburgh for the sale of them,
and the chance of the topical hit was one which
the last lines show he could not pass over without
a good-humoured laugh :—

> " A cottage stood by the side of the sea
>   Upon the wave-lashed shore,
>   And the wind was sighing drearily
>   In through the open door ;
>   A maiden lay on a pallet there wasting wearily,
>   And fading away from this world of care
>   Like foam from the rocks of the sea.
>   And Death through the open door he glowered,
>   Advanced with cautious tread ;
>   And 'neath his frown the inmates cowered
>   As he sidled up to the bed.
>   And he hugged his ribs with a skinny arm,
>   And said, with a leering grin,
>   ' The clothes are upset and you cannot be warm,
>   Allow me to tuck you in.'

> And he straddled stealthily on to the bed,
>   Her throat his fingers felt,
> But she looked at him sweetly and softly said,
>   '*I've got a magnetic belt.*'".

Yet this irresistible sense of the ludicrous was not inconsistent with deep thoughtfulness regarding the world to come, and we are constantly reminded of this by verses in which he keeps himself well in hand and speaks seriously of the problems of life. Of this we have a specimen in these weird lines on "Memory" put into the mouth of Æneas when he returns from the land of the Shades, which, though showing imperfections which are evident enough, yet betray considerable power for a lad of sixteen :—

> "And on, and on, I journeyed on
>   Until I came where shore there was none,
>   But only a great wide rolling sea
>   With never a rock nor an isle to free
>   Its lonely sad monotony,—
>   And the name of that sea was Memory.
>   Nothing can swim in that bottomless sea,
>   Nothing can o'er it fly swift and free,
>   And nothing can on it steadfast lie ;
>   But all must sink down drearily,

Sink, sink, for ever sink,
With nothing to do save only to think
Of why they once slipped over the brink—
Lost! Lost! Lost!

A mournful cry wailed over the deep,
And the Great Spirit sighed as along it did sweep,
And I heard it moan and I heard it weep,
And I looked and I saw but a poor soul asleep,
And it tumbled over the edge of the steep
Into the cold, sad, bottomless deep.
And the Great Spirit told me to go away back,
And tell all I met of the dangerous track
That led to the dark sea gloomy and black."

Another charm of the magazine in its early days was to be found in the sketches with which Scott enlivened its pages. He never had lessons in drawing or painting, yet his sketches were full of suggestion and their execution very artistic. I have before me a water-colour which he has named "Loch Trool and Tam o' Shanter"—the Tam o' Shanter being his school-cap stuck on a walking-stick in the foreground. The distinctive characteristic of the marshy ground in front, the deep blue of the loch, and the autumn glory of the hills capped by masses of clouds behind which the sun is passing, are all strikingly re-produced, and the work itself is far above the ordinary level of an amateur. He said himself that it seemed to him the most natural thing in the world when one saw a landscape he liked to put it down on paper; and our admiration of these rapid clever sketches is tinged with regret that his life should afterwards have been so busy that he had no opportunity of cultivating this talent, and producing work which would have appealed to a wider public than the small circle of friends who possess these valued relics of a genius prematurely removed from earth.

The great attraction of the magazine was in his contributions, whether these were the prose nar-rative of a trip to Mars, which was written by himself and a schoolfellow as a parody on the works of Jules Verne, or the more serious poems like "Death's Despair," or the John Gilpin-like "Mr Speedie's Run," or his "Farewell to an Old Cap,"—the Tam o' Shanter mentioned above—which is too good to be passed over without quotation.

"To an Old Cap.

And must I say Good-bye, my trusty friend,
My friend without a bow, without an end ?
Your nap's half off, your lining seedy grown,
And only half a bob stands all alone.

You served me mighty well in every fashion,
'Mid hats of low degree or of high station,—
In Princes Street 'mid tiles genteel and tall,
Or in the labours of a football maul.

You've served as drinking-cup on an occasion,
You've been an instrument of castigation ;
Your tails have been the mark of every schoolmate's spite,
From the fifth classic to the awful Gyte.[1]

We've travelled many a mile, we two together,
We've clambered up the hills and through the heather ;
We've seen the shining birks upon the banks of Dee,
We've seen the mistful mountains on the lone Glenshee.

We've passed through bright Braemar, and o'er the great
    Glas Mheall,
We've passed the Devil's Elbow where the mountains reel ;
We've seen the long Loch Tay upon a cloudless night
Shining and shimmering in the cold moonlight.

But now at last you're done, inside and out you're seedy,
No student of divinity looked ever half so needy ;
So I must bid farewell, but my regrets I'll smother,
And think, 'This was a hat — when comes there such
    another ?' "

---

[1] New-comer to the lowest form.

We have already mentioned the illness that seized him during his school-days. A neglected cold proved too obstinate for his usual defiant treatment; serious symptoms of lung disorders supervened, and work was forbidden. As his letters show, he had the prospect of an early death to look full in the face. In the hill air of Berwickshire and the salt breezes of Troon he breathed new life. He fought the dread foe of threatened consumption with cheerfulness and confidence, and shows by his letters that his high spirits never left him. The winter months were spent in the house, and he employed the time in manufacturing along with a companion a canoe which did good service to his friend at Musselburgh in the following summer. To him he wrote frequently—once only giving the least hint of weariness :—

"It is a beautiful frosty morning just now, and I can see the people in the Gymnasium 'skating double geese and shadows,' and all my big sisters and one big brother have gone off to skate. I am left to sit at home and bite my nails like Giant

Pope in the 'Pilgrim's Progress,' and I wish I could eat some of them. I only mouthed a piece of Xenophon, however, and, as you are in the same box, I send you my heartfelt sympathy."

Another letter he begins thus: "This house at present does not possess a 'J' pen, so I have had to take the toes off a Waverley pen with a file. The above and following writing is the result, but I know you will excuse it, being a lover of ingenuity."

Later in the year, after the danger of his illness was past, we find the following postscript in a letter to another friend: "Tell Fred he does not know how to get into the canoe. This is the way "—

Position I
Half in
Pos. II
In the well
Pos. III
Well in!

To this time also he traced a new departure in spiritual life. His influence at all times lay more in character and action than in what he said about religious matters. He was one of those who, carefully nurtured and trained in religious principles, grow up into the Christian life without any evidence of the rapid and sudden changes characteristic of most men who attain to eminence in the Christian world. Pure in thought and life, open and generous in character, thoroughly boyish in his pleasures, he was totally devoid of the unnatural pietism which would have repelled his contemporaries. He was religious; every one instinctively felt him to be good. Probably it was the near presence of death which made his religion now more personal, and brought him into that close communion with God which was so strongly marked in his university career and in his mission-work in town; at any rate we find now in one of his letters the earliest mention of his conscious entrance upon a newer and higher relationship to God, and from this time all his work and energy were devoted to preparation for entering the ministry.

He thus announced his recovery to a school-friend who was studying for the Civil Service :—

"10 Royal Crescent, Edinburgh.

"My dear Charles,—Mr Phlegm is dead at last! I have been doing no study this summer, but spent my energies in fighting the gentleman aforesaid.

> I fought him with driver, and iron, and spoon,
> I fought with my toe and my heel ;
> I fought him at Arran, I fought him at Troon ;
> But he fought me in bed, the cowardly loon,
> For oh, he's a stubborn chiel !
>
> I fought him at cricket with bats and a wicket (!!),
> I dozed him with salt sea-air ;
> I laughed and grew fatter, and bathed in the 'watter' (!!),
> And he's gone to,—we need not ask where.

If you were a doctor you might understand this, but we need not go into particulars ; the plain meaning is that I am strong again, and hope to stand the winter all right — 'Not to die, but live, and' (I may finish the verse) 'declare the works of the Lord.' It may be absurd for me to talk of dying, but I was just at the head of that avenue which conducts a great many young fellows to the other world, and I had to look that full in the face. It should not make one gloomy, but it does make one serious.

" It was not for what I have been telling you just now that I began to answer your letter so soon, but somehow that came first which was secondary. Charlie, give me a shake of your hand. We are rather far off, but make a long arm and we'll have a good shake. If I may ask something for you, may God give you a pure faith and freedom from doubt. The way to be free from doubt is to keep close to God; many men to escape doubt have thrown themselves into the arms of Rome,—it is safer, I think, to throw oneself into the everlasting arms of God. He has the clearest faith who has lived nearest God all his life. I should have had far less fighting had I not been so wretchedly bad till I was sixteen years old, before which time you did not know me, I am glad to say.

" 'Trailing clouds of glory we may come,' but how many scatter away all the glory before their boyhood is over!   Few men dare say they do not require to be ' born again.'

"We must all be missionaries, and I am glad you are going to make the Civil Service a missionary scheme.   From all I have heard, the lives of ungodly Christians abroad do more than almost anything else to hinder the spread of the Gospel.—I am, your affectionate friend,

"C. A. R. PENTER."

CHAPTER III.

STUDENT LIFE IN EDINBURGH UNIVERSITY.

THE illness of which we have spoken in the last chapter cast a cloud over his university career, as for three years he had to "take things easy," and refrain from all study except what was absolutely necessary. He passed the usual examination for bursaries in October 1880, and his name appears nineteenth on the list—a position not at all low, when one considers that he had been away from school for nearly the whole of the previous year. The summer of 1881 he had to devote to a long rest in order to regain lost vigour. He spent it in Abbey St Bathans amongst the Berwickshire hills. An invitation to New Abbey brought the following reply :—

" If you could manage to transplant me to New Abbey without my will, or against my will, it would be splendid; but as it is I can't do it noways. You'll have to take Miss —— as a companion, and I daresay the world will not be too hard upon you, as you are young and very lonely. By the by, talking about your age, as I won't be writing again before Monday, I must wish you many happy returns of the day on which the great event takes place. Long life and prosperity, a happy age and a good old wife, and many of them, and heaps of the blessings which sometimes illumine our hard lot, and very few of the ills that flesh is heir to. What do you say to concoct an ode on the occasion? Perhaps you don't know how odes and suchlike are brewed,—it is not such difficult work as one might imagine. The first thing to do is to find a termination which suits a good many words—' ed ' is a particularly fine one, and a great favourite,—thus: spread, head, fed.

THE ODE.

Verse 1. May blessings thick be on him spread,
   With oil and butter on his head ;
   With laurels green may he be fed—
     The dear wee Charlie !

Now didn't that go off well?   I think we might take 'eat' as a termination for the next verse,— so: eat, meat, feet.

> 2. Give him as much as he can eat—
>   Potatoes, cabbage, good roast-meat,
>   And haggis, greens, and porker's feet,—
>   The dear wee Charlie!

Another favourite ending is 'all,' and it strikes me as being rather suitable,—thuswise: withal, small, all.

> 3. Let him be stuffed with cake withal,
>   And ragamuffins chopped up small;
>   Oh! how will he digest it all!—
>   The dear wee Charlie!

It begins to get hard work when you get to the fourth verse, but three verses are not enough, so we'll try 'un,'—so: one, gun, bun.

> 4. May he have gifts a hundred and one,
>   A hobby-horse and a little gun,
>   A stick of rock and one more bun—
>   The dear wee Charlie!

That last verse would not do for a farewell, so we'll try one more—something about 'life,' which, of course, suggests 'wife,' and that naturally suggests 'strife':—

> 5. May he live long a happy life,
>   May he obtain a tough old wife,
>   And win in each domestic strife—
>   The dear wee Charlie !

I can't write any more after that exhausting effort, and post time is approaching.—I am, your affec. friend,   W. A. Scott."

His second session was devoted to Mathematics and Logic.   At its close he passed the examination in the former for the degree of M.A., and during the summer of 1882 he acted as tutor to a family in Perthshire.   He wandered with his pupils among the mountains, drinking in their inspiration and revelling in their grandeur.   Several of his letters during the early summer months have been preserved, and in them one gets the picture of a youth who thoroughly enjoys his life.

> " *May* 15, 1882.

" Whenever you feel inclined to write, the address below will find me—

> *W*. *A. Scott, Esq.,*
>   *Drumore,*
>   *Blairgowrie.*

I ventured to put Esq. at the end, seeing 'as I hold a lofty position' in the community. I think you forgot to congratulate me upon the completion of my mathematical education, but as I have congratulated myself as much as I could, it does not matter much. It is no use congratulating you, of course. . . .

"The only difficulty I have here is in making amusement, but that is not bad for, as perhaps you know, *Dulce est desipere in loco.* We have been busy at the youthful occupation of making balloons lately, and did not find the work at all distasteful, especially as they went very satisfactorily. We have lessons in the morning, and then are out the rest of the day—fishing or shooting, or looking for eggs, or following some other occupation not less pleasant. We climbed the Glas Mheall on Saturday, and had a fine day of it. Our barometer gave about 3500 feet at the top, which is a very respectable height up in the air. We had a grand view of the Cairngorms, and away round to Ben Gloe, Schiehallion, Ben More, Ben Lawers, and the Lomonds of Fife.

On the road down we had to cross a ridge of snow
about 30 yards wide and as steep as the roof of
a house. It was great fun trying a glissade,
seeing the snowballs running away down in front.

1 was down first, and so had the fun of watching
the others coming down. It looked quite Alpine
seeing the keeper at the top creeping down at
a dangerously slow rate, a steep bank of snow
behind him showing against the blue sky."

"Drumore, *Wednesday.*

"I should like to have seen you acting 'Dominie,' with a long and serious and stately visage, and a 'leather assistant.' Next time you try it, when there is a little, pale, anxious face in front of you, and a little white hand below you, and the 'leather assistant' lies dangling over your back, just imagine that Bill Scott, or F——, or J——, is looking through the keyhole, and keep your gravity.

"I have some news for you, however—of course about myself. Last Christmas I sent a portrait of my trouser-leg and shoe protruding through a door as a first-footing card to Mrs M——. Your uncle saw it and writes to ask me if I have any objections to his printing it off for next Christmas. Of course I have not, especially as it is to bring me a 'honorarium.' (I am not quite sure what kind of a plant that is. I shall need to look up old Woody,[1] I think.) I wrote to ask if they had any more of these rare plants, as I should be very glad to cultivate a few for

---

[1] Professor J. H. Balfour.

winter consumption, but I have not got an answer yet.

"I have not been doing much in the study line. The essay, I am afraid, is knocked on the head, as I have no time to hammer it out. I have been doing a little Homer so as not quite to forget Greek, and I have read Milton's 'Areopagitica' through, and a few more odds and ends. The 'Areopagitica' is just splendid. You should read it soon, if you have not read it yet.

"I am coming back to the land of books in the beginning of July, I think, so perhaps I shall get a little more work done then. Tutoring won't stop, of course, till the end. I have forgot all about mathematics. Trigonometry and algebra lie far removed in the perpetual past. Like Pope and Pagan in the 'Pilgrim's Progress,' they may 'gnash with their teeth and clutch with their fingers, but they can by no means come at me any more.'"

"*17th August* 1882.

"I have been down near Dumfries for a fortnight with C. W. He is going up to London this

Wishing You a Happy New Year
First-footing it.

month to commence being stuffed by 'Wren's patent' in view of the Civil Service exam. in June. It must have rather a demoralising effect, I should think; but I suppose there's method to be learned by it, which is always the excuse for everything mechanical.

"I had a jolly time of it there, sketching the most beautiful avenue of trees, which arch over the public road, and make every one upon the road look beautiful.

> Naught but suffers a tree-change
> Into something rich and strange.

(I found out what makes the strangeness. The light gets in *below* the trees, not from the top, and throws the shadows up instead of down—as I noticed when painting the branches, whose dark side was on the top.)

"Ruskin is fine. He does *slash* into Claude, and raises Turner up to the skies. (He was up there before, however.) I think all who lecture or write books ought to be mad about something or somebody—even though it be a delusion. It's much more interesting than impartiality as it is called. I am getting sceptical somewhat in regard to impartial philosophers. I don't believe Descartes ever did 'hing on' by that wee 'ego' of his without any other support. He may have thought he did, or thought it would be a fine thing to do, but I don't believe he ever did it. There's too much of us ever to be rested on the top of a rail, and it's not easy to sit down on a needle, and stools are always made with three legs and not with one. . .

"I had a letter from —— yesterday; he's groaning over the small amount of work he has done. Since I am through mathematics I don't care a dump for pheelosophy."

In the late summer of 1883 he spent a few weeks in Galloway, sketching, swimming, boating, &c. He gives a humorous picture of a not uncommon experience of those who have the misfortune to bathe on a coast where they have to wade for water :—

"Next day we travelled a good number of miles, including a few in the Solway. You've heard of men running away from the tide. We ran to catch it, and were very fatigued with the exertion. Bob had to take a pair of opera-glasses out of his pocket to find at what part of the coast we left our clothes!"

In the November of 1883 Scott entered the Divinity Hall of Edinburgh University, and speedily made his mark amongst his class-fellows by winning the Eccles bursary of the year. In the shade of great sorrow he began his theological studies, for a week or two earlier the mother who had been to her children a living impersonation of holiness was, after the cruel torture of a hopeless disease, called to rest. He spoke little of his sorrow, but her memory remained bright in his life. Frequently he used to quote her sayings, and with him all his life a question of conduct was settled when he could say "Mother said so." He was a man who repressed almost sternly all expression of his emotions, and the only reference we find to his loss is a short one in a letter replying to an expression of sympathy: "The stewing for that bursary kept me from at once answering your letter, for which I should like to shake hands with you. 'Men must work and women must weep.'"

This appointment as Eccles bursar was peculiarly timely, occurring as it did when circumstances made him enter on that form of Scottish student life which has operated most strongly in developing all the resources of men. It was necessary for him now to support himself entirely, and there began that noble struggle with fortune which issued in his double qualification of an ordained medical missionary. Private tuition —the resource of so many students—was undertaken, and the expenses of his Divinity and Medical courses were all met by his unending industry. Whatever may be the habit under the New Ordinances, there existed, I believe, a kindly practice amongst at least some of the medical professors of remitting the fees of those who were training for the mission-field. At any rate so he was told. We used to urge him, in order to guard against the risk of an absolute collapse, to try whether, on the strength of his prospective service of the Church, the Foreign Mission Committee might not relieve the burden to some extent. But his resolution remained to offer himself to the Church without permitting the shadow of any claim upon him for mission-work except the call of God to it; and of the opportunity which he might have had through the practice mentioned as common amongst the medical faculty, he also, with much less reason, refrained from taking advantage. He believed that God had given him resources to meet His own call, and that duty called him to use these resources to the utmost. However wise or unwise the course he adopted may seem, it certainly had the immediate effect of a training in self-denial and self-reliance which was an invaluable preparation for his future career. For weeks continuously he allowed himself only five hours' sleep—yet a strain like this, which would have been impossible to many, never affected his natural cheerfulness. Though towards the close of his college life he began to show by his fagged appearance signs that his constitution was being tried to its utmost extent, his cheerful greeting had its old hearty ring, and a good work for any one found in him a ready instrument.

His many works outside of his classes will demand a separate notice, for in them his natural characteristics received full scope; but in this place we may recall the impressions received by him in one of the early "Hall" days. In the Missionary Association, of which he was a member from 1880 till his death, a letter was read on Saturday, 8th December 1883, from his brother, pleading for men for the missions in Africa. Few of us will forget the younger brother as he rose to speak on the subject. He was now of tall commanding appearance, his features were such as arrested attention immediately, and the charm of his steady, kindly blue eyes won for him at once the sympathy of a listener. His utterance was quick and nervous; probably the fact of addressing a company of students — the most critical audience in the world — increased his tendency to stammer,—a tendency due more to the rapidity of his thoughts, and his inability to make them keep pace with his speech, than to any other cause. His wish "to throw a bomb into every heart that did not feel the burden of the heathen, and shatter every obstacle to the realisation of duty," was so evidently the sincere expression of a heart consecrated to a life's work that one could not hear it unmoved, and one at least of the company can trace to that day his recognition of the duty of the Church to those who dwell in the lands of darkness.

To the circumstances of his work was due the fact that he did not take as a student that prominent place which his position on entering the Divinity Hall seemed to promise. But, indeed, it did not follow in his case any more

than in many others, that the absence of his
name from honour lists implied that he simply
walked through his classes.   Whatever fell to
be done by him was a *duty*, which therefore
had to be performed thoroughly, and in every
branch of his work he took a real interest.   An
accident to his knee in a football match laid him
aside for so many weeks that he " lost his session."
He bore it with his usual fortitude, as we see from
the following :—

" 1st March 1885.

" I began a letter to you two weeks ago, but
it has gone somewhere, so I will start again.   You
asked me for news of myself; I shall put you up
to that.   I played one match at football this
session.   It was in the middle of November.
At that match I got a smash on the nose which
I found, a week afterwards, when I could examine
it without fear of making it bleed, broke the
cartilage away from the bone.   It has joined
again all right, and has forgotten all about it.
But I got another injury which has not forgotten
all about it.   I got a blow on the side of my

knee which made me lame, though I did not stop
going about till the Wednesday after. Then the
old thing would go no longer, developed synovitis,
and here I am hobbling ‘vix’ about on two
sticks. I was in bed for three weeks, and have
been spending a heap of half-crowns on cabs up
to College. It is getting better now, I think,
though still an almost useless appendage. ‘Oh,
I’ll never do so no mo’, I’ll never do so no mo’.’
I really did not intend to play this year, indeed I
did not, but they were hard up and sent a deputation to get me out again, and I could not refuse.

“In some ways I have felt this a burden,
although I have found it good too, for it is good
to have to lie still and think. It makes you look
to your bearings. I don’t know whether you
have found it, but I find one is apt to drive
through work without ever thinking what one’s
hold is below water on the things unseen. You
make no way. I don’t believe on Carlyle’s ‘Produce, Produce,’ unless you know you are not producing rubbish. We don’t belong to ourselves at
all. We are God’s property, because He bought us.

That gives us the right bearing, don't you think ? You must excuse me speaking in this style, because you asked me news of all my doings, and that has been my chief discovery for some time back. I hate talking 'goody,' for it often goes along with a disagreeable expression of face, thorough meanness, complete want of kindness, and general lowness—and therefore properly, to be fair, I ought to tell you all the lowness and meanness, &c., &c., which also discovers itself; but perhaps it will be enough if I thoroughly acknowledge the presence of that and let it go with that. I most thoroughly appreciate Mr Glas's protest against the preaching TRADE. It is a dangerous profession.

"A somewhat serious result of my knee is that the Divinity Faculty will not count my session. I was absent eight weeks. They are rather an obstinate set, with precedents to go by. I have done most of the work for them,—98 pages of essay for Flint, &c.,—but they hold by the 'bodily' presence, as H—— talks of. They don't seem to see that precedents are things which multiply, each one becoming harder than the last. Now, they have decided that, however much work a man may do, it makes no difference against the 'bŏdily' presence. There are no examinations which a man *must* pass in the Hall except the almost nominal presbytery exams., so there is nothing they can hang on to but the 'bŏdily' presence. But they seem to me quite incapable of understanding what a rule means. The medicals are going to count my session all right I expect. I was there a fortnight sooner, as I had to take my choice between the two, but then I am better known at the Hall. I don't know if I told you I am taking Medicine. I wish to be a medical missionary, as I believe I shall be more useful as such than trusting to my tongue simply. It is pretty hard work doing both and making your living besides; but I believe I am right in taking this course, *so it has got to be done.* The decision of the Divinity Faculty hampers me considerably, however. I shall need to take Hebrew again; if he makes me pay the fee a second time, I shall request you to send up some dynamitards to do a little affair for me—a little piece of retributive justice, you know. This letter has been lying in my note-case for about a fortnight, as you will see by comparing dates: I didn't forget the poor thing, but have not found time to finish it. Since I began it my leg has strengthened considerably. I have dispensed with cabs altogether, but still go on four legs. If it goes on as it is doing, I expect soon to chuck away one stick and go on three legs. My two fore-limbs are getting immensely strong with having to do more of the work of progression. I have been a baby in arms, you see, for some time back. Going at snail's pace is very trying; not being able to beat a nurse and perambulator is most humiliating. I have got to the 'retired-from-business-old-gentleman' pace now, however, and hope in no long time to be as 'fast' a young man as ever. My little injury has cost me pounds of money and pounds of flesh. If you have any aims in life that will harm by laying by for a few months, *don't play football.*—I am, your affec. friend,

"W. A. SCOTT."

He was, however, by special permission of the General Assembly of 1888, allowed to proceed to trials for licence. Yet at the time his mind was undisturbed by the prospect of the extra year of university life, and with characteristic energy he occupied the period of enforced leisure in reading the work for the degree of Bachelor of Divinity, to which the pressure of medical studies afterwards prevented him from proceeding.

In the summer of 1884 he became increasingly convinced that his work as an African missionary would not be fully efficient if he were not licensed, as he said in his own happy style, to "practise as well as to preach." Indeed he believed that his talent did not lie in the direction of preaching at all, and he then definitely determined to acquit himself as a medical man. His own explanation of his new departure he thus expressed :—

"You see God has not given me a ready tongue, but He has given me a ready set of fingers, and if I can't do folks very much good by what I say, I'll be able to help them at least by patching up their bodies and making them more ready to hear other people speak."

To the objection, that by taking up medical studies he would be prevented for three years longer from entering the mission-field, he was always ready to retort that, by his work as a doctor, he would be able to crowd two years into one, and thus soon make up for lost time.

Scott bore about with him the atmosphere of true religion. In his rooms there was ever in the midst of hearty, happy fun an earnest recognition of the claims of God upon the lives of men. The day was begun by reading with his fellow-students a chapter of the Hebrew Bible, and closed with another of the Greek Testament. He had the singular faculty of bringing men into close contact with the divine, simply by his life. When needs must, speak he could and speak well; but in his life more than his words lay the secret of his power. We never came across any man of whom it could have been said more truly than of him, that "men took knowledge of him that he had been with Jesus."

His friend Dr Rankine says of these days: "I can never forget his zeal and enthusiasm for his work—his physical strength employed only for what is good, his saintly character soaring high above ordinary mortals such as I, his mental agony if he thought he had done anything to injure any one, his noble self-reliance based on his faith in God and love for Christ. This, as you will see from his letters, was increased in later years."

CHAPTER IV.

MISSION WORK IN GREENSIDE.

WHILST he was engaged during his university career in a task that usually is considered sufficient for two men, Scott did not consider that the demands on his time from an educational point of view in any way excused him from doing his utmost to assist every good work that lay at his doors to be done. He was a member of the parish church of Greenside. The parish lies to the north-west of the Calton Hill, and when you go down one of the side-streets off Leith Walk, or look down upon the district from the slopes of the hill, you discover that though within a stone-throw of Princes Street, and nearer still to the broad thoroughfare of Leith Walk, the parish really consists of very closely-packed dwelling-houses containing a dense population. Amongst these people Scott found a fertile field for manifesting the many-sided character he had. In 1881, when his eldest brother left for Africa, a congregational class of boys taught by him was in danger of dissolution, when Willie stepped into the breach and offered to continue it in order to keep it together. He was about the same age as the lads he undertook to teach, and in the first year he read with them through Bunyan's 'Holy War.' He also suggested that as a class they should enrol themselves with him in the Fellowship branch of the Young Men's Guild, of which Lord (then *Mr*) Pearson was President. By his own influence he solved the very common difficulty of keeping lads for the older association after they are too old for the Sunday-school. Later on in the Guild's history Scott became its President, and threw himself into its work with his wonted energy and vigour. If a paper were wanted and a writer awanting, he was always ready to step into the breach; and we well remember the energy and scorn with which he set himself, after reading 'The Larger Hope' of Archdeacon Farrar, to rend his ideas into pieces for the enlightenment of the Young Men's Guild on the dangerous teaching it contained.

He succeeded in a marked degree in overcoming the stiffness there is very often found in such meetings—a stiffness due probably to the fact that the members do not understand how completely natural a man must be in his religion if he is to converse about it in a natural fashion. Scott being himself nothing if not natural, managed to infuse his own naturalness into other people, and so the meetings had perfectly frank interchange of ideas without any of the "debate" aspect about them. One member of this class and Fellowship Association says: "Dr Willie Scott's influence on me personally was probably greater than that of any other man I have met. He was one of the very few who attempt to carry out to their logical conclusion in practical conduct the doctrine of Christ. He seemed to me to love his neighbour always better than himself."

To his brother's work in the Children's Church
in Greenside he also fell heir. For children he
had always a very great affection, which was
reciprocated fully by the young people.   In a
letter written when he was *en route* for Africa
he says: "I left my old landlady not without
deep feelings on both sides, poor old body! in
the beginning of October, and went to live
at 2 Merchiston Bank Avenue for the winter.
Molly and I grew very chummy—it makes me
home-sick to think of her. Molly is my brother
Andrew's little girl, you know."

His vocal gifts enabled him to do much to
train his mission-boys well in the singing of
their hymns, and his artistic powers were put
to use in this work also. He usually painted
an illustration or illustrations of the text for the
day, and presented them to those who answered
best.

But the work in Greenside that called forth
his best qualities was his Sunday evening class
for boys. Regarding this class a fellow-worker
closely associated with him writes:—

" This work was carried on for the benefit of those boys in Greenside Church who lived, generally speaking, in the most neglected and often most miserable circumstances, who were under little parental supervision, and therefore attended Sabbath - school of their own freewill. From amongst these Mr Scott gathered round him what were often termed the 'worst' boys, and it was plainly evident that the bond between him and them was of a marvellous sort.

" To know the case better it should be remembered that these boys had to fight the battle of dear life almost from the moment they entered it. Frequently orphans, or the children of drunken parents, or in many instances the incorrigibles of otherwise well-conducted households, the most of them had become hardened in a ceaseless war with care, in which every man's hand also seemed to be against them.

" Numbers of them were miserably clad, and often went without food for days, perhaps; and hunger, or poverty, or ill-treatment was plainly

their inheritance, while they were often destitute
of the soothing encouragement of family life.
Plainly at times their young hearts could not
but feel that they were outcasts of society, and
little better off than the stray dogs that hunted
in the gutters for a livelihood and for whom
no one cared.

"It was such boys that Mr Scott sought out
and invited to the Sabbath-school—some of them
bold and brazen-faced, some sly and suspicious,
whilst others again appeared to have given up all
hopes of better things or times, and it seemed
from their prematurely dejected appearance that
despair and desolation had settled down on them.
It is needless to say, however, especially to those
who are experienced in this kind of work, that
there were those in the classes on whom their
surroundings had as yet no bad influence, and
whose personal character was all that could
be desired—sometimes, indeed, refined by misfortune like pure gold, or rendered precociously
courageous by the fight for existence. In Mr
Scott all these boys found what he earnestly

strove to be —- a dear brother who was ever thinking of them, knew all their circumstances, their dispositions, and their temptations. In a way new to them he was faithful to point out their faults when they failed to do what was right, and no doubt at first he found his hands pretty full! But he was careful to make the transgressors feel in his own singular way that, although he detested the transgression itself, it yet increased his affectionate solicitude for the offender, and made stronger his desire to leave the ninety and nine to help the lost sheep out of dangerous places. He became as one of themselves in their amusements, and in organising and providing physical recreation he sought to evoke in them a desire for healthy amusement and fair rivalry in all such games as boys naturally love. In short, he sought to teach them to enjoy their games with gentleness as distinct from rowdyism, and in this he succeeded. The boys crowded to his class, and came to regard him as a peerless hero whose slightest word was law to them, and who, strange to say, made them respect themselves by the respect he had for them."

He was able at all times to make his "boys" feel that there was no condescension in his attitude to them. They were his friends, and he would put his arm through theirs quite as naturally as he would through that of a university class - fellow. His rooms were always open to them, and he was not content with merely teaching them. On one occasion most of them were unable to attend the annual picnic of the school—a disappointment hard enough for those to whom this was perhaps the one outing of the year that was easily within their reach. Rather than disappoint them wholly of an afternoon's pleasure, he determined to take them to Portobello at his own expense and give them an afternoon's boating. They could not all arrange to get away together, and then he decided to have a strawberry feast for them in his lodgings. He brought a fellow - worker to help to entertain them, and a jolly night they made of it—all the merrier because Scott was able to interest them in games very different from the usual horse-play of their leisure hours.

His method of teaching the class was, as we may imagine, quite original. He met them once a-week to enable him to "chum" with them, and in these evenings his carefully trained tenor voice was requisitioned for the singing of hymns and songs, and for the teaching of music to the boys. With his own keen insight into nature and appreciation of the beautiful, he was always anxious to use the eyes of the class to assist their hearts. Cheap pictures of the terrible order which too frequently deface the walls of mission premises, with their senseless colouring and false representation of the facts they are intended to illustrate, he could not endure, even if he could have afforded to buy them.

For the purpose of illustration, however, he procured a sheet of ground-glass and several sheets of paper of different tints. With these he was able to make a background of any colour he desired, and then with the coloured chalks he drew for the boys the particular illustration he wished. One does not wonder that he became to them a " peerless hero."

As we have seen, he was not at any time in very easy circumstances as regards money, but to his boys in Greenside he was often banker as well as teacher. He frequently bought for them clothes and food, and it speaks volumes for the worth of his work that he had very few of the experiences (common enough amongst mission-workers) of being duped and deceived in his charities. When the surroundings of the boys seemed hopelessly bad he often advised them to enter the army, believing that the discipline of the soldier would in great measure lend to their characters a fixity of purpose which would not be readily attained at home. After his medical studies had advanced a year or two he became surgeon and physician in ordinary to the lads and their friends — taking friends of his own to the cases that were beyond his experience. Food and medicine he supplied himself. One of his patients was a poor fellow who suffered from asthma. As usual he was unable to get any rest in a reclining position. To help him Scott manufactured a sort of table, which he put across the bed, so that the sufferer was able to lean forward on it in such fashion as admitted of more rest than he had ever known since his attack began.

One night after ten o'clock, when walking with a friend from the east end of London Road to his brother's in Merchiston, Scott was very anxious to dismiss his companion at Greenside. The latter discovered that he wished to go down to Greenside Row to visit one of his patients. This was a lad who had formerly been a scholar—a young man far gone in consumption. He was supplying the patient with everything he needed. He grudged no time to sit at his bedside and speak of the things of the kingdom, and his conversation had all the more force and power from the fact that from his hands came every comfort the sufferer had on earth.

It was his habit to give out his washing to be done in Greenside by some poor woman or other whom he wished to assist. It was no small sacrifice, as any one will understand who takes the trouble to look down from the Calton Hill upon the Greenside rows and closes, and ask himself how it is possible in the midst of the smoke to have anything thoroughly white. Scott was as fastidious as most men, but he considered it unworthy of him to allow his taste to interfere with the chance of doing some good.

He has been known to seek out an old cobbler, take him his shoes to mend, find it necessary to give him leather for the purpose, pay him for his work, and after all require to hand them over to another.

What he did in that parish was unknown to any but himself and God. His bright, cheery, hopeful face, his ready purse, and his deep piety must have left influences that will never fade. One who knew him well declares that in one year, when he earned £150 by his varied energies, he spent only £20 of it upon himself and gave the rest away. Probably this is an exaggeration of an admiring friendship, but the fact of the amount stated shows that what he spent was very considerable.

CHAPTER V.

WORK IN THE UNIVERSITY MISSIONARY ASSOCIATION.

SUCH work as this we have just noticed would give any man a very good claim to be considered a devoted mission-worker. But this was only the work which represented his duty to his congregation. He was a member of the University Missionary Association, and felt he had a duty to it. In the early days of his theological studies the University Missionary Association was forced to consider the question of their field for Home Mission work, which, besides effecting much good for the district in which it was pursued, also supplied in some little way a means of training the students who carried it on in pastoral and parochial work. In 1884 the Old Kirk Parish, the scene of their operations for several years, was equipped with an organisation of its own, and it seemed doubtful whether it was possible to carry on successfully the mission in Blackfriars Street any longer. An application to the presbytery to allocate to the Association a portion of the High Street, which had been overlooked in the last division of the city parishes, was unsuccessful—the "no man's land" being allocated to those parishes on which it bordered. There seemed sufficient room also for work amongst a stratum of the population lower than any yet reached, and the Home Mission superintendent of the day was anxious that during the summer of that year the Association should remain in their old field and endeavour to "dig deeper" amongst those whom poverty or sin, or both, had sunk into a pit whence it was difficult to raise them. Three fellow-students—Scott, Dr Rankine, now of the China Mission, and Mr A. G. Thomson, representing the Faculties of Divinity, Arts, and Law— came to his rescue with promises of assistance, and he was thereby enabled to carry on the work in

the name of the Association, without any charge
on its funds for the summer.   All did yeoman
service, and the experience Scott had gained in
Greenside proved a tower of strength to the little
band of workers.   Two departments of the work
he made specially his own—the class for young
men, and the meeting on Sunday nights for all
who would attend.

A motley crew they were—labourers, scaven-
gers, performers at "penny gaffs," rag-pickers,
street-loafers of every description, fallen women,
were found around us, with a sprinkling of those
who had "gone under" in a real struggle for existence.   Amongst them he was, as in Greenside,
engaged in work which called forth his best gifts.
His purity attracted while it reproved ; the manliness of his religion was a living testimony of its
power; his athletic well-developed frame showed
the young men that strength and vigour were
far from inconsistent with godliness and virtue.
Whilst the sin with which we came into contact
was a constant sorrow to him, he had a boundless
confidence in God, and a no less boundless con-

fidence that every man had in him the possibility of being like God, and that these people only needed to know the love of God to rise out of their hopeless life into true manhood and womanhood. The Young Men's Bible-class received a new lease of life when he became its teacher. Few others could have secured as he did without any effort the quiet and reverence which attended his opening prayer. He won as few could win the confidence of such men to a degree that made them speak to their teacher quite frankly of the relation of divine truth to their own lives. Yet he was too essentially in sympathy with them to shut his eyes to the fact that, by becoming all things to them, he might by some means save some. He was distressed by their profanity, and also by the thought that amongst these lads—some of them not out of their teens—the taste for strong drink was rapidly being acquired. To counteract this, and to win their confidence still further, he organised a flute band amongst them, and constituted himself their teacher. That he could not himself play was to him only an unanswerable reason why he should learn. He arranged the music himself, and copied it for the various instruments. The conditions of membership were these : attendance at the Bible-class, refraining from profane language, and total abstinence. Once one of his best players broke systematically the first and third conditions, and after a week or two was ruthlessly dismissed without a thought of the cost to the music, and another was trained in his stead. Latterly, I believe, the services of a bandmaster were engaged, but that happened only when the pressure of his work made it impossible for him to continue to conduct the band himself.

One of the proudest days of his life was Christmas Sunday of 1884, when he brought his band into the Children's Church, and heard them lead the hymns in the musical part of the service.

One morning a friend of his was near the Waverley Station, when he was attracted by a flute band of from fifteen to twenty members, composed to all appearance of what are termed ragamuffins when the souls of men are valued by the bodily appearance, marching down Canal Street to the Station in good order, and playing a simple air with great spirit. In their midst he discovered Scott playing one of the instruments with all his might, as if he had no greater satisfaction in the world. He was off with his boys to a place in the country for the day, to give them an outing that would be a " red-letter " experience in their existence.

Another of his organisations was the Mission Football Club, of which Dr Rankine and himself took the control. Here the one condition of membership was that no profane language was to be heard on the field—quite a sufficient one in the eyes of those who know the frequent associations of the game. There was amongst us a not unnatural apprehension lest those men — great strong fellows — should take advantage of the facilities the game offered for asserting their superiority of brute force over students whose intellectual and moral power over themselves they had to recognise, however unwillingly.

When this was put before them as a reason why they should superintend and not play, we got the answer, " Oh, it's all in the day's work.   If a few kicks at us will ultimately land them in the kingdom of Christ, it will be a cheap price."   As a matter of fact, in one of the first games one of the students was brought home disabled by a " charge " from one of the men and crippled for many a long day ; but the result showed that the accident was the most profitable occurrence we had experienced, as the men were so ashamed of it that their attendance was henceforth regular at the meetings, and their attention to the message of salvation most marked.

The writer remembers of one occasion on which Scott asked him to intimate that next Sunday he would preach a sermon for football-players.   The club was urged to bring all they could persuade, and we had a large congregation of those whom outsiders would have called the " roughs of the Cowgate."   Some came to see the fun, and to hear what text the Bible could give for football-playing. Scott spoke from the eighteenth Psalm—" By thee

I have run through a troop; and by my God have I leaped over a wall. . . . It is God that girdeth me with strength. . . . He maketh my feet like hinds' feet, and setteth me upon my high places."

He impressed upon the young fellows that strength is from God, and is to be cherished as a divine gift. They needed not to fear that religion would make them unmanly; on the contrary, God must be pleased to see the powers He has given us carefully nurtured. A young man who, for the sake of being a servant of God, seeks to have his body as strong and active as possible, is doing what is pleasing to God. But then this strength is to be used for God. It is not given us to enable us to trample on the weak, but to protect them—and especially, he said, must young men use it to protect and guard, as they would their own mothers and sisters, those who are the mothers and sisters of others.

The perfect manliness of the whole address, the freedom from all appearance of pulpit style, only added to the force of the sermon, because it was so thoroughly like himself—a young man speaking as a good comrade to those who felt he was really a friend.

The recollections of those associated with him are the only source from which information can be had, as in the nature of things those who came under his influence could hardly attain that prominence which enabled students to keep sight of them after college days were over, and the workers were scattered over the world. Had our university life been on the model of English student life, and Scott been compelled to live amongst his class-fellows, we cannot doubt that, as in the cases of Wesley, Martyn, and Heber, pleasing records of his influence on men who afterwards made their mark on the world would have been very numerous. To say that his work was less prominent is not to admit that it was less noble. Rather, surely, does it borrow a sacred beauty from the fact that, though in great measure it could never be remarkable, it was performed with the whole-hearted devotion of an earnest soul. It was, too, peculiarly suited to his genius and temperament. He was attracted by misfortune as by a magnet. That a man was down was sufficient reason for Scott being a devoted friend. He had the faculty beyond most of seeing the good in all men, and of unearthing gems of true manliness from the mass of sin and street smartness, which repelled those who had not the secret of looking at them through the love of God.

One can see from the foregoing that much of the influence that Scott had was due to the fact that he had the faculty of throwing himself completely into the position of the people amongst whom he worked, and of looking upon life to a certain degree with their eyes. Hence he was at pains to know them, and approach them with a friendship which had in it nothing of the aggravating condescension which workers of less tact might have betrayed, but which was simply the love of one who knew them quite well and was as one of themselves. A fellow - worker of his states strongly: "The incidents of his mission-work are not easy to remember, as Willie avoided anything like publicity. But the inner working of his life was easy to judge by what one saw; and to see him, and the Holy Spirit working in him, made one as sure of that Person in the Godhead as of the existence of Arthur's Seat."

The spirit which led to his "march out" with his band-boys is that of the truest manliness. We are accustomed enough to societies and organisations for the betterment of the poor, but we feel very often that the societies have more prominence than their work—indeed are forced for very existence' sake to keep *themselves* in evidence. But his action was an action of self - effacement. Accustomed to the best society in the city, a schoolboy of Edinburgh with friends to be met at every turn, and a prominent athlete known in that capacity to everybody, he had certainly attained the virtue of complete self - effacement. In so identifying himself with those who loved him, he succeeded in proclaiming to the lads the true relationship the Christian has to those in circumstances due as often to misfortune as to wickedness. His actions were not intended to *proclaim* a truth, but were simply the natural outcome of the thoughts he had about God.

Without thinking anything about the matter, Scott put himself on the true lines for meeting the despairing cries of socialism as it exists in the lowest classes. He had very little belief in legislation doing much of permanent value, except in the way of diminishing the temptations to drunkenness; but he *lived* unostentatiously a brother amongst them, and raised them by the mere contact of his own noble, pure nature.

It will be no surprise, in view of this sketch of his work in Edinburgh, to learn that he was terribly dissatisfied with Church life as it showed itself throughout the city. He had no sympathy with the system that is too general in all the Presbyterian churches in Edinburgh, which forces the minister to devote most of his time to his congregation, and leave the "mission-hall" in the charge of an assistant or a missionary. He often spoke of this as a disgrace, and a state of matters which the Church ought to rectify. He quite recognised that the selfishness of the ordinary congregation would be a very serious obstacle in the way of any minister who attempted to make his chief work lie amongst the "submerged tenth." Still a minister's business, he considered, was to be found mostly in the places his Master would frequent, and, rightly or wrongly, he thought that Christ's work in Edinburgh would have made men find Him most frequently among the poor.

The following programme of his Sunday work at this time will give some idea of his manifold energies :—

1. Guild meeting, Greenside   .   10   A.M.
2. Bible-class, Blackfriars Street .   11.15 A.M.
3. Afternoon service, Greenside .   2.30 P.M.
4. Boys' class, Greenside .   .   6   P.M.
5. Mission meeting, Blackfriars Street   7   P.M.

Add to this his frequent share in services in the wards of the Infirmary, and, oftener than not, visits paid to the sick after the mission meeting in the evening, and one sees that, however much his Sunday work was rest to him, it certainly was not idleness!

CHAPTER VI.

LAST DAYS IN EDINBURGH—ORDINATION—DEPARTURE FOR AFRICA.

As his university life sped on Scott became more completely identified with Africa and its needs, whilst, as the foregoing chapters show, the work that lay to his hand was not allowed to suffer because he looked forward to the greater that awaited him. His industry embraced four hours of tutoring daily, besides the execution of other work which afforded to him some means of livelihood. In 1888 one of his water-colours was given a place in the summer Exhibition of Water-Colours of the Royal Scottish Academy, and, when one considers that it is the work of an artist self-taught, his early thoughts of devoting himself to art do not at all seem an extravagant dream. In his artistic powers he suddenly realised that he had struck a rich vein in the execution of microscopic drawings in water-colours. This work demanded not only an artistic faculty, but also the knowledge of a microscopist who understood physiology and pathology. In this work, as he became known, his services were much sought after and were very remunerative.

He found it extremely difficult, however, to produce the drawings accurately with the brush, and at the best the work was slow. The need of painting little cells in exactly the same form and of the same size demanded time that he could ill spare. In order to save his time he set his wits to work, procured glass tubes of a certain size, held them in the gas-jet of his lodgings, pulled them out to the requisite fineness, filled them with his colouring matter, and by simply dotting his drawing with the tubes secured the uniformity he desired.

He drew the illustrations for a work on surgery,

and proved to have complete command of the human hand for artistic purposes.

In the midst of all this work his personality impressed itself with ever-deepening power on every one who employed him. Perhaps this will be best illustrated by the following quotation from a letter to the writer from the author of a medical work for which Scott drew the diagrams :—

"I was only too glad to put any illustration I wanted done into his hands. His rapidity, and at the same time accuracy, astonished me, and I always look back on it with admiration. He used to come with a pencil and a large sheet of paper. We then fitted on (say) some apparatus in its first stage; with our hands in position where the manipulation was difficult to follow, we would stop for him to make his sketch, and in a very few minutes he would have a vivid outline complete. Next day he would bring a reduced pen-and-ink drawing full of life and action and expressed in simple telling lines. That was in 1889. Since then I have watched other artists at work in the hospital, and have seen none so rapid and at the same time so accurate. Dr Scott always seemed to me to see the outline of what he wanted on the white paper, and he had nothing to do but trace it with his pencil. Until Dr Scott began these drawings for me I had known him only by sight. We worked together at them only for a few weeks, yet, after he had gone out to his mission-work, I could never hear of Africa without thinking "That's where Willie Scott is." We never corresponded, and I never saw any of his letters, yet the news of his death was one of those shocks which I can never forget. When I heard that he was dead I felt that the world was poorer for his loss—not in any commonplace way, but as if a permanent blank had been made, and the year that has passed since then seems to make no change in the feeling."

In the last two years of his Edinburgh life it was evident to all his friends that his spiritual life was becoming deeper and fuller. He was readier to speak of what he called the things of God, and, generally, the true strength of his devotion began to assert itself. We cannot doubt that the hardships of his life had much to do with this, and the prospect of danger of war in Africa with Portugal was also a factor in renewing his boyhood's experience in looking into the "long avenue."

In 1887 Major Pinto was suddenly seized with a desire for the extension of Portuguese territory from the coast into the interior of East Equatorial Africa, and headed an expedition which planted the Portuguese flag in a position so close to our mission there that it was evident Blantyre and the Shiré Highlands were the prize to which he aspired. The Portuguese claimed that they had "allowed" our countrymen to prosecute missions in the interior of their lands, and that now the flag of Portugal should wave over the country instead of the union-jack. It is unnecessary to give any account here of the really dangerous position in which the Blantyre Mission stood at the time — a danger which might have been aggravated by the fact that this mission occupied a rather solitary position—the others in Central

Africa being more directly connected with the lake; and to have conceded Portugal's claims to the Shiré provinces would have put Blantyre and the other stations of the mission under the baleful influence of Portuguese rule.

Pinto's expedition caused no small excitement in this country at the time. Scott's first thought was that the mission would need men, and he wrote to the Convener of the Foreign Mission Committee as follows:—

"27th February 1888.

"You will know better than I do the state of matters at Blantyre, but I wish to say that, if you think there is any immediate want of men there at the present crisis, I consider myself under your orders. I hope to be ready at any rate by July if I pass my examination, but I do not know whether a man or two more might not make a great difference at present. I want to have my degree before I go, but if there is a present need, I am ready.

"At any rate, is it not the fact that if a good many of us young men went out there soon it might be the means of saving the country from slavery and Mohammedanism? We might make a strong appeal on that ground if it were so."

It was not deemed necessary to accept this offer, for the danger was considered less to the life of the agents than to the whole existence of the mission in Africa. Yet the very fact of the troubles could not fail to impress an imagination and a spirit like his with the nearness of eternity, or to prove a warning of the light tenure by which life might be held in the mission-field. More trying to him by far was the not impossible event of the Church being unable to accept him at all, or perhaps of his being sent to some other field than Africa. Finance—the bugbear of every missionary society whose work extends faster than the interest of the members—seemed to forbid that any additional missionary be sent to Blantyre for some years

If there were no post in any field, then he determined to go to Africa in spite of the Church, if not for her. He was certain to be able to work his passage out as a ship's surgeon, and with his resources it would go hard with him indeed if he could not pick up a living, and on the 8th January he offered himself thus :—

"To Rev. J. M'Murtrie, D.D.
"*8th January* 1889.

"In again presenting myself for mission-work in Africa I wish to lay before you the particulars of my training for such work.

"I entered college in November eight years ago, took the degree of M.A. three years later, and have since studied Theology and Medicine. I took the University degree of M.B., C.M., in July last, and have to pass only the examination for licence to complete my Divinity course. That I hope to do very shortly. Since last October I have been studying diseases of the eye and throat, as well as dentistry, at the several dispensaries.

"I am now earnestly desirous, if God will, to be sent to work as soon as possible, as I feel that, humanly speaking, my training is done. My training and physical and mental capabilities are, I think, such as fit me for Africa rather than another field. I dare not be absolute on the point, for, if God sends me elsewhere, I am His, but it must be God's will and not a trivial reason. I have been engaged in Home Mission work during all my course.

"I need scarcely say that mental training I count for nothing unless one be trained of God; but, on the other hand, one cannot hold back as unworthy even of this high office, since God has decreed that in no other way than by the lips and lives of sinful men can the love of Christ be spread abroad; and therefore (trusting to His grace) 'Here am I, send me.'"

There was a feeling in the Committee that he should be sent to China, and a proposal was laid before him to that effect. He felt that personal preference had nothing to do with the matter, and gave to the suggestion the following reply:—

"*15th January* 1889.

"I have prayerfully considered the proposal which your Committee has made to me. I have endeavoured to lay aside all personal preference in the matter. I desire to look at it as a member of the Church of Christ simply. When I do so I think that in Africa there is the greatest need at present of an ever-increasing missionary influence. It is there that there seems to me to be the greatest danger of the enemies of the Cross gaining the day, and that to counteract their influence ours must be ever extending. There seems to be a crisis there such as exists in no other place. This conviction points me to Africa still. But though such is my belief, I leave it entirely to you to say what my destination is to be. I only ask that you will give this matter your prayerful consideration, so that what is done may be so planned as best to advance our Master's kingdom."

This was followed a week later by another letter :—

'22d *January* 1889.

" I am afraid you must have misunderstood my last letter, though I thought it was clear. I felt that my *feelings* had no place in the question, and said that, therefore, I laid them aside. I stated my conviction as to the needs of Africa just now, and my conviction remains. But if the Committee are not of the same persuasion, I am perfectly willing to go where I am wanted to go, and I shall go with as whole-hearted desires to China as to Africa. I am vexed to hear it said I should go in a half-hearted spirit to China, for it is not the case. There is a grand work going on there, as I very well know—a work in which any one would be proud to have a share. I just repeat that I lay aside personal preferences in the matter. My conviction of the critical state of missions in Africa keeps me from offering myself on my own responsibility for China, and I feel bound to leave it to the Committee to decide. If the China Sub-Committee were told that my *feelings* pointed me to Africa, that was exactly what I did not want to be said, as I am convinced that my feelings have no weight in the matter."

Three days later he wrote :—

" I desire to put in writing the gist of our last

conversation. If the Committee decide to send me to Africa, I offer to go for just so much as will keep me in working order for the first two years. I think, from what I know of life in Africa, £100 will do that—that sum at any rate to be definite. I have some diffidence in making the proposal, as the offer of salary should come from the Committee; but feeling that the Committee would not like to offer me less than the ordinary salary, and knowing the difficulty in which the Committee is placed, and also that the difficulty does not exist in the case of the China Mission, I venture to do so. I trust that this will not pass beyond those whom it concerns in the course of business."

Ultimately by private individuals a salary of £150 was guaranteed him, and (we blush to record it) it was for that sum that the Church of Scotland sent out one whose place amongst her missionaries is, in genius, character, and devotion—second to none.

In these years, too, he gave himself over largely to pleading the cause of missions throughout the country in the name of his University Missionary Association. He was specially interested in the Foreign Mission of the Young Men's Guild, and frequently accompanied their missionary, Rev. J. A. Graham, M.A., to meetings intended to stimulate interest in that new venture.

It was the writer's privilege to hear Scott preach on two occasions — once in the parish church at Slamannan, where he spoke about Foreign Missions, taking as his text, "If thou forbear to deliver them that are drawn unto death, and those that are ready to be slain; if thou sayest, Behold, we knew it not; doth not He that pondereth the heart consider it? and He that keepeth thy soul, doth not He know it? and shall not He render to every man according to his works?" (Prov. xxiv. 11, 12). He expressed himself in terse, telling sentences whose effect was hardly marred by the utterance. He impressed upon us that, if we were ignorant of the needs of the heathen world, it was wilful, sinful ignorance, and that our responsibility was not covered by our ignorance,

but by the way in which we availed ourselves
of the sources of information which God gave us.
In the evening of the same day he preached in
the little iron church in Limerigg, a village in
the same parish, from the thought, "Saved by
his life." His habitual rapidity and stammer
that night forsook him. We see him to-day
still, in the glow of the evening sun which
illumined his countenance, radiant with the
mystic light of the kingdom of God. He was
undoubtedly pouring out his own experience
of the life that walks with God. He spoke
absolutely without notes, and told of the things
of the kingdom with the air and authority of
one who was dwelling "in the secret places
of the Most High." The little church was
beautiful with the light of God's love and
holiness.

This was in 1889, in which year he was
licensed as a preacher by the Presbytery of
Edinburgh — but not without a careful study
of the Confession he had to sign. Some parts
of it seemed to him to be stronger statements

than he was prepared to admit, and it was only after careful thought and study of the Confession as a whole, under the direction of one he trusted, that he consented to sign it. Ordination followed apace.

On the evening of 7th April—nearly nine years after his university career began — the Presbytery of Edinburgh met in St George's Church and ordained him to the holy ministry in the presence of a large congregation. The Rev. Archibald Scott, D.D., gave the ordination charge to the new missionary, who, as he stood with the writer in the vestibule of the church waiting to bid good-bye to the people whose prayers had risen on his behalf, remarked of it, "It does one good to get one's marching orders as straight as that." Indeed his ordination was to him a very solemn thought, and he regarded it not as the seal of the Church on one who had "got a church," but as the seal of God on Himself setting him apart for labours that might be unto death. The ordination address did not call him to services higher

or nobler than those he cheerfully offered, and
of his work abroad the preacher said : "It is
the very noblest service to which you have
been ordained, that to which all true Churches
will ever devote their best men, and of all
service in our mission-field you are called to
what at present is acknowledged to be the most
responsible.   The post of difficulty to which
you are called may before you reach it be a
post of danger; but we know the material of
which God has made you, and we have only
to remind you that not just the honour of
your Church and country, but the honour of
the Saviour whom you love is intrusted to your
keeping, to incite you to be faithful to the
utmost, even unto death."

The hymn that followed closed with this
verse :—

> " Toil on, and in thy toil rejoice ;
>   For toil comes rest, for exile home ;
>   Soon shalt thou hear the Bridegroom's voice,
>   . The midnight peal, ' Behold, I come ! ' "

Alas ! how soon—how very soon—mercifully none

of us suspected. He looked that night like a man who had come through a long illness. The iron will had sorely tried the iron frame. Yet the hopefulness of his own nature cast its glamour over his friends, and none of us imagined but that he would live a life of many days and conspicuous honour in the mission-field.

It is too often perhaps a characteristic of those who devote themselves to the evangelisation of the heathen that they fail to see why any man should choose a different sphere of work, and indeed will hardly admit that the work of the Church at home is Christian work of any value at all.

Scott's mind was too great for this. He had views of the kingdom as broad as the love of God within his own heart. One evening just before his ordination he met in his brother's house a band of friends—boys from Greenside, old class-fellows, prospective missionaries, and others. He spoke then of his ideas about the kingdom. He considered that the Church at home required to lose the sense of "foreign" in her mission-work, and missionaries to lose the idea that they were engaged in work different in kind or degree from men at home.

Probably the complete identification of himself with his night class in Greenside or his morning class in Blackfriars Street made him more ready to recognise and declare the work for the kingdom as God's work, and honourable, whatever its sphere. He instanced work he had seen done at home, and asked us how we could imagine work in Africa nobler or more useful. In some respects he recognised that Africa was an easier field—at any rate there he would be sustained by the prayers of the believing Church, for he would be recognised more as belonging to the whole Church than the ordinary minister at home; and in Africa, at least, he would be free from men who were Gospel-hardened. He sang and spoke well, and remarked once, " Well, you fellows, I can't tell you how it is, but to-day I find myself singing at one moment and praying the next."

On the morning following his ordination a small party of us met to send a cheer after him as the Flying Scotsman bore him off to London. His happy, brave face, as it shone its loving good-bye to the past and its welcome to the unknown future, remains as the last we saw on earth of the purest, bravest soul we ever knew or hope to know.

The next day he wrote to his future wife regarding his ordination :—

" The ordination service was in the evening. It was awfully solemn. I am beginning to realise what it means now, and I must tell you what it means. It means that God has called me to work there, and I can never leave that work till He calls me away. So there is no hope that I shall come home from Africa (except on leave) as long as health lasts. That is my ordination pledge. I professed that zeal for the glory of God, love to Christ, and desire of saving souls are my only motives for going. I was charged to love Christ beyond all else. I am pledged to be His, and to be done with by Him entirely as He pleases— absolutely to be His, and to care nothing what becomes of me so that His kingdom come. I was charged to be faithful to Him and His work ' even unto death.' . . .

"I do not surrender common-sense or worldly prudence, but I would use them to the full—only, however, to carry out His will, never *in place of His* will. I shall take care of myself because I belong to Him, and therefore must take care of His property. But wherever He sends me I shall gladly go."

The following narrative of his late work and life in Edinburgh was written, during his voyage, to a friend in Canada :—

"I have to begin at last September and note briefly the order of events in my case up to a short time ago. I got all my drawing done for H—— in September, and got £33 for that job. I got all the drawings done for C—— satisfactorily, and got £15 for that one. I was drawing for W——— all winter, and got I don't know how much for that. T———'s drawings were for his thesis on tubercular diseases of joints, and I learned something from them. I stuck into my drawing pretty hard, as I did not know what the low state of the funds of the Foreign Mission Committee might compel them to say to me at the 'hinner end.'

" As regards study I have not such a successful report to make. I got only a week's holiday after the final on account of H———'s work, and as a consequence found, when I started to work in October, that my head said, ' No, no, old chappie.' I submitted, and went north to Loch Carron to paint for ten days with E——— N———. We had a very jolly time together, and I saw the folk who keep the Sabbath and believe in the doctrine of Election, in which I also believe, but not quite in the same way. It was the ' Fast ' week when I was there, and though the sea was crowded with herrings so that it smelt of them, and the loch was packed with boats, and men went down with carts and hand-nets and scooped up the herrings till the carts were full (we sat up late one night helping our landlord to get his lot), yet not a boat would go out on Wednesday night as next day was the Fast-day. Our old landlord did not like E——— to sew a button on his trousers on Sunday morning, but fetched a pin to fasten them instead! I was there only one Sunday, but I heard an old minister say in an awful tone that it was ' an

awful thing for men to be sealed for damnation.'
I do not know where he got that doctrine—not in
the Bible, I think.

"I got a little painting done, and came back to
Edinburgh; but my head said again, 'Na, na, old
chappie, you're too soon yet.' So I went to see
Professor Greenfield, who forbade speaking at meetings or working much till Christmas. So I enjoyed doctor's orders as a man should, and went
to dispensaries (throat and eye) and to the Dental
Hospital, took singing lessons, and practised
Schubert's songs with Lizzie, and generally enjoyed myself.

"I shied at the Confession of Faith at first, but
after due consideration, and having told the Presbytery in a letter what I meant by signing it, I
signed it. It is a composite document, and you
require to know something of its history before
you understand it. I find, however, the nearer
I get to the Truth, I get nearer to thinking as it
thinks, although it dogmatises about things I
cannot dogmatise about. And of course, beyond
all formulas of man's devising, I am pledged

as every one is to search for and be satisfied with nothing but the truth, wherever it is to be found. To think otherwise is to be a Roman Catholic at heart, whatever the outward profession may be.

" The Confession was the most difficult part of my theological work. I started to work in October at the mountain of work prescribed, and got all my discourses written but one before my head told me ' to bide awee.' I did not appear again till February, having done no work for the exam. in the meantime. I was then summoned to appear on very short notice indeed, so with becoming modesty I appeared. . . . I passed with flying colours, and we shook hands up to the elbow. . . .

" The chief event that stands out in my recollection before Christmas was the Conference of the Guild at Kirkcaldy, where Graham was set apart for the mission-work of the Guild at Kalimpong. I got a piece of advice there that I have not forgotten since, and that was to set apart at least half an hour in the morning for prayer.

I find that as time goes on half an hour is far too little. We must give God time to speak to us if we want to learn of Him. That Conference was the greatest event of history that has happened for a long time. . . .

"Since New Year my daily life has been much as usual. My preaching engagements came thick and fast, however. I preached in Greenside Church before I left. It is strange that, ever since I gave more time to prayer from last October, preaching, which was like murder to me as you know, has become a delight. . . .

"I was ordained on the 7th of April, and sailed from London on the 10th, so no time was lost. Dr Scott gave the ordination charge. It is an awfully solemn thing to be ordained to a post,—to be charged to be faithful unto death. But I believe, Davie, that every Christian is exactly under the same vows. If we read the Gospel rightly, we must believe that if we follow Christ we give our lives and all we have, because we are redeemed, to Him to be used simply as He wills, and our duty is only to find out what His

will is in regard to us, and then set about doing
it. That is what makes 'counting the cost' so
hard in one way. But if we fix our eyes on Him
who says 'Follow me,' we shall soon forget what
is behind in the joy of being His and His only.
And more than this—He cannot receive us at all
unless we do this. Read 'the Rich Young Man.'
We must give up our wills to Him, and let His
will rule. Looked at from the outside, it is hard,
hard, but from the inside it is most glorious, is it
not ? The only trouble is that we try to do it in
a half-hearted manner, and the result with me is
that life becomes miserable. One feels hounded on
to do God's work just because one is not willing
in the day of His power. If I pleased myself
entirely, I daresay I should be quite comfortable;
if I pleased Him Whose I am, I should be infinitely more at peace; but between the wind
and the tide the water is troubled. Still I
have had much more peace lately, because I
have got a little nearer doing as God wills.
I can see that the life of a child of God should
be one of glorious liberty. Let us reach out and

seize that. All we have to do is to open the door and Christ will enter. We do nothing but stand by and see what the Lord will do. To try to do anything without abiding in Christ is fruitless, like a branch trying to bear fruit without the vine.

" I got a lot of presents before I left Scotland —a very great many; people were very kind. I got a writing-desk from my Bible-class, a medicine (travelling) chest from the Children's Church, a purse with £33 from Greenside and other friends, and a great deal more besides.

" I have not put on clerical clothes, chiefly because I do not see reason to change my ordinary dress. I am a doctor, and therefore do not require to. There is no law of the Church in the matter. It is not a suitable dress, as regards collars and starch, for Africa. Carlyle taught me to hate clothes as such. People say that I am ' ashamed of my cloth,' but that is not Scriptural. The only thing we are not to be ashamed of is the cross of Christ, and the two are by no means the same. I find at least on board ship that I am much freer in the same clothes as the other fellows. And, lastly, our Church is paying far too much attention at present to clothes and odds and ends of services and all the machinery of religion, and seems tired of the simplicity of Christ. People are playing at being religious nowadays, and it is a waste of time."

CHAPTER VII.

NOTES OF THE VOYAGE TO THE CAPE—VISIT TO THE TRANSVAAL—IMPRESSIONS OF THE BOERS.

AFTER two days spent in London with an old schoolfellow, Scott sailed for the Cape in the Drummond Castle. The voyage passed in the quiet and soothing monotony of the sea. He regarded himself now, however, as a missionary, and though he was pursuing his way to a definite field, he had the spirit which made Wesley say, "The world is my parish." He regarded all with whom he came into contact as the objects of God's love, to be won for Him through love of Christ.

At last, too, in his busy life he found time for communion with God in more unbroken meditation than it had hitherto been his fortune to enjoy; and the waves bore onward one who was earnestly seeking to have his life leave marks behind it not of himself but of his Master. His fellow-passengers and the crew became the objects of his solicitous affection and prayers, not that he regarded himself as *better* than *they*—far otherwise, indeed. He saw amongst them noble fellows with whom he would not compare himself, yet he knew that he possessed a treasure which would make their lives divine. His one regret ever consisted in his feeling that he was unable to help them spiritually to the extent he wished, and he mourned the fact that, whilst every encouragement was given to amusements on board, religious meetings were not recognised to be in any way an essential part of ship life.

"*April* 29, 1889.

"We had service as usual yesterday, Sunday, in the saloon (first class) at 10.30. I can't get on with the English service at all, at all. All my time is occupied hunting up the place, and they read so fast as to give you no time to think. I suppose their wits are nimbler than ours. We had service on the fore-deck in the afternoon, and on the third-class side of the deck in the evening. We sang a lot of hymns afterwards at the piano. It was the most homelike Sunday I have spent since I left.

"Except one of the officers, those in authority seem to think that the fewer religious meetings there are the better. They are very obliging over balls, or concerts, or games, and it is a strange ungracious way of treating religion. I think what must grieve our Lord most is the little we care about Him. He lived for us, and we care little. He died for us, and still we care so little. He rose again and pleads for us, and yet we care so little. We are even ashamed of Him, although He is not ashamed to call us brethren, and He might well have been."

Christian fellowship with kindred hearts proved a source of unalloyed delight.

"I am travelling second class, perhaps I told

you.   I have met a fellow who is going as teacher to Bandawe, Free Church Mission—Stewart by name—and another fellow, Thomson, who is going in the same direction.   I am very glad that I have met them.   We have had much Christian fellowship together."

He was ever seeking opportunities for speaking to others about the divine life.   Although we have been unable to trace any of those who were influenced by him on board, we cannot, in view of the magnetic influence he had over men, doubt that he was the means of leading some to aspirations after God, which resulted in their becoming "missionaries of light."   He found eternal life in the knowledge of God, and consequently sought wisdom at every hand.   Probably none but himself would have dreamed of the advisability of admitting in a missionary meeting in the saloon that, as he had never been in the mission-field, he could offer no authoritative opinion regarding the methods or value of mission-work amongst native races.   It was simply his own humility and anxiety for knowledge that led him to ask any old colonials to give their opinion in the matter. New missionaries, who had less common-sense and not more devotion, might have lectured the older men of experience with the assurance begotten of a common and natural feeling of young men, that the world is out of joint, and that they possess the only grand remedy for putting it right. No man was better qualified than Scott to put right the particular sphere in which he himself was placed, or at least to devise some means to that end, but none ever distrusted so much his power to do so.

"I have asked their permission for the use of the saloon to hold a missionary meeting there to-night to consider our duty in relation to Africa. I spent as much time in prayer as I could all day. There were not the same preparations made for the meeting as for the concert of the previous evening. All the better, perhaps,—we are too apt to trust to machinery in religious matters nowadays, forgetting 'For Thine is the power and the glory.' I came into the saloon at eight o'clock as intimated, and at a quarter-past we began. The 'Patriarch,' one of our passengers, informally introduced the speaker. Among the audience which filled the saloon there were numerous beer-bottles, and empty tumblers, and cards, and some little piles of money. (Henceforth I am teetotal as regards cards.) Most of these unintelligent auditors were removed, however, but the Kings, Queens, and Knaves remained, and the Queen's heads too, in little piles. I rested my eyes upon the last-named auditors till they hid themselves. I told them why I was going as a missionary, dwelt on the fact that we are all missionaries either of light or darkness, spoke of the need of asking ourselves whose missionaries we were, and then said that gambling and betting were not the best preparation for being God's missionaries. I was bound to speak out, though it was like being sent into battle with a bayonet behind you,—to some extent at least. There was plenty of encouragement, however, and it was a much easier task than it would have been in some other boats. Then

I called upon any old colonials to give us a word about things on which we wanted advice. Three others spoke. A Methodist spoke first, especially about the drink question in Africa and other places. Then the 'Patriarch' spoke—that is all the name he got in our cabin. I think he is professor of something somewhere. He has been over a lot of the world, and away up in the heart of Africa. He was most amusing, and also dealt with the effect of drink amongst the natives, told us a long story with a point at the far end of it, and was greatly cheered. Then a lecturer spoke about fair dealings with natives chiefly. He has been in India for a long time. No one else spoke, so we closed with prayer, as we had begun.

"I hope the meeting may make the fellows think, for to see careless Christianity going out to meet heathenism, darkness going to make the darkness deeper, makes one tremble for the ark of God. Let all Christians at home who are interested in missions pray for the passengers of every vessel that leaves for South Africa, for in each the fortunes of Christianity in Africa are wrapped up. There is, so far as I can see, an awful need of Christian life at the borders (Kimberley, Johannesburg, &c.)—more than in absolute heathenism, I think. The fellow with the fine tenor voice and beautiful musical taste who was singing hymns on Sunday night, knowing and liking all the best ones, and was playing Gounod's ' Nazareth ' on Thursday morning, came in rolling drunk on Thursday night. He is going to Kimberley—whose missionary ? "

His schoolboy diffidence in speaking of personal experiences of spiritual life clung to him in his later years. He kept no diary, and whilst on many grounds this is to be regretted, we have the consolation of being able to regard the confidences made in some of his letters as real expressions of his thoughts about divine things, unalloyed by introspections often far from healthy. The letters written during the voyage to his future wife and to two medical friends reveal the inmost depths of his heart. None save his intimate companions would have suspected the thoughts which these show to have been uppermost in his busy life. As his letters written from Blantyre are more or less of an official nature, he shows in them less of this side of his character; and whilst later chapters will show him as a man of action, the reader must judge here what he was as a man of prayer.

"We had a service to-night which was very good, but I want more of the love of Christ for men—oh, much more—very much more! How poor we are in love! How cold at heart —almost incurably so! O Lord, our Saviour, help us to be more and more filled with that deep broad love of Thine."

Evidently he thought much of his responsibility to others, and of the proper method of discharging it. He had learned that there is a time to be silent as well as to speak, and the well-meant but often ill-timed "button-holing" in which many indulge was utterly foreign to his nature.

"God gives me a voice for preaching now; therefore I must use it for that and that alone, else it

is a perversion of the power, is it not ? I must
not use it for public speaking otherwise than
the purpose it was given for. I got it only
for that. That is only fair. But we want
more grace and more charity to all. I think
we get more into the way of doing nothing but
simply asking God to use us as He pleases, and
to take His own way with us. So don't you
think that you are *bound* to speak, or teach, or
say anything. All we have to do is to give
ourselves to God to do what He wishes. If
He needs your voice He will give you the words
and the opportunity, only let us wait at His
gates. That's where I meet you, and I really
feel as if I do meet you there and take your
hand almost. For in Him all the family is one,
and in prayer we all meet together. . . .

" I scarcely ever felt so impotent before speaking. God made it true, however, that when we
are weak then we are strong, for I never had
so much freedom before in speaking of the love
of Christ. It is not because I like to shove
myself forward, for it is sometimes like going to

execution, but I must. May God keep us from all pride which breeds vainglory and presumption, and then we fall."

We have constant evidence that he endeavoured so to order his life that Christ might be commended to all men. On one occasion he was asked to take the chair at a concert on board. After it was over he writes:—

"I had to confess with shame at night that I had not taken Christ with me. I could have gone, I daresay, if I had,—I do not know, but I was not conscious of His presence, and therefore had no right to be there. You will see that what I say is true from the fact that the gentleman who honoured (?) me by asking me to take the chair did not honour the Master by attending service in the afternoon, even though I invited him. Perhaps they think I wish to push myself forward. I would far rather hide myself in the cabin. God grant that we may determine to know nothing in the world but Jesus Christ and Him crucified. Is it not fearful to think how often we are ashamed of Him who was not ashamed to die for us? Oh to live under the powers of the world to come! How different the world does look in the light of those powers!"

The kindly appreciative view he took of his fellow-passengers, and the readiness with which he acknowledged every good point he could discover, as well as his thoughts about poetry and character, are shown in the following description of the concert on board:—

"The concert consisted mostly of songs—all good and healthy. One I do not care for, 'The Storm Fiend,' because I think it is a false view of nature to talk of the power of the storm as a fiend; but the man who sang it is the jolliest, frankest, truest, heartiest Englishman, with a laugh most unfiendish,—a man you would fall in love with if you saw him, I think, so that it was quite easy to forget whatever was unworthy of the singer. Perhaps you will think this hypercritical, but I consider the first requisite of poetry is that it be true (Ruskin, you see!). Then a man sang about 'Other Lips'—a beautiful song, and he has a beautiful voice, but I do not think from the look of him that he is a beautiful character. I don't think you would fall in love with him. Then we had a recitation from a Mr Y——, a fine-looking fellow, a man you admire even from a distance, a true-born Englishman, tall, good-looking, sincere, not stuck up, dressed in cricket clothes, with a cricket hat on the back of his head, and a blue flannel jacket. He recited the ' Charge of Kassassin,' a fine true battle-piece. I like men who are fond of noble pieces and not parodies. There were other songs and a piece by the band, and there was dancing after at which I was not required to be present, and I was glad.

" A good deal of gambling was going on to-day in the cabin amongst three fellows at nap. Whether to say nothing or to speak I do not know. I did not say anything. May God give us more love for our fellow-men, so that we shall grieve for sin more, and be led into the fellowship of the sufferings of Christ. How far we are from that ! How little we care ! People sometimes call men to the Christian life because it is a *happy* life

It is a *blessed* life, 'always rejoicing,' but it is or should be 'as sorrowful,' for we have fellowship with the Man of Sorrows. I am awfully ashamed of myself sometimes. May God keep us from being ashamed of Him.

"I long to be at my work at Blantyre. I almost grudge the time in the Transvaal. I must not spend more than a month there. I begin to long after those brethren whom we have not seen yet. Oh, it's a more difficult thing to live the Christian life away from home! If you don't live constantly with things unseen they grow unreal, and after you have preached Satan whispers to you when you are tired, 'What a fool you are! people don't care a bit. They will go and gamble to-morrow again.' Ay, and so they do—the very man with whom you were pleading to answer the question, 'What think ye of Christ?' at it again to-day. We need to be filled with the Spirit, for we have to trust to nothing but the simple Gospel of Jesus Christ and Him crucified to win the world for Him. Be with me here, for I see it will be a hard battle, especially for me, for I am not good, and am very prone to be half-hearted.

"I was down in the depths reading M'Cheyne's life. My life has been so worldly and selfish. 'As a branch cannot bear fruit of itself except it abide in the vine, no more can ye except ye abide in Me.' Therefore it is no use trying to bear fruit unless we abide in Christ. Again, 'If ye abide in Me, and My words abide in you, ye shall ask what ye will and it shall be done unto you'; but we cannot get what we ask for unless we abide in Him. How much of our work is an attempt to bear fruit without abiding in Christ, and is in consequence like a withered branch. I feel like a child that has not learned to speak, and scarcely even knows its own mind."

The Drummond Castle reached the Cape on the 2d of May, and he spent a few days on shore before sailing for Durban. He there made his first acquaintance with natives, whose occupations brought forcibly to mind his mission - work in Edinburgh.

"There is nothing very remarkable about Cape

Town. There are a great many different classes of natives. I saw Malays, and Kaffirs, and Basuto boys, and negroes, I think. They take the place and do the work of Greenside people at home. It was queer to get the offer of the ‘Argus’ or ‘Cape Times’ from a little brown boy with dirty white legs (dirt is white in Africa, I find). They drive the hansoms, and cabs, and bargains of that kind, and all the carts, and do the lading of the vessels. It is rather amusing to watch them working—such a jabber! They do not seem to have much head for managing affairs, and require pretty constant oversight I should think.”

En route for Blantyre he spent a week or two in the Transvaal on a visit to a favourite sister, Polly, who was married there. The visit afforded him the greatest delight, and its memories were afterwards the more valuable to him owing to her early death. Here, too, he had his first real contact with native races, and his letters show that the problems of mission-work were being carefully considered. That the settlers did not do much, if anything, to lead the Kaffirs to a knowledge of Christianity was a fact which did not escape his keen insight; but he entertained at any rate the thought that some of the blame of the hostility of the whites to the idea that the natives should be Christianised might conceivably be due to unwise missionary methods, which resulted, not so much in the change of will and disposition effected by a real apprehension of the love of God, as in a bastard Christianity, which was only a caricature of the genuine religion of Jesus Christ.

" I do not know what to think about the native question here.   One hears such contradictory opinions.   I've come across very few people, indeed, who believe in sending missionaries to them, and not a single colonial who does what we would call mission-work among them.   These two facts of course go together; but whether it is that missionaries begin to build by working from the top downwards in dealing with natives, and so produce nothing but conceits and caricatures of Christianity, or whether Christianity would necessarily alter the relations between Kaffir and white man, to the intense disgust of the latter, I do not know. The relation of master and servant is a very difficult one to sanctify anywhere, and that's the relation between white and black here. It is rather curious to hear some opinions from those who know (?). One well-educated man said to me that the way to treat a Kaffir is to be fair with him and give him a good licking now and again, and there your duty begins and ends. I do not say that the licking is wrong if it be deserved. It may be the right way; but if you do the parental on the Kaffir's skin, it seems to me you are bound to do the parental all round, and with the same intentions as parents have. People are always slow to see a duty which costs pain and trouble.

"The law towards the Kaffirs is parental too. If a Kaffir steals or offends in any way, he gets licked. At the same time there is a law that no one is allowed to sell drink to a Kaffir. There is, however, one little hitch. If a Kaffir steals, as far as I hear the law catches and licks him pretty quick ; but the Kaffirs who are so inclined get drunk as much as they please, and the law takes no trouble to find out who sold the drink. I am just a little doubtful if the wisdom of the colonials is true wisdom."

In Johannesburg he was asked to preach by the Scottish minister there. He did so, feeling that if the congregation were to maintain itself in any worthy way, it must not be satisfied with services for Scotsmen alone, but must devote itself actively to mission-work amongst the natives. He had no belief in a Christianity that does not show itself possessed by the spirit which seeks to embrace those who are without the knowledge of God.

"There are a great many Kaffirs at Johannesburg working, but as far as I can see scarcely any one cares about them as men. English ideas about natives are perhaps sentimental, but colonial ideas are certainly prejudiced even amongst religious people. It shows what a skin-deep thing religion is. If God, who is in character infinitely higher than we are, humbled Himself to the cross to serve us, shall we think ourselves so infinitely much better than Kaffirs that we consider it folly to think of living to serve them? With such an example I think we should gladly be fools for Christ's sake.

"I could not get hold of a sermon on Saturday night, so went to bed, awoke at 4 A.M., and got one then. I find that it is only when you are emptied of all natural powers that you get a message which leaves no room for boasting. I got a good many good wishes from some of the people. I have one fear for the Church at Johannesburg. If they do not start mission-work among the Kaffirs there they will drift like M—— into formalism, which is like opium-smoking."

Wider views of the hope of Christianity in Africa were forced upon him whilst he was in the Transvaal.

"I had a short talk with T—— on Saturday. He wished to know what means of transport, &c., there is up the Zambesi to Tete. A good many people's eyes are being turned towards the Mashona country. It is a splendid country, well - watered, rich in minerals of all kinds.

Selous, the great South African hunter, is, I believe, organising an expedition to that country, and I should not wonder if very soon it be opened up to Europeans, with perhaps a richer gold-field than even that of Johannesburg. If so, we missionaries should make a push there too, for I believe that at the meeting of the waters missionaries are most needed."

In view of the interest aroused in the Boers by recent events, some of his notes regarding them may not be uninteresting.

" They have the Dopper Church, which I expect is something like our old Cameronians, and two other Churches differ much, I expect, as our Free and U.P. do—quite unintelligibly to outsiders. Their monthly gatherings are something like the Highland preachings. They sing as slow as would please the 'pest Hielant man that neffer wass,' and it is nearly as difficult to make out the tune as it is sometimes in the North. I recognised Old Hundred by remembering well what note came last. The Dutch are very like Scotch country-people, even in face. I have seen typical Scotch faces, with high cheek-bones, &c. They seem a good deal like in character too, and are just as fond of their independence. They are much liker the Scotch than English people are."

"It gets so cold sometimes at night in this country that the sheep are killed by it, or at least very much damaged. George found that in the Free State it made a difference of 20° F. between a thermometer placed on the grass open to the sky and one with a covering from the open sky. He tried to persuade the Dutch farmers that if they would simply have a shed, however rough, open on all sides but covered overhead, for their sheep, they would save them. But the Dutch are 'dour' (that's the pronunciation, I don't know the spelling). They call any one who does not know Dutch 'dom,' they themselves being 'dom' to everything but Dutch. New ideas take a very long time to force their way into their heads. Railways even have not yet (1889) found their way, though they would increase the value of Boer property to a very large extent."

I

CHAPTER VIII.

QUILIMANE—NATIVE MUSIC—FOURTEEN DAYS ON
THE KWAKWA.

THE mission party arrived at Quilimane on Sunday, 15th July, and after the usual delays incident to the African coast, proceeded up the Kwakwa towards Vicenti. His stay in Quilimane, though short, was sufficiently long to give him very strong opinions regarding the capacity of Portuguese officials there.

" Quilimane is a really pretty place. The chief street has a pavement no less on one side, and an avenue of acacia with long black pods hung all over them—plenty of cocoanut palms about, and some very good houses. The one we were in was large with lofty rooms, a very large verandah, and

walls 3 or 4 feet thick ; for Quilimane was a
flourishing place in the slave-trading days not
many years ago, and the town was built by slaves.
The punishment the Portuguese have to suffer is
an incubus of laziness and incapacity all round
this coast. They seemingly cannot do anything
but squat at the mouths of the rivers and collect
as much toll as they can get, and I expect it will
not be long before the course of the river alters
and leaves them on the mud with their laziness
for company."

He has left a racy description of a future journey
up the Kwakwa in an Arab dhow which we shall
quote in this chapter. The present experience was
to Scott something of the nature of a picnic. His
long-looked-for work was at hand ; he was among
the natives to whom his life was to be devoted,
and his keen eye was busy noting every particular
that came before him which in any way would
assist him in understanding African life.

"The boys use, not oars, but spoon-shaped
paddles, and (where the river is shallow) poles.
They are as jolly a set of fellows as ever I saw.

Their wants are small, being limited to a small piece of cloth.   All they need for dinner utensils is a set of clean fingers.   You should hear the laughing and chattering and joking that goes on round the camp-fire at night, and indeed during a large part of the day too.   The world has not grown old yet with them anyhow.   All crabbed and inhuman theologians should take a journey up the Kwakwa with a crew of ' naked savages.' It would do them much good.   People at home may talk about the hardships of a missionary's life, but between you and me it has been just the most delightful and prolonged picnic I ever had."

The dangers of river-travelling in Africa are well known.   An experienced traveller once remarked to the writer about them : " If you are going to live in Africa you should avoid the lakes and the rivers.   They are very pretty so far as scenery is concerned, and very useful so far as transit goes, but if you wish to *live* stick to the hills."   The malarial poison that lurks along their banks has been the death of many a friend of Africa.   Scott escaped fever on the way up the Kwakwa, and he speculated a good deal on plans by which other people might escape it as well.   He went to Africa to teach the native, but he thought that in matters of health the native might quite well be able to give his white brother some useful lessons.

"We took tea in one of the boats.   That's not a good plan though.   There's a damp malarial smell near the water at sundown.   The proper way is to squat round a fire as the natives do. There is no smell there at all.   The natives *always* light a fire and sit round it at night; they say they would be sick if they did not. White people are always stupid—some to an incredible degree, but all to some degree.   When you come up the Kwakwa you will have a fire lighted at sundown, and take tea round it and not in the boat."

At Mopea the party met Mr Selous waiting for his carriers to come together, and there they got news that a man-of-war had arrived at Quilimane with Consul (now Sir H. H.) Johnston of Mozambique—an evidence that Britain at last had awakened to the fact that she had interests in that part of the world which were worth preserving.

"The Portuguese have been going a little too far lately. I hope Britain is going to step in. What is the use of spending men's lives in opening up a country if it is only to allow these scamps to come in and blight it? That's all they do, and nothing else. Everything that can debase a country they bring in. On the side of the oppressors there is power, and the only use they make of it is to force taxes from the natives, so that they raise about £1600 from one of their tax-farms at Mopea, in return for which the natives get nothing. They are at present sending 300 Zulus armed with Martini-Henry rifles to get more country among the Makololos. I understand the so-called vindictive Psalms of David now."

He was very much delighted to find real musical talents amongst the natives who acted as the crew for the expedition. Probably visions of future work like that he had left among his Greenside boys floated before his mind, and he promised himself many happy times in training them to sing the praises of God when he was settled among them.

"Some of the canoe - boys sing very well—mostly minorsort of chants, often with a chorus and refrain. They dig their paddles into the water with great force, sometimes with a quick stroke, sometimes with a long and short alternately, and when they are in very good spirits, a clap with the paddles on the boat between the strokes. I tried to take down some of the chants while Mr Hetherwick took down the words. I will not vouch that they are quite correct, as it is very difficult to know what note of the scale they start on. They have the same scale as we have—at least the few gourd pianos I have seen have our scale, generally starting with Soh of the scale and going up to Fe of the scale above—rather a curious arrangement. I give you the result of our investigations. The Mazaro boys who live about here are much better singers than the Quilimane boys, and the Lake people are said to be better still. They have a good many variations of their own which I could not pick up, and of course you want the accompaniment of the stroke of the paddle to make the music sound well at all, but when you have all that it is very pretty. The second part I have not been able to get correctly. There is a queer interval in it which is taken by a single voice.

Chorus—*Sen-sen senenka muno.*

Verse 1. *Kwatu kuli nyama.*
At our home there is food.

2. *Kwatu kuli mbusi.*
At our home there are goats.

3. *Kwatu kuli ng'ombe.*
At our home there are oxen.

&c., *ad infinitum*, with the chorus after every verse."

A month after their arrival at Quilimane Scott and his companions reached Blantyre, after vexatious delays, unintelligible to those accustomed to the promptness and regularity of civilised modern travelling. A year and a half later he came again over this route, the delays then being, if anything, in an aggravated form, and calling forth the following humorous letter :—

" I am going to write a book and call it ' Fourteen Days on the Kwakwa in an Arab Dhow,' and the impression left on the reader's mind will be that the Kwakwa is a majestic continental river, and the dhow a slaving craft captured by us and put to a nobler use. Anything about Central Africa pays just now. I don't see why we should not be in the swim. The real fact of course is, that ' Fourteen Days on the Forth and Clyde Canal in a Barge ' would be just as interesting and impressive, and a very close likeness too; but people at home don't know that, if you don't or can't tell them. It is a fact though ! We were fourteen days on the Kwakwa in an Arab dhow. It would take too long to tell all the odds and ends of circumstances that produced such a historic event—we will leave that for the book and begin :—

" The 2d day of April 1891, at sunset, saw us

leaving the pier at Quilimane in a dismasted sea-going dhow of —— tons burden, with all the drunkards of Quilimane for a crew. They had been paid beforehand, just in time to allow them to go home to say Good-bye to their families and friends, and fortify against the start. Some had over-fortified, but we quickly enrolled ourselves as volunteers, and with the help of those that were fortified to the fighting degree, we slowly, silently forged ahead. It was not promising. Unknown dangers and difficulties lay ahead, a faithless crew, &c., &c.; but we yoked to, and so did the mosquitoes. The fourteen days and nights that followed we shall sample only.

"Of course we suffered all the incident of African travel. Our men deserted us—four out of the twelve. It had been found necessary to chastise one man, but only slightly and informally. He did not run away, but on the spot two others did. Being in a hurry we had no time to pursue. That same night two others deserted, and escaped in the darkness. The name of one was Mr Feather-both-ways. He had learned to feather his oar in his young days, and he always did so when no one was looking. The influence of the other three also had always been down-stream, so that their loss really was our gain. Our loss was their gain on their side (always look on the bright side!). Besides, we were in a hurry, and had to work so hard ourselves that it was difficult to look after all the laggards.

"Some day those men will be taught deportment, but as yet there is only a Portuguese school for it.

"We ran aground twice in mid-stream, but fortunately the vessel's timbers were very strong, and the pace we were going about ·5 knots an hour, so no one was hurt. We all landed to get the vessel off, but she was no 'lighter'—she was a dhow. The second time we struck was just within sight of our destination, almost within buckshot of it, or, according to our calculation, not more than a day off with fair poling-ground, or less than a day off rowing.

"So near and yet so far! We were never more than two days from our destination all the time.

" All those days the ducks and geese flew by us, sighed after, but unfollowed. Being in a hurry, hard steady work being our only hope, we could not go after them, even though food was getting scarce. There had been a slip in the commissariat department; we had provision for one man for six days, while we were at least twice that number of men for more than twice that number of days. We were reduced to pouring hot water on old tea-leaves before the relief expedition found us—*i.e.*, before a canoe we had hailed on its way down passed us again on its way up. One old Banian trader was touchingly kind to us. He had no tea for sale, but he shared his last two private tea-spoonfuls with us. We gave him some of our last tin of sugar in return. Unfortunately his resources were limited, and none of his richer brethren would help us. The inhabitants too were unfriendly : we could buy nothing except at prohibitive prices. Portuguese officials too made a show of helping, but said aside that they did not know ' istos gentos ' (it was bad Latin and worse manners) ; ' those gents ' being in their shirt sleeves, one at the helm and the rest at the poles, perhaps they were to be excused.

" No novelist could imagine a more unprogressive way of working—on the outside oars no rowlocks, but bits of *nkuni* (firewood) rammed in for pins, to which the oars were tied with *maluzi* (native string), or anything, and on the shore-side poles mostly forked at the end. Being a sea-going boat she answered her helm and gripped the water, $3\frac{1}{2}$ feet of it, beautifully; at the same time the water beautifully gripped her, so that if we rounded a corner where the stream ran fast, and neglected to hold grimly on with both hands to the trees or grass at the side, out went her head, and off we went to the other side. Time elapsed before the *maluzi* could be untied, the *nkuni* pins extracted, the oars shipped, shifted, and fastened at the other side, while the polemen in the meantime struggled across between them, and it was a wonder if we did not dine where we had lunched. It would not have been so bad if the river had had any bank or any bottom, but for days and days (by our reckoning) the deep grass at the side kept us from both, giving about as good a hold for a pole as a pile of loose hay; and if there was not grass at the side there were loose bushes.   We tried all sorts of inventions to help the speed.   A sail of course was the first, a good-sized sail too, for an ordinary craft.   I almost think it saved us a day or two, but as every time it was hoisted or lowered all the work stopped to look on, and while it was up it was expected to do wonders—the problem is not an easy one.   A tow-rope on the bank was another idea, but a clump of trees at the water's edge where the men could not get under, nor the rope get over, soon put that light out.   Then we tried a canoe out ahead with a long rope.   It did fairly well; but if the rope got away under the floating grass, we had to pull a lot of things up besides the dhow, rather like a dredging excursion.   On the whole, too, the crew did not take kindly to innovations; they had to have a day or two to learn each new one.   One good thing at least they did—they kept one's brain working, which is all-important for a man who does not smoke.

" But, looking back, what a delightful panorama of Kwakwa life we witnessed—the canoes with their piles of native produce, ground-nuts, and fowls, and vegetables, or demijohns of rum for Portuguese territory-up country, passing and re-passing us on their way to the coast. Every now and then a Portuguese family boat would pass us, or we would hear in the still night the chant of the sugar-company's boat's crew swinging up the river, and then, days later, the same chant of the same boat swinging down the river again. And then the animal life!—egrets greater and lesser, kingfishers little and big, geese, ducks, cranes, herons, adjutant-birds, snakes that almost fell on us off the trees as we passed,—all these *outside* the boat. The lesser egrets were the commonest. One we passed must have had a nest or something hidden on the bank. A member of our party who is a naturalist said he never saw one behave so strangely—flying in front and behind, and then in front again, then settling for a moment most un-easily. I am no naturalist, but I guess she thought we meant to stop, and could not make out whether we had stopped or not.   We had no reason for stopping there—we were going full pace ahead.

"We passed a barge with a crew of four men on its way up, and we were proud.   It was the only thing we did pass except what was actually stationary like the egret's nest.   But it passed us again, like the rest of the panorama, so our pride was short-lived.

"However, the longest entertainment comes to an end at last.   So did ours, and we arrived at Vicenti, hungry for news of the outside world."

CHAPTER IX.

THE OPENING UP OF CENTRAL AFRICA.

BEFORE we proceed to follow Dr Scott through the work of his six short years in Africa, it will not be out of place to bring before our readers the condition and nature of the scene of his labours, in a very rapid survey of the present state of the country to which he came.

If one wishes to estimate the rate at which discovery and civilisation have advanced in the Dark Continent, he cannot have a better object-lesson than in a comparison of a map of Africa as it appeared in the atlas he used at school with one published within the last year. Then we had a fringe of territory round the coast pretty well defined ; the supposed courses of the rivers,

however, marked by broken lines, indicating that
we did not know positively whence they came,
and showing now that our guesses were very
wide of the mark.   The interior of the map was
filled in by the suggestive title written from the
edge of the Sahara to the borders of British
territory in the south, DESERT.   But our map
of to-day shows that this supposed desert is
in reality a country of great resources and marvellous wealth.   The gold-fields of the Transvaal
have opened a new chapter in the history of the
south ; Rhodesia spreads away up to the Zambesi,
and the development of this province under the
Chartered Company we may expect to proceed
with phenomenal energy.   The continent now
from the Congo to Zanzibar is being developed
by the Congo Free State and the European
Powers, under whose influence its several parts
lie.   What was charitably supposed to be desert
has been proved to be a land of "mountain and
flood," with a teeming population, and the world
has suddenly awakened to the part Africa may
play in the history of progress and commerce.

The change which has been brought about in British Central Africa can be best explained by a rapid survey of the map as it now appears. The river Zambesi flows in Portuguese territory from the 30th parallel of longitude to the coast. Of this river the Shiré is a most important tributary, navigable for many miles. On the course of this river, a few miles from its junction with the Zambesi, British Central Africa in its eastern portion begins. From this point inland, at Livingstone's death, the land was named from the chiefs of the several districts, except in the few instances where Mackenzie's expedition had left its imprint in a name, or a solitary traveller had succeeded in doing the same. Now, as we sail up the Shiré, we have Port Herald and Blantyre; to the east, Fort Lister and Mlanje; Fort Sharpe on the Upper Shiré, and Fort Johnston keeping guard at the south end of Lake Nyasa at the point whence the Shiré issues. Beyond the British Protectorate, but within our sphere of influence, we are met with Fort Rhodes at the south end of Lake Tanganyika, Fort Rosebery on the Luapula at a distance of over 1000 miles from Quilimane north of the delta of the Zambesi. Communication was always a matter of months, and, as Livingstone found, it might be of years. To-day we are already in telegraphic communication with Blantyre, and within a very short time the line will be extended from Blantyre to Zomba, thence again to a point on the Shiré, along the left bank of which it will proceed to Fort Johnston.   Communication is maintained by steamers between the various points on the lake, and the telegraph line will again start from Karonga at the north end of Lake Nyasa ; it will be continued to Abercorn at the south end of Lake Tanganyika, and steam communication will then bring Ujiji, the place where Stanley found Livingstone, within ten days of London !   In place of the old river-boats paddled by natives, which were the curse of all travellers on the Zambesi and Shiré, steamers run regularly from Katunga's (thirty miles from Blantyre) to the Chinde mouth of the Zambesi, and bring up their passengers with a despatch that mitigates to a considerable extent the risk of the terrible malaria of the route.

The slave-trader at one time held as his own all the fair lands in the lake district; the slave-route to the coast passed near Blantyre, to the sorrow of missionaries, who were powerless to help; but now, under British administration, the Arab trader will be speedily forced to betake himself to lawful trade, or to depart, for the traffic in "black ivory" is put down by the strong hand of the military.

The land was twenty years ago the habitat of the lion and the hyena; the Angoni from across the Shiré came down on the tribes inhabiting the hills, and these again were at constant war with the river-men. Zomba, Chiradzulo, and Mlanje—familiar names in African mission story — were centres of the Arab slave-trade. And now, all over the Shiré Highlands we find flourishing coffee - plantations, roads well made, wars at an end save in the interests of slavery. There is now a Resident Commissioner of the British Crown with the necessary officers, and a force of Sikh soldiers who have done great service in the expeditions against the slave - traders. On Zomba there stands a British Consulate; its slopes are marked by the coffee - plantations of the late Messrs Buchanan, and at its foot nestles the mission station of Domasi. We may expect wars rapidly to cease, and the development of the country to proceed steadily.

To what, then, is all this change due? We may answer unhesitatingly that in the first place it is the direct result of Christian missions. It is well known that the work of Moffat and Livingstone was distinctly a missionary work, undertaken in the case of the latter for the purpose of saving the African from the human vultures that preyed upon him in the guise of Arab slave-traders, and from the superstition which made him prey upon himself. The favourite dream of Livingstone was the foundation of Christian colonies amongst them which would suffice as centres of both religious and educational work. Explorer and statesman though he was, he had the firm conviction that nothing but Christianity would save Africa — the scheme of the colony being, as he thought, the most suitable for accomplishing the Christianising of the natives.

He claimed to have made an open door by which the Church could enter to save Africa from its double burden of slavery and superstition. The first response to Livingstone's appeal for men to open up for Christ that magnificent interior, with its inland seas, its wooded heights, its navigable rivers, came from the universities of England and Ireland, who sent out a party under the leadership of Bishop Mackenzie—a fellow-countryman of the traveller. This party Livingstone himself led to the Shiré Highlands, his long experience telling him that, amongst the generally unhealthy conditions of life for Europeans in Central Africa, the elevated situation of this part would present fewer than most others. Death soon thinned this little band; war broke out amongst the tribes—or rather it continued in its usual intermittent fashion—famine supervened on its ravages, and the survivors were forced back to the coast. Livingstone himself followed Mackenzie to the grave in 1873, and the story of how his heart lies in the Africa of his love, and his body in Westminster, to which an admiring and mourning people consigned it, is one of the triumphs which the love of God in man can accomplish.

Hannington, Mackay (another Scotsman), and many others have made Uganda's name as familiar in the ears of Anglo - Saxon Christians as Iona, or Tara, or Canterbury. At Lake Nyasa the Livingstonia Mission of the Free Church of Scotland is stationed, and in the Shiré Highlands that of the Church of Scotland, which attains its majority next year, having been founded in 1876.

The centre of this last mission is Blantyre— named after Livingstone's birthplace — and likely to become the capital of East Central Africa. This is now a thriving town, which, as the Commissioner in his report to Parliament (1894) acknowledges, owes its existence to the mission. With the party that went to prospect for the Livingstonia Mission of the Free Church of Scotland, there went also Henry Henderson, the pioneer of the Church of Scotland Mission. He forsook the rivers and lakes as being probably good enough as means of communication or travel, but inexpedient for the residence of Europeans, owing to the dread malaria. His inclinations led him in the direction of the Shiré Highlands—the old choice of Livingstone—and there he decided his Church should begin work. The first missionaries went out in 1876 with the purpose of carrying out Livingstone's policy, which in practice did not work well, and in 1881 the mission was reorganised on its present basis. Until the missionaries went no white man was seen there, with the exception of an occasional explorer or hunter, or perhaps some Portuguese half-caste hunting for slaves. The Gospel opened the way; then followed the trader. The African Lakes Company was formed to combine trade with sympathetic action towards missionary work. The natives were found to be sunk in superstition, idleness, and slavery, and the mission-work has proceeded largely on the lines of undoing the evils of the situation as seen in the native mind. Superstition has been made to face the facts of the Gospel and of science through the medical mission; idleness is met by the teaching of trades and the employment of men in the industrial work; and slavery, which would, one cannot doubt, have died, but with a harder fight for life, is met with the Christian truth of the love of God to man, and it has now to reckon as well with the force of arms under the Administration.

Once at least, in 1884, the personal influence of the missionary saved the European residents from destruction—the Rev. David Clement Scott being able, through the friendship of the Makololo chief, himself to turn back the war-flood. The raids of the Angoni were stopped by the influence of the same missionary. In British Central Africa the missionary undoubtedly opened the way for the trader, and the development that has taken place is certainly due in the first instance to the influence of the Gospel. Amongst the earliest planters were those who were originally members of the mission staff. There may be to-day between 4,000,000 and 5,000,000 coffee plants in the Shiré provinces. Coffee was first imported and planted by one of the industrial missions, and when it had been once demonstrated that it could be grown to profit there was no lack of settlers. The claims that Britain could urge upon the right of protectorate over this portion of Nyasaland were beyond all question. Without reckoning the expenditure of capital outside the Church, that of the Church of Scotland had already been very large when Portugal claimed the territory; and it was unquestionably the right acquired over all the district through the possession of it by our Churches for Christ that made Lord Salisbury say " Hands off!" to Portugal in 1891, and declare Nyasaland a protectorate under the Crown. The future in store for the country seems undoubtedly a very bright one. The conditions of health may improve, and as Christianity spreads amongst the natives, many customs which operate against the elevation of the African will be removed. Indeed Sir H. H. Johnston, in the report already referred to, states his conviction that it is safer to leave such customs as that of the *unyaga* dances "to die out by the spread of missionary teaching."

CHAPTER X.

EARLY DAYS IN BLANTYRE.

BLANTYRE was now fast becoming a most important centre of commerce and population. Very rapidly its whole character was changing. Till recently the only white people there were the members of the staff; the officials of the African Lakes Company and a few travellers, or members of the Livingstonia or University Missions proceeding inland, had been their only visitors. But by the time Scott arrived planters had begun to settle, and there soon followed him—as Consul-General —the future Commissioner of her Majesty. Till this time the mission had been the centre not only of the religious life of the district, but also of the administrative life as well. Native causes were

constantly brought to the missionaries for settle-
ment, and the chief of the mission staff was the
"father" of the people. Henceforth, in a few
months, all this was changed. The Administration
became the centre of executive power, and the
disputants in legal causes were now forced to
bring their cases before Government officials, not
altogether to Dr Scott's regret. On its prominent
site was rising the beautiful church at Blantyre—
a triumph of patience and genius, and a monument
to the energy of the senior missionary, who taught
first himself and then the natives to make the
bricks ; who drew the plans and acted as his own
master of works, his colleagues, Messrs Buchanan
and M'Ilwain being his builder and carpenter
respectively. At no time had they more than
eight native artisans—none of whom, it is said,
had at any moment the least idea of what their
work was to produce. Scott came to a station
where now there were the rudiments of a native
church ready for organisation, with native teachers
and preachers. The foundations were already laid.
He had to help to build upon other men's

foundations, to aid in the reaping of what others had sown, whilst at the same time he was called upon to sow in new soil, and to open up the way for others.

The native printing press was now constantly at work. The carpenter's shop and the gardener's work were holding an important place in the education of the native; and the translation of the Bible into the native tongue was proceeding apace, the Rev. D. C. Scott having already, by his Mang'anja Dictionary, reduced the native language to writing.

Scott was among friends at Blantyre. His brother—the Rev. D. C. Scott, B.D.—was already there; his old Edinburgh acquaintance, Dr Bowie, with his wife; his class-fellow, the Rev. Robert Cleland, was at Mlanje; and the Rev. Alex. Hetherwick, B.D., in charge at Domasi. There were, besides, the industrial members of the staff.

To all he proved himself a willing coadjutor, whilst, on the points of mission polity regarding which he differed from them, he clung with his wonted persistence to his own opinion.

His first Sunday in Blantyre must have been a red-letter day in his life, because then for the first time his mouth was opened to speak of the things of the Kingdom of God to the natives of Africa. After morning service he accompanied all the white people of the staff to a native village belonging to a chief—Maundi by name. An address was given first by his brother, who then acted as his interpreter. The line he took in speaking to them was the one which might have been expected. He had around him men whose lives only wanted one thing to make them great. They believed in spirits; but the good spirits did not obtain from them any love or reverence, as they needed not to fear them. The whole effort of their religious rites was to defeat the purposes of the evil malignant spirits who brought trouble upon them, or to propitiate these by any possible means. Their troubles and superstitions he knew could be overcome only by the knowledge of the love of God, and at once he began to speak to them of the love of God. He carried his old Edinburgh feeling towards men to the mission-field, for he proceeded to tell them that the black man and the white were equal before God, and that the missionaries had come to do them good. God had given the white men something that would be useful to the black, and he hoped they would be received as brothers, and that they would listen to the Good News which was brought from the far-off land.

He thought rather much time was taken up in deciding disputes among the natives, although probably the missionaries had been drawn into the position of arbiters almost without seeking it. Still one would hardly expect Scott to take the trouble of inquiring how what he considered an error came to exist; and as he thought, whether erroneously or not, that it did not conduce to the bringing of men to know Christ, he took the first opportunity of his preaching in the English service to sound what was believed to be a note of warning on the subject, taking as his text, "Man, who made me a judge or a divider over you?" One can do justice to the frank manly spirit that made him speak of what seemed wrong, not so much with others as with that particular work with

which he was specially identified, whilst at the
same time we entertain a real doubt of the
possibility of his having had long enough experience to pronounce an opinion on the matter at all.

His energies for the first months of his stay in
Blantyre were concentrated on the language, the
want of the knowledge of which was a terrible
trouble to one of his active temperament. In
the times between study he seems to have turned
his hand to anything—making a sketch of the
neighbourhood, manufacturing a mould for a brick,
or attending to a patient.

“ I have lots to do and cannot do it till I have
Mang’anja, so I am ‘ wiring in ’ as hard as my
stupid castle-in-the-air-building head will allow me.
I am going to hire a native with a *chikoti* (whip)
to give me a lick up every time I am caught
building in the air, and I have printed up on
my wall, ‘ Ugwire nchito pamene pantawi pausana
chifukwa usiku utodza pamene muntu sangate
kugwira nchito ’ (‘ Work while it is day, because
the night cometh when no man can work ’).”

The church at Blantyre was drawing towards

completion when he arrived, although it was not opened till 10th May 1891. The most of the finishing touches in the way of painting, &c., were given by his own artistic hand, and he recognised that his fears about a sermon in stone and lime had been groundless.

"The church would remind one very much of Sweetheart Abbey—of course on a very small scale. It is a sort of miraculous thing to me. David is architect, Mr Buchanan the builder, and Mr M'Ilwain, carpenter and brickmaker, &c. . . . It has taken an enormous number of bricks, all made here by natives. . . . I am busy at odd times with a mould to put an ornamental line round at the level of the top of the arches. We have thought of a sort of arcade of pine-apples.

" . . . I was a wee doubtful about the justice of a swell church like this when the Church visible is so deeply invisible as yet—individual determination for God being scarcely more than a wish as yet—but it brings more men to the place, and that from far and near; it teaches them work and the fruits of work—beauty. And they hear the Gospel every day—and see it too; for I have never come across a more Christian life than Mr M'Ilwain. He has all the charge of the workmen, and the brickmaking, and the carpentry in the place, and so he is 'weel kent.' I do not mean to sound his praises abroad, for that's not a useful occupation, but of course I tell you what strikes me."

His early letters abound with lamentations over the hindrance caused by his ignorance of the language, and with kindly notices of all and sundry about the station. For a lady specially interested in one of the mission girls he wrote:—

"Ndendemera is a good-looking, nice little girl. I should like to get a sketch of her if possible. She is of the richest chocolate colour—almost black. Those horrid photographs give no idea of the natives. You would think that they are uglier than ugly—especially the girls. The native African is very often a beautiful creature, as you might expect—large black eyes like the eyes of a deer often, and the ruddy chocolate is a beautiful colour (when it is clean!!), though it turns to an ugly whitey-blue-black when dirty —which it sometimes is."

Only one health note regarding himself appears :—

" Fever has not caught me yet ; I hope to have the language up before it does, so that I shall know what to say to it."

The question of his own particular sphere in the mission-work was well canvassed during these probationary months of linguistic study. Already the mission was working at three centres — Blantyre itself, Domasi at the foot of Mount Zomba, and Chiradzulo, which was regarded as a stage on the way to the Mlanje Mission. Scott had for six or seven years regarded himself as specially preparing for work amongst the warlike Angoni—a tribe of Zulus who at an unknown period had migrated from the south, and settled in the northern part of the land lying between the Shiré and the Zambesi. His own adventurous disposition made this work a peculiarly happy prospect, and as a friendship with Chikuse had been formed in 1881, and a promise made by the mission to fix a station amongst his people, everything seemed favourable. Twice he made a journey to the Angoni country, and he assisted in founding a small out-station there; but his own hope of settling among his soldier friends was never realised.

Another scheme occupied much of his attention too. South of the Angoni country lies the land of the Makololo, who will be ever remembered as the faithful friends and carriers of Livingstone. Mission-work among them could be carried on only by residence on the river—an extremely risky process so far as health was concerned. It was thought that both projects might be carried out together, and the prospect of the arrival of his friend and class-fellow, Dr H. E. Scott, now of the Domasi Mission, seemed to him to point to a way of accomplishing this. This was the subject of his first official letter to the home Committee and he suggested that a hill-station should be formed amongst the Angoni, and that this should be wrought alternately with the river by two medical missionaries.

"It would not be wise to keep the same man working on the river continually on account of health considerations. Therefore we should require a man to exchange from the high country at intervals. Blantyre is at a convenient distance from the river to allow this, but Blantyre needs one permanent head; and, moreover, if we start medical work on the river, it must be continuous and not intermittent. That being so, the question arises, 'Where should the other station be planted?' The solution that commends itself to all of us is that we plant a station among the Angoni which would be two or three days' journey away, and exchange between that and the river as required.

"It is perhaps more than a coincidence that Mr H. E. Scott, who is taking the same kind of preparatory course as myself—viz., Medicine and Divinity—and who independently, so far as he himself is concerned, has determined for Africa, is to be ready in July. . . .

"I do not know yet how the work on the river will shape itself. I think we should require a permanent station at some considerable centre, and work up and down by boat to a considerable extent.”

His official letter closed with a reference to his troubles with the language, which is interesting, as it contains one of the very few remarks he ever made about his own struggle to make ends meet :—

“I have been doing scarce anything but grind at the language since I came up, and I foresee a good many months’ work yet before I shall be able to speak it. Half-grips will not do in the matter, so I shall not think of other work until I have mastered it. I am in that sort of despairing condition which I suppose every one experiences while trying to learn to speak a native language. One cannot be expected to speak while climbing a hill ; at least I cannot till I get to the top. As far as I have come yet, life has been one hill after another, sometimes with five minutes to take breath, sometimes without, but not much time for talking.”

CHAPTER XI.

DOMASI—CHIRADZULO—AFRICAN LAND QUESTION—
PROSPECTING TOUR IN ANGONILAND.

EARLY in this year Scott was sent to the mission
station at Domasi, where he continued his studies
of the native language, and acted as medical officer
for the station. A fellow-worker there tells me
that he never actually knew of the Doctor having
his room to himself overnight, and that on many
occasions he must have slept sitting on his chair.
His bed was one that could be converted into an
arm-chair during the day; his apartment was a
very small one, and it was quite a scientific
business to steer one's way over the floor at
night without trampling on some native boy

for whom the Doctor had turned his own room into a hospital. Frequently there were so many of them that there was not room on the floor for the bed—but this was of no concern to Scott so long as his "boys" were comfortable.

His mechanical gifts were of considerable service here. Across the stream, which in the rainy seasons was impassable as it came rushing down from Mount Zomba, he threw a large tree, smoothed it with an adze, and put a hand-rail across it, thus making the road such that it could be used at all seasons.

His great feats of walking were soon a matter of wonder all over the district. The *machila* (hammock carried by bearers) he despised, except when he was ill. Once he started from Blantyre with a party—himself in a *machila* like the rest; but in the course of half an hour he got down in disgust, walked on foot the rest of the way, with his carriers panting after him, hardly able to keep up. Here is an example of the conditions under which his work was often done :—

"MLUNGUSI, *April* 1890.

" If it had not been for the rain I would not have started this letter at this particular place and time, but should have gone right on to Domasi. . . . I have been here for an hour. I left Chiradzulo this morning (call that thirty miles), carried a gun all that way, and would have gone on to Domasi (eight miles more), but, as I said, the rain met me just as we were about an hour from here, and came on like a flood. It rained like the heaviest home thunder-shower. It makes crossing streams and getting drinks easy for one who is so wet that one can't be wetter. So we just walk through the streams and take a drink in the middle. It takes hard work to get tired. I am far too well."

Chiradzulo was then in charge of the Rev. Robert Cleland, who was holding it as a kind of advance-guard for a missionary assault on Mlanje. During this year Scott had much to do in aiding Cleland in peculiarly difficult cir-cumstances. For three years Cleland had held

this outpost alone, in the midst of wild surroundings—with a slaving robber-chief just beside him, who had great hopes that the presence
of the missionary might aid him in securing power
over neighbouring tribes. In his letter just
quoted, he continues about this station :—

" Yesterday (Sunday) I spent with Cleland at
his menagerie at Chiradzulo. He has no show
of lions just now, however — chiefly baboons.
He has been doing some missionary work in
shooting them. They are at present perfectly
swarming now that the maize is ripe. Fathers,
mothers, and children come down to feed, and the
poor human women have no chance. The baboons sit round them and munch; when they
have to go away they carry with them a bundle
of maize-heads, slung over their shoulders with
the ends of them in their mouths (Cleland has
actually seen an old male do that). He keeps
the snake part of his menagerie in his food-store
—that which opens into his bedroom without a
door between. His cat was killed by a bite from
one specimen the other day. . . . His worst ani-

mal, however, is one that lives far up the mountain. It has kept a woman in a slave-stick for the last two years. Cleland has not got him tamed yet.

"We were round the parish on Sunday upon the hillside, and had three services at three villages in the forenoon. Cleland is a real nice fellow, made of Livingstone kind of stuff. He is all alone there, and he told me he sometimes talks to a native boy as if he were his dearest friend,— in an incidental way he did so—only to me, for he does not say much in that way."

While living at Domasi he gave the Blantyre people a surprise one night by walking in upon them just after evening service—minus coat, vest, and bed-bundle, which did not arrive till next day with his bearers. He left Domasi at half-past three in the previous afternoon, stayed at Mlungusi overnight, left at 6.15 next morning, and walked straight into Blantyre, a distance of fifty-eight miles.

All kinds of work fell to his lot. Cases for his medicine shelves he made himself. "It has to be done," he writes, " and I have to do it, so the sooner the better." No doctor at home ever expended more care on a good patient than those natives experienced from Scott. " I had a boy bad with fever in my house here. I was afraid about him one night and did not undress. He is a very nice boy, with a pretty refined face, but it was terrible work getting him to take medicine. I never had such bother before. I had another bad case of fever away up on the hill—5000 or 6000 feet up. I was rather afraid of him, but he got all right ; and the next thing I hear is that one of our station boys who has a sore on his leg has gone home to that same village to get medicine there ! They are very stupid indeed."

Orders came from home that Scott should be sent on a pioneering expedition to determine the direction in which the mission should extend. This was quite to his mind—the more so because he had begun to fear that his medical knowledge was to be used in such a way that personally he could have no share in evangelising the natives in a district of his own. The thought of this was rather a sore one, and finds expression in several of his letters. The desire so to use him did not exist — the order against immediate extension being due to the financial straits of his society.

"I am on a prospecting tour to see where we shall set our foot next. The Committee at home want us to huddle together—five ordained men in three mission stations—to which, as you may imagine, I say with all due respect, 'Not for Joe,' —or any other clerical expression of the same import. I don't tell them that, of course, but I just do what has to be done, and when it is done I tell them. They don't dismiss a man for a first offence. I am not going to muddle, whatever they say."

As we have seen, the question of evangelising the river was kept in view by the mission, and Scott's first pioneering journey was towards the river in the Cholo district. It was thought that there he might find a spot sufficiently elevated to be healthy, and yet nearer the river than Blantyre, and thus more easily reached by the river agents whenever need arose. He succeeded in winning the confidence of his carriers to an unusual degree, and round the camp-fire his presence was the signal for general merriment. The African dearly loves a joke, and they suited each other exactly. These journeys opened his eyes to the way in which the native looks at native questions, and gave him the power to look at both sides of the question—an ability which it is no want of charity to say that settlers and Administration officers are apt to lack in a new country. Africa has a land question as well as Ireland. In the following we have the statement of the African land question from the side of the native :—

" I asked Masea to drink tea with me. He is a big, fat, kindly man. He wants a missionary to build beside him and have a school, but he thinks that land - buyers are *ochenjera* — *i.e.*, ' sharpers ' exactly, and I quite agree with him. One sees how very wrong it is to be ' sharp ' here when the sellers are not, and *cannot be sharp*. I explained to him as well as I could about buying land ; all the difference between our idea of owner-ship of land and theirs, and how we must have

everything written down and not left to chance
promises.   Let me explain to you how it goes.
A man here has bought land from the chief.   He
says to the people who are at present hoeing
gardens on part of it, 'You may reap this year,
but next year you must not.'   But the chief from
whom he bought it never would or could say such
a thing.   His people live where they please, except
where the chief's own gardens are, and change
their gardens to new ground when the old is done.
Now if a man buys ground from a chief, he buys
only the rights which a chief has—in the name
of justice surely.   How can he buy from the
chief the rights that the people alone actually
possess ? "

Just at this time the politics of the river (Shiré)
were in a very unsettled state.   When the Portuguese came up on their land-grabbing expedition,
Mlauli, a river chief, would put no confidence
either in the African Lakes Company or in the
mission, but went to fight the invaders.   He was
defeated and fled to Cholo, close to the spot at
which boats unload for Blantyre.   He was not a

popular man amongst his people, and they elected another in his place. It was not the most propitious time to make a missionary expedition amongst them, but, so far as making friendships was concerned, it was eminently fruitful. But Scott found that Africa has a national sin which is already so prevalent that it must not be encouraged by the facilities which European commerce could easily give for it.

"There was a beer-drinking at the village. I don't take it, and my two mission boys do not either, just for the same reason that made me teetotal at home. 'Teetotal, eh? and stuck-up, stand-aloof, and-so-you-think-we-should-not-take-it-either, no-good-fellowship-about-you, and so on,' and it must be a little trying, in fact considerably so. This country must somehow find the power to say 'No' to *kachasu* (brandy), for it is almost sure to come, and it is being 'tempted above that they are able' to have it offered them just now. They could not resist it. God does not tempt *us* beyond that *we* are able, but we have the power so to tempt our younger brothers here. You can imagine what kind of devil's work it is to do so. I have heard people talking about the survival of the fittest in such a case. You might as well offer a child poison in a lump of sugar and talk in the same way. You can offer Mwembe the brandy if you like, and I don't think he'll take it; but if he had not been at Blantyre, I would not answer for him. At Kumpata's it was like a pot-house at home when we went up—women joking with half-drunken men, and all that's nasty. We were glad to be away."

He returned to Blantyre from the Cholo expedition with a clear idea of the natural course a mission should follow as regards that part of the country. He had thought that a station might be founded on the hills near enough the river to enable him "to jump back to it before fever caught him." However, he found "the jump" was too great. The question then arose as to the next direction in which he should look, and his own inclination, as well as the old promise of the mission to visit Chikuse, pointed to Angoniland. Just as he was getting up the expedition messengers arrived from Chikuse asking for help against his nearest neighbour, a chief, Chifisi by name. These messengers had been sent to purchase guns and powder at the stores, but found that the trader would not sell. Scott regarded this as a good opportunity to get guides to their own country, and perhaps avert the war. He was thankfully accepted as a companion, as the warriors knew their lives were not very safe if they returned without the war material. He started, then, with an escort of Angoni warriors, whose dress reminded him not a little of that of the Highland regiments at home. He was puzzled at first by the circuitous route they followed, but later he discovered that one of the expectations of his host was that the Doctor would give him poison to poison all his enemies' wells, and thus dispose of his foes with a minimum of trouble to himself. Among his escort was the chief's executioner—Kudambo—" with a face that would stick at no devilry." They arrived at Chikuse's in due course.

"I came in here mysteriously and silently in

the dead of night, stepping softly, with a silent black guide in front; but it was not half so eerie or bad as walking up to the pulpit behind a Sunday-faced beadle!"

He found the people here had a sort of national look about them—one of the *bambos* (councillors) had a real pawky Scottish face and a voice like a crow. They were industrious—forges were to be seen in many of the villages. His energies were at once directed to the bringing about of peace. Chikuse was determined to have poison, and would not content himself with a refusal in which Scott told him that God gave him medicines to cure men and not to kill them. The chief executioner pressed him for it, and said it was *mlandu* (sort of case at law) because he refused.

When the *mlandu* was spoken, Scott explained his desires, saying he wished to go to Chifisi, and asking a guide. This was refused, as the last messenger they had sent was killed; and Scott, thinking that Chifisi had probably heard of Chikuse's little poisoning game, thought it better to return, and approach Chifisi from Blantyre direct.

He explains this " political " enterprise in a long letter home :—

" You may wonder what all this politics means, and what I have to do with it ; but we have to do a lot of things here, and on what seems a big scale. If you found all the boys in New Abbey just going to batter each other with stones, you would not say it was meddling with politics to stop them if you could. So here. So as soon as the world goes round a bit I am going back again to Blantyre, and thence I expect to Chifisi, and perhaps we'll stop Angoni fighting with Angoni."

The interminable delays of African life were a great trial to him. One refusal never convinced Chikuse of the hopelessness of getting the poison, and Scott was practically a prisoner, as he could not, consistently with etiquette, leave without the chief's permission. Here is a picture of the chief :—

" Chikuse came back again to-day to talk, and sat a long time. He is about as big and fat a man as ever I saw. He said he wanted me to come and stay, but we'll see about that. I showed him a lot of my medical instruments—all the tooth-forceps, and the amputation-knives, the laryngoscopic mirror, which makes your face like 'coming back from Lipton's,' and as his face is already like 'coming back from Lipton's for the second time,' I do not wonder that he laughed at his own picture. He looks to me like a big spoilt boy, who unfortunately has the power to kill an enormous lot of people. There is much need of a man of God here, if such a man exists."

Seven days he had to "squat," doing nothing, his men grumbling, and the delay making the prospect of peace more and more remote. The inaction was to Scott unbearable.

"I do not like sitting still with nothing particular to do—as here. How an African chief or courtier, or a Princes Street man at home, manages to exist I don't know."

At last he got permission to leave, with a guide back to Blantyre, where he arrived with many strangers in his train, following to be treated for various ailments when he got home. Regarding the whole mission prospect he sent home to his Committee a report which gives a clearer view of the district and its needs than any paraphrase could :—

"The knowledge I have gained in this journey has made my ideas as to the mission campaign perfectly clear. Blantyre, as you know, lies in the centre of a plateau that falls away on all sides, and is about thirty miles from one end to the other. Towards the east it falls away to the plain between us and Mlanje. South-east it is flat; then the Cholo district rises from it with a quick descent to the river. Then boxing the compass south, we go gradually down to Katunga's for thirty miles. Then come the cataracts; and north-west we fall away gradually to Matope's, on the upper river, which flows nearly north and south. Then, lastly, about north we fall but little, and travel along the flat as one would think, but really along the top of a range of big hills, as I saw, from Matope to Zomba—good forty miles. Chiradzulo lies on the way. Blantyre is the platform or stage, the body of the hall stretches to Zomba—the back gallery. The stage is well filled, but the body of the hall is only empty benches because of the Angoni sweeping in at the side doors. The back gallery is well filled, as it has a lock and key and all manner of trap - doors in Mount Zomba, so that the Angoni cannot sweep it.

"Now the parishes here are plain—Blantyre is one, and there can be no other close to it except the river itself. Zomba is the next on the north, Mlanje the next on the east, and Angoniland the next on the west—for between Blantyre and Angoniland it is again a case of empty benches. Our main-door looks Westward Ho ! What I feel very strongly is that we should get one foot on to the Angoni plateau to keep that main-door open : when the Church awakes we can draw the other leg up. The fact that I have a knowledge of medicine gives me confidence in urging this, as precisely the way in which that knowledge ought to be used. Besides, ordination means either a separate or a collegiate charge, and I cannot take a permanent post in any station without that being distinctly understood. To send out two ordained men, and at the same time forbid extension, is to make a dilemma, for the one implies the other. We dare not hold ordination cheap, dare we ? "

Probably the day will come when the churches will recognise that a good medical training is as great and proper a qualification for ordination to a missionary's work as an indifferent theological education—but that time is not yet ; and it was a touch of nature we can well appreciate, which made him resent the idea that his double qualification should after all give him only the inferior position of a medical missionary.

CHAPTER XII.

MLANJE—DEATH OF CLELAND.

A MEETING of the Mission Council at Blantyre in the beginning of September took up the question of Cleland's work at Chiradzulo, and the prospects of getting a station commenced in Mount Mlanje, where with much difficulty Cleland had secured by purchase a site from Chikumbu the chief. The original tribes—the Anyasa—lived in constant dread of their formidable neighbour, who hoped to make use of the mission-work to secure his own ends of conquest; and on one occasion Cleland, hearing that war had come, rushed to the mission-ground and withstood the violation of treaty by protesting against the fighting going on there. His opinion was that circumstances might easily occur in which the mission must temporarily retire from that district, and as the strain was too great for one man, Scott offered to go for some months to work alongside of him till better times should dawn.

"I must say I don't like all this temporary style of work, but Cleland has had to be at it three years alone, so I need not complain."

The two young men did not find their task an easy one at all. Chikumbu was not an easy problem. He stole the crops of the hapless Anyasa, fired upon them sometimes, and took some captives, of whom he made slaves. One Sunday he sent his wives and families to morning service and despatched his men to steal. The missionaries, however, went up to his village immediately after service and found all the men gone. In answer to their inquiries the chief informed them that they had all gone out walking, indicating with a grand flourish a direction away from the homes of his victims.

"Things are not improving—they are becoming more and more misty. Chikumbu the chief is—

well—a 'nice wee deil,' as perhaps M—— would say with her universal sympathy. Eleven years ago he lived at Chiradzulo, and was such a 'nice wee deil' that the people would stand him no longer and turned him out. He came across here and burned and slew to the Ruo, and at last got the land he holds just now. Our mission-land lies between him and the Anyasa, who are no fighters, and of whom he wishes to possess himself. They naturally don't want the devil for chief if they can help it.

"Before we came home we sent to Chikumbu's to ask about the captives, and he said that as soon as the *Asungu* (*i.e.*, we) came he would give them up. When we came he said in Chi Yao practically, 'I'll see you far enough.' We waited a week and then called on him again, saying we should need to go if he did not surrender them. 'Then he was vexed to see that our heart had changed,'—in plain terms, that we had not been his tools — and said he did not want us any more.

"We are just a little uncertain about what the

chief may do next, for he is a mad man and a bad man together. This uncertainty has nearly brought things to a standstill in the station, and the school is nearly empty. Luckily, I brought medical books enough, so I am getting some reading done in this favourable chance.

" This would become a very nice place if things would only improve one tiny bit, but if people will not receive you the old command is to go. This seems an intolerably stupid letter, but my brains are all scattered, and I am looking at things with no speculation in my eyes, as mother used to say. Things are all in disconnected units in my head: *e.g.*—

" 1. I shot a big water-buck on the road here, and hunted it for miles till the sun went down, but it got away.

" 2. The canary sings gloriously in the woods: it makes quite a home sound.

" 3. I have several patients down at the Anyasa —one little boy shot in the head by Chikumbu's men, and a man shot in the hand.

" 4. We have a sort of influenza among us—

nearly all the boys have been ill, and Cleland has been down with it too.

" 5. If you hear any one say that Mohammedanism is a preparation for Christianity out here, just tell him it is not true ; if he says it is better for the people, that is not true either.

" Really it is no use struggling to write until things go a little smoother."

Things did not improve with Chikumbu. At last he threatened that, if the missionaries did not bring the Anyasa under his rule, he would put an end to all their work, and he promptly carried out his threat. School was emptied, services deserted, and everything at a standstill. Of course his plan was unsuccessful, as Scott and Cleland immediately took steps to seek another station. They found by experience that if a chief was really great, it was a help to be near him and under his goodwill and protection ; but if he happened to be small and mischievous, it was good for nobody to be in his vicinity. He would have been ready to throw hindrances in their way, but the frankness with which they told him their plans disarmed him, rendering useless the spies he set upon their movements. They had, besides, many friends among his people, who acted as their carriers; and one of the chief's sons decided on accompanying them on their *ulendo* (expedition), so that they felt they had sufficient hostages both for their friends the Anyasa and for their goods.

They were unwilling to leave the mountain altogether, and prospected just in the neighbourhood. About eight miles from their station they found at a higher elevation a promising piece of level ground. It was outside of Chikumbu's territory, and appeared healthy, being much drier, and supplied with beautiful water. This they determined should be their headquarters henceforth, their old station becoming an out-station. How Chikumbu might like it they did not know.

"We are a little curious to know how he will take our removing just outside his country, but I think the 'hit-him-in-the-mouf' principle will suffice now."

On they marched through many villages that afforded evident scope for mission-work—sometimes well received by the natives, sometimes with suspicion. They went as far as Chilomo, at the mouth of the Ruo, whence they returned to Mlanje.

"We have Cleland's donkey with us in case of emergencies. He is a most ridiculous beast—a very nice beast, but very fond of a joke. During morning service he took to scampering round the houses, and when the women and children ran away he was all the better pleased. Then he careered down the village, braying all the way. I don't know how the boys kept their gravity."

One purpose they had in view was to open up a road (direct) from the Shiré to Mlanje, in order to save the delays caused by going round by Katunga's and Blantyre.

A day in the bush we can picture from his next letter :—

"We left Chilomo with Mr Marshall, who is sort of Vice-Consul on the Ruo, and Mr Mitchell, one of the Company's men. We sent the men round by the path to a village six miles out of the road by which we had come, telling them to take the road to Cholo, and build a *masasa* (grass-hut) when they got to a sleeping-ground. We went round by the edge of the Elephant Marsh, through the bush, to see if we could get any game. Mr Marshall used to be an elephant-hunter, and has a native name that means a 'regular swell at it.' We saw a wild boar—I had never seen one before—but he smelt us and was off. We saw also a herd of black-buck about the size of ponies, but they were also to the lee of us and too far off; saw no buffalo as we wished, and, after losing our way, got into camp about sunset.

"The boys had made a beautiful *masasa*, so well built that even though it rained somewhat during the night scarcely a drop came through. We had some glorious porridge and tinned milk, cut up a biscuit tin to make a frying-pan for the sausages, and had a regular 'Boys' own Paper' time of it out in the bush, with, I suppose, wild beasts all around."

N

Cleland and he parted company on the way back—the former returning to his station and Scott going *viâ* Blantyre, arriving there in the last week of October. A few days later he was again at Mlanje assisting Cleland in founding the new station. He was left to see to the building of the house, and Cleland returned to Chikumbu's for the goods which they had left. On the 2d of November Cleland was stricken by fever, which showed itself at once to be of a virulent type. Scott moved him farther up the hill, to a hut which he got built, despatched messengers to Blantyre for medicines and assistance, and tended him as he loved him—like a brother.

The messengers brought back a *machila* with them, and into this Scott hurried his patient with all speed and set off for Blantyre. His journey was one which demanded all the resourceful energy of his character. He had to throw bridges across two streams and to watch his patient, who collapsed very rapidly. He got into Blantyre in marvellously short time, soon enough for Cleland to take farewell of his friends and pass away. The shock would at any time have been a great one, but for Scott it was peculiarly so. Cleland had "thirled" himself to the Doctor by ties of common work, tastes, and spiritual sympathy, and his death produced on his friend a depression which he seldom showed.

"BLANTYRE, 12·10·90.

"All the home people will be very sorry to hear of Cleland's death. It came so suddenly. We were staying together at Mlanje, beside the Linje. Cleland went to Chikumbu's to send along the stuff we had left there. I built a house for the boys while he was away, intending that we should put up in it till the bigger house was ready. He came back on Saturday night a week and a half ago. On Tuesday we moved up to the little native hut we had been staying in. On Wednesday we were clearing the ground for the larger house and a road to the stream, but in the afternoon Cleland became seriously ill. It was one of those virulent forms of malaria which are fortunately rare here. . . .

" I did what I could for him, but it was a case like some you may have heard of at home in measles or scarlet-fever, where the disease takes the form of an acute blood-poisoning. I got him into Blantyre on Monday, but he died the same night.

" It seems a cold bare statement of the fact this, but after the struggle of the waters comes the wilderness always. Don't be over-troubled about this, for I was exposed to the very same during our stay together, but had only slight fever. I do not even know whether it was Mlanje that gave him this last attack, or whether it was the *ulendo* on the river we had together. It is almost the regular thing to have the fever eight or ten days after one comes back from the river, and it was just about that period when the fever came on.

" I have not much heart to write just now. It will be better to wait for a little till the depression passes away. It was a great shock to all the people here, especially as there have been so many deaths among them from influenza."

The trying circumstances of the past fortnight told very severely on Scott. The journey resulted in a very sharp attack of fever too obstinate to be neglected. Dr Bowie advised him not to return to Mlanje till after New Year, and the next six weeks he spent at Blantyre, taking a share in the services of the station, assisting in the medical work, working with the choir, and finishing the painting of the church. His stay lasted over Christmas, which all the Europeans in the district hold as a holiday, on which absent friends in the old country were especially in mind.

"Like all English people, we took an immensity of trouble to get ourselves amused. The Blantyre people invited all the white population to dinner on Christmas eve, and all the ladies had a share in the preparations therefor. Mrs Scott roasted the turkey, Mrs Smith the duck, Mrs Bowie did the jellies, and Miss Beck, Mrs Fenwick, and Mrs Henderson were up to the elbows in it. There were thirty-three at dinner, so you may see that the community is growing at any rate in size. I can't count them all up, but there are some outstanding figures—Mr and Mrs Fred. Moir, and at least six of the Company's men ; Mr Shearer, Mr David Buchanan, Mr Pettitt, and others who would be only names to you. The dinner passed off most successfully."

CHAPTER XIII.

A TERRIBLE MARCH—DEATHS AT BLANTYRE.

THE New Year of 1891 dawned very hopefully on the mission, which, notwithstanding Cleland's death, was still strong, and confident in the prospect of speedy reinforcements. Scott's health was now re-established, and he started on the first Monday of the year to Mlanje to redeem a promise made that he should return there. It was intended that he should be absent for only ten days, and as he bade good-bye to Mrs Henderson, she remarked it was hardly worth while bidding him good-bye for so short a time. He travelled over the old road with its sad associations, but the grass had grown green and the mourning of the country was past. Things were brighter when he reached Mlanje. He sent a message to Chikumbu to ask about the old question of the slaves, and on the Saturday he had a *mlandu* which was very satisfactory. He found the people so well disposed and anxious to have the mission settled amongst them that he promised to go back himself, that Cleland's work should not die.

He was just starting on his return journey when messengers came in from Blantyre saying that little Henry Henderson had died of diphtheria, that his mother was ill, and asking him to come on at once. The little fellow had died the day after Scott left, but the speed with which he travelled had enabled him to cross rivers which a day later were impassable for the natives, and he had been thus prevented from having the news more quickly.

He started at once, and soon reached the Likabula, now swollen with the rains. After an hour's search he found a place where he and his party were able to cross, and at two o'clock in the afternoon they reached the Tuchira to find it a roaring flood—very broad, and several times his own depth. He sent off his men for *maluzi* (bark) to make rope, and looked about for a ford. The men delayed long—they could not swim, and were terrified to think of crossing the flood. Darkness fell upon them before anything was done. He spent a sleepless night cogitating plans for getting across the stream, in which he heard the hippopotamus grunting—an evidence of the great depth of the water. Before dawn he roused his men, sent them off shivering and shaking to get more *maluzi*. With his native boys, Kaliaté and Misco, he decided on a spot at which they would cross. He knotted the tent-ropes together, tied the line round his body, waded to a tree in the river, and then swam to another. Clinging to the branches, he fastened his rope while his faithful followers had the other end made fast to a light tree on the bank. This he drew across and fastened securely by means of *maluzi.*

They had, however, another "span." For this they had provided a bridge of bamboo. This was worked along the tree by the two boys, who then swam to another tree nearer the opposite bank. To them Scott heaved the tent-rope, and securing the bamboos by means of a noose through which they could run, he allowed them to pull it across the tree which acted as a pier, and he then fastened the other end, after a second swim, on the Blantyre side of the river.

Hardly waiting for more than a biscuit by way of breakfast, he reached the spot where he intended to cook about four in the afternoon. There another messenger met him with the news that Mrs Henderson had died of diphtheria, and that Dr Bowie was also stricken with the same disease. Cooking was out of the question, and on he marched — through tropical rains and thunderstorms most of the way, all the streams rivers, and the pools ponds. He found amongst the natives great interest being taken in Dr Bowie's illness, and at one village got the news that he was somewhat better. He arrived at Blantyre at 2.30 in the morning, having done a four days' journey in little more than forty-eight hours.

His colleague he found in a low condition owing to previous influenza, but not hopeless. When Scott entered the sick-room Dr Bowie remarked, "There will be no need for tracheotomy before morning, so you will have time to read it up." Rest was impossible, and the hours till dawn were spent reading for the operation and watching the patient, but they decided it was not a case for tracheotomy.

"The symptoms both in his case and in that of Mrs Henderson were strange and indeed terrible. I was forced to conclude in Dr Bowie's case that there was a central paralysis of the inspiratory centre, with paresis of the centre for deglutition, giving symptoms similar to those of hydrophobia and much of its terror. He was able at all times to respire quite freely, and there were no symptoms of laryngeal obstruction to respiration such as would be caused by membrane. There was never any membrane coughed up except once before I saw him. . . . I almost hoped that with stimulants and regular artificial respiration he might pull through; but, on the evening of the day he died, a terrible paroxysm came on—a noisy, utterly incoherent delirium, ceaseless restlessness and fearful distress, so that I gave him a whiff of chloroform, which I knew would relieve him and would not hasten the end. It was like gripping a rope that a friend holds by in deep tumultuous waters too strong for both."

The mission band was soon broken up. Many of them under the strain were at breaking-point, and seven were immediately despatched home to recruit. Scott was sent down the river in charge of them, and saw them on board their steamer at Quilimane, at which place Henry Henderson, broken in health and spirits by the loss of his wife and son, followed them to the grave. With that party Scott despatched a letter to the Missionary Society, in which the needs of Africa are forcibly put :—

" Now there are three of us left for Blantyre. You can imagine how ashamed of ourselves we feel. I expect I shall need to search in holes and corners for David and Mr Smith when I get back, for they are even thinner than I am, having lost a half each. Being, then, as meagre as we are, we take this chance of parading our leanness before the eyes of the Church, not that we mean to beg for *pity* only; for though we are lean, we aim at wiriness. But we want men badly, not only to hold our own, but to meet the responsibility our charter contains. We want men for Mlanje, the river, Cholo, Angoniland, and, to speak as desperate men, we must have them. We have been personally more than once to all these places, and have virtually promised the people that we will come to live amongst them.

"So many people are flocking into this country, that if we are to be beforehand we must be sharp. The advantage of being first in a place cannot be overestimated. It gives the mission a voice as nothing else does, and it does exasperate one to see the Company with a station at Mlanje, while we cannot fulfil our promises to them. I do not know what effect the news from Blantyre will have on people at home.

I hope it will tend to stop playing at missions and praising missionaries, and make people yoke to as to a real business."

His place was now at Blantyre—a position which he never intended to be a final one. The hope of a station of his own in which he would be "preacher and healer" both was one to which he clung all his life. One of his first duties as medical officer there was to defend the mission site against charges of unhealthiness owing to unsanitary conditions, &c. This defence he wrote with a vigour and scorn of which one would hardly have deemed him capable. The statement was sent home by one writer that he was never well at Blantyre. Scott replied :—

"The writer was here for a few days. The health of a place, I need scarcely point out, must be judged of by the health of those who live there—not by that of those who merely visit it. Blantyre district is at present the health resort for north, south, east, and west. There is practically no malaria at Blantyre."

In his medical reports for the year he writes, regarding the risks of diphtheria in the district :—

"There have been in former years other cases of diphtheria in the Shiré Highlands among the English population. I know of no clear evidence that it is found among the natives. It broke out at a house about a mile from Blantyre a good number of years ago, when two English children died. I do not know what the disease was traced to, but I believe its origin was unknown. Another case which occurred in Zomba at the consulate, a few years ago, is most instructive from a medical point of view. It was so inexplicable that medical authorities at home would scarcely believe it was really diphtheria. But a post-mortem examination satisfied Dr Bowie it was really so. . . . . The case of Mrs Henderson's child was similar to this one. The stream at the place where the water is drawn is pure, and, moreover, the water was always boiled before being used for any purpose, as was also the milk.

There was nothing epidemic about the disease, as the child's mother caught it in trying to make the feeding-bottle draw before the disease was recognised. Dr Bowie sucked the tracheotomy-tube. The disease spread no further.

"If we could think the disease was due to a removable cause, we should be less anxious. As it is, we have to reckon with the fact that diphtheria is not unlikely to attack British children in this country as it does in Natal, and perhaps all new countries, and that it is more to be dreaded here than at home."

After his return from Quilimane, Scott was for a short time at Blantyre working at his medical practice, and hoping that now he would have the opportunity of continuing for a little in one station. His kindness and unselfish devotion to others were soon well known. A fellow-worker in the mission-field gives me a personal experience he had of this :—

"On our journey in to Blantyre from Domasi, our halting-place for one night was to be Chira-dzulo, which was then unoccupied by white men.

On arriving there in the evening we were pleasantly surprised to find Dr Scott waiting for us. He had come out fifteen miles to meet us, and had brought with him tea and milk, besides a dinner which he had prepared at Blantyre. While the dinner was getting warmed up he made us tea with his own hands, and would not let us do anything to help, although he had walked the fifteen miles from Blantyre that afternoon after his usual morning's work. He thought we had done enough, seeing we had already come thirty miles.

"We soon retired to rest, and the Doctor spread his blankets on the top of an old table that had been left in the house by Mr Cleland; but with him the case of the willing horse getting the heavy load was being constantly exemplified, as during the night some messengers arrived, having followed him from Blantyre, with the news that a white man was ill. He simply got up and walked away with them through the bush. I went to call him in the morning, and found his blankets on the table. When we reached

Blantyre, he was going about as fresh as if he had been in bed all night, and cracked a joke with us about his moonlight flitting."

The new church was opened on the 10th May 1891, and Scott took part in the services. Then reinforcements came for Mlanje, and he was required to go to start the new station.

CHAPTER XIV.

FOUNDING A NEW STATION—HIS FIRST LION—PURSUIT OF CHIKUMBU—SPECULATIONS REGARDING MALARIA.

THE lessons of the past had been well learned by the Doctor, and a good substantial bridge of two spans, bolted with iron, now crossed the Tuchira. August 1891 saw him again on the scene of his old labours.

"I have been knocking about a good deal, and am back here till Christmas. I wanted to be at Blantyre, but had to come back here to help to start the station. I seem to be the unfortunate Jack-of-all-trades who have to give a hand here, there, and everywhere."

Of a flying visit to Blantyre he says:—

"I walked into Blantyre in a day, and it's a long, long walk. If you are putting the news of it in the 'Christian,' you may say it was because I did not want to travel on Sunday; if it is to go to 'Tit-bits,' you can say it was pure 'cussedness'; if to my big brother, say it was all his fault, seeing I got news on Friday that he was going home and that I was to come in straight; so thinking he might start on the Monday, I went in straight. I came out straight again—not in one day though."

In the midst of the building and other operations necessary for the founding of the station, Scott kept the missionary idea prominent. Before work, the workmen were assembled and he conducted service with them—some of them being dependants of his old antagonist, Chikumbu. The people were eager to hear the "News of God," as they called the Gospel. He made a long excursion up the mountain with a planter of the neighbourhood, and fancied himself at home again among the Pentlands or Lammermoors. His letters often state that of course he had no adventures—" of course I never have." He had seen something afar off which might be a lion, but he had not made a closer acquaintance with the king of the forest. On this expedition, however, he did, and his own racy words tell the result :—

" There are other things in the bush besides bridges. The following statements we certify from personal experience. When one hunts game on the Tuchira plains it is quite possible that a lion may be up to the same game. When one is sitting in a wide *dambo* (plain) just after sunset, with one native attendant, waiting for the men to come to carry the hard-won meat to camp, one cannot be sure, because there is no cover or long grass near, that a lion will not come to demand a share, or more than a share. Lions do not always creep close up stealthily and then spring. Our one came up like a horse at full gallop, with a bass growl that grew alarmingly bigger, till he stood five yards off, with only a hartebeest between us. Lions do not seem to mind being looked at either by a white man's eye or a black. We had both these, though of course we cannot certify the quelling power of either. Perhaps eyes differ. If one take a towel and a hat and a handkerchief and wave them at a lion in such circumstances, the lion may bolt off thirty yards and stay growling there behind a scrap of a bush. Ours did. If then one take a rifle and fire after him he may not go any farther away. Ours did not. Then when one sees the black shapeless mass, which is all that stands for the lion in the mirk, growing bigger again at an alarming rate, we shall agree that an orderly retreat is safest. We thought so, and went without soup that night. We were as glad to give that lion his game as any native could be to pay the Administration his taxes.

"If any one asks if we were not dreadfully frightened, we can only say that if we had only been one-half as frightened as we were, we should probably have bolted at once and been no better for it. We have always had a kind of wish to see a lion, for very few have the chance. We are quite satisfied now."

In this year Chikumbu got into bad relations
with some of the neighbouring planters, who
probably were not quite able to appreciate the
doings of the "nice wee deil" so well as Dr Scott
could. They complained to the Vice-Consul, who
decided on an expedition to catch Chikumbu.
Scott got a hint of it, and foresaw that the
native boys who had been left in charge of
Mlanje might fare badly without a protector.
Loyalty to the Administration prevented him
letting them know what was at hand, but he
despatched a messenger, telling them to meet
him at the Likabula. They failed to do so, and
another messenger sent for them came back with
the news that "war had come," and when they
reached their destination they found the houses
burned, and all Chikumbu's people fled. So far
as catching Chikumbu was concerned the expedition had failed. To pursue him among the
rocks and cliffs of the mountain was impossible
for the expedition, and Scott offered to follow
him and endeavour to bring him back. His
offer was accepted gladly by Captain Maguire,

who gave him a message to Chikumbu, and orders to try and get the people back.

He very quickly found Chikumbu's brother, who promised to go down, but refused to give a guide to the chief's hiding-place. Scott was afraid if he returned to camp that the officer might not let him start again. By persisting, he at last got the guide, and, soon after starting, met his mission boys safe, although the station had been burned. On he pressed, without food, till it was quite dark. Fires were lit, and by means of one at the head and another at the side, he was kept tolerably warm. When the moon was well up he roused his guides, and followed the track of the fugitive chief and his people.

At last he overtook them in a ravine of huge pine-trees and rocks, and delivered his message, offering them safety if they came in, and saying that if they did not come back he would return without telling where he had found them, as he was no spy. He succeeded in bringing in the women and children and a fair number of the men, but the chief fled elsewhere for the time.

While at Mlanje he gave the following humorous picture of himself as regards dress :—

"J—— wants to know what colour of stockings I like. I can't help laughing as I look down at my limbs in their present condition. Here is a diagram up to the knees :—

(*a*) Knickerbockers Joseph Thomson left behind.

(*b*) Silk stockings—sunburnt a good deal.

(*c*) One mustard-coloured sock.

(*d*) Another sock—pale pink.

(*e*) Boots—used to be long, but were too heavy for the 'constitution,' so they were beheaded.

" *N.B.*—Feet of the socks not shown in the diagram, but they have feet—some of them."

He returned finally to Blantyre in the end of 1891, and took up a permanent post as medical missionary there.   He got a parish of his own—the Ndirande Hill, in which he laboured as a preacher. He took the greatest interest in the choir of the church, saying that since they had the finest church in Africa they should also have the finest choir.   He succeeded in getting the four parts well sung, and people who have been in the church say that the singing of the choir, even without taking into account that it was in Africa, was wonderful.   He felt strongly that such a life as was spent in an African mission was one which demanded all the best powers of men.

" Don't let any one pity you for coming out here to a wilderness.   Tell them there are ever so many boys here who know what a demi-semi-quaver is, and can sing any reasonable tenor off at first sight, and ask cute, difficult questions on various subjects—*e.g.*, ' Why won't water burn ? ' Then we have started a bank, to keep the boys from spending their money on tinned meats. They were buying sardine-tins at a shameful rate.

"We have also on hand a scheme for teaching English—not to mention a monthly paper on scientific subjects, such as the boiling-point thermometer, translation of the 'Pilgrim's Progress,' recreation-room, &c., &c.

"So if any man thinks he is in danger of losing his intellectual acumen by coming to Africa, let that man know that he thinks much more of himself than the circumstances of the case warrant. He will find that all he can give will be thankfully received, and more will be wanted."

His translation of the 'Pilgrim's Progress' into Mang'anja was finished in January 1892, and despatched home for publication. He became increasingly anxious for additional men to join in healing Africa. Every letter speaks of the need.

"I had a brotherly greeting from the 'Guild' Council. There are thousands of members, but we can't get three teachers out here from our own Church. So it is a case of 'greeting.'"

Again : " I can scarcely say how glad I am you have thought of coming out here. If you knew what a fight one has, both in one's self and outside, with sin and all that's bad and mean, you would be doubly glad to join in and give a hand. Two are ten times (not twice) stronger than one. We are sorely in need of men here —never more so, never half so much so. I don't know how many fellows at home are waiting for some internal ' call,' which is the same as to stop one's ears when the bugle is blowing, and listen to one's own semicircular canals. In very deed this land is in danger of going to the devil by the three paths—the lust of the flesh, the lust of the eyes (wanting to grab whatever you see worth grabbing), and the pride of life (contempt for those that are weak and prejudice against them). When one finds all three in one's self, and feels the power of them, one longs for more men out here who know the wrong and hate it."

The subject of malarial fever occupied his attention very much in his work. Its prevalence, the various forms it assumed, the possibility of being acclimatised against it, were all matter of careful inquiry. His medical report was hardly an orthodox document. The usual plan of keeping the number of cases, and tabulating them, was not congenial. Instead he sent home his theories regarding malaria :—

"Fever has formed a large part of the practice here, both amongst Europeans and natives. Natives, especially children, seem even more susceptible to it than Europeans. . . . The idea of acclimatisation is nonsense—the natives even are not acclimatised.

"Side by side with fever cases are cases of ulcers—both native and European. These, too, I am coming to think, are cases of malarial infection. Just as the half of a home practice deals with tubercular cases, medical or surgical, so here, the half, or more, of the practice deals with malaria, and malaria has its surgical side, though unrecorded, so far as I know. In the case of Europeans the connection is quite clear. A case I had illustrates this. The patient had been troubled with small irritable ulcers for some months. There was one especially painful corroding ulcer on the middle finger of the left hand which resisted treatment. One day it and its neighbours began rapidly to heal, and coincidently an attack of fever developed, from which he had been free all the time the ulcers troubled him.   Ulcers and no fever, or fever and no ulcers, is the rule amongst us.   I do not remember having seen them together.

"We have not the same clear proof of the relation of native ulcers and malaria, but a good many facts point in that direction.   A Blantyre boy accompanied me to Mlanje last year.   He has hitherto always had an attack of fever on returning from a journey to the low ground.   He went with me on both my journeys to Mlanje last year, had no fever either time; but on both occasions an ulcer developed, which ran its course, and healed. At other times he is not troubled with ulcers."

The reader will probably have come to the conclusion ere this that, whatever faults Scott had, he was free from the more obnoxious forms of "professionalism."   He was proud of his position as medical preacher in an African mission, but was one who valued good work and good workers wherever he found them. His tendency to rollicking fun, however, never left him, and occasionally he gave it vent when he imagined that people were going beyond their province and speaking of what they knew nothing about. The mission boys printed a monthly magazine called 'Blantyre Life and Work,' and to its pages many contributions were sent by members of the staff and others. A series of "Practical Health Notes" were written by one of the European settlers, giving his own experience of the means he found best for the preservation of health; but in one of them he was betrayed into the use, or rather misuse, of technical terms. The next number contained from Scott's pen the following laughing protest, which reminds us irresistibly of his schoolboy productions :—

PERISCOPE.

" This magazine usually abstains from using technical terms, because most that it has to say can be said in plain English, and it is taking an unfair advantage of lay readers to speak in an unknown tongue. When an engineer speaks of

' cams,' and ' trunnions,' and ' throttle-valves,' one
is as much alarmed as when a liturgist speaks of
introits, matins, complines, or vespers.

"Plumbers' technical terms would probably be
even more terrifying, and architects' would need
to be hushed up.

"Of course if you want us to talk trade we can
do it. We need only mention the Klebs-Loeffler
bacillus, or the Staphylococcus pyrgenous aureus,
or the Liquor Arsenici et Hydrargyri Iodidi, and
I think, with the voice of history back to Galen
behind us, we could match even a plumber at
technical swearing. But it is not good form, for
it is not that my intelligence is inferior to the
plumbers' that I don't know what he is giving
me, nor do I think myself superior to him
because he is nettled to know what I am at.

"Now the strange thing is that as soon as
a body gets a little way 'ben' into some other
body's business, the first thing he shows is all
the dictionary words that belong thereto. We in
Blantyre here build, and we can all talk of
' ogees,' and ' gargoyles,' and the ' clerestory,' and

'thrusts.' The deacons even will soon be lisping in 'liturgies,' I believe. Here, where every man is his own doctor, and architect, and carpenter, and veterinary surgeon, the chances of making some literature must not be neglected.

"You see, sir, you must write Bacillus malariæ, if you write it at all, and you must not even write that, for the thing is not a bacillus.

"Germs are of many kinds: there are 'cocci'— *i.e.*, little round bodies; and 'bacilli,' little rod-like bodies; and there are also 'amœbæ,' little jelly-like bodies.

"Now the malarial bodykin is an amœba-like form, though to what particular class of amœba it belongs is not quite settled. The germ that occurs in smallpox and vaccine lymph belongs to the same large class, and so probably does the germ of cancer.

"In temperate climates, the 'three-days',' 'four-days',' &c., paroxysms of malaria are due to the swarming of the amœbæ in their natural life-history, and not to chills, getting wet, worry, excitement, indigestion, &c. Laveran, who discovered this malarial germ, thinks there is just one, as there is only one, say of smallpox; others think that there are more than one.

"The reason why the habits and structure of the B.C.A. microbes are still a mystery is that none of the doctors out here have a lens that magnifies 600 times, and you cannot study it with a less powerful one. Probably, too, as they call 'hæmaturia' hæmorrhage, and are mostly 'missionary bodies,' they might not be able to find it. So one's own conclusion as to the nature of malaria is of no value whatever till one gets a microscope that magnifies 600 times and studies it. Specialists never allow their own conclusions to sway their judgment.

"By all means let us have his experience of native medicine from the author of 'Health Notes,' for all our medicines were native to start with, and a new one may turn up any day as good as, or better than, the old. But let him keep to the beaten path of common English, for he will make our little paper ridiculous, and we can stand anything but that."

CHAPTER XV.

THE NATIVES AND NATIVE QUESTIONS.

In every new country one of the great problems is the question of the true relationship that ought to exist between settlers and the native tribes. In America fire and sword were the arbiters for many generations, and even in the territories set apart for the North American Indians recent years have seen revolts and all attendant cruelties. Our own experiences of the mutiny of the Sepoys in India, of the Maories in New Zealand, and at the present time of the natives in Matabeleland, have shown us how important the solution of the problem of ruling conquered races must be. There are, of course, two plans between which all others must oscillate. There is the method of brute force, which regards the native as having no rights except that of having none, looks upon him as an inferior being, pestilential, indeed, if no use can be made of him by way of service. To those who follow this method every suggestion of the rights of the native savours of cant or weakness. It necessarily follows that with such views of the native there should be found deep-rooted contempt for all missionary effort which does not result in more subservient acquiescence in tyranny or cruelty.

If by becoming a Christian a native is more easily managed, then Christianity is a good thing for him; but if it has the effect it usually produces on white people—if it makes him think for himself—if it opens his eyes to the true brotherhood of men in Christ, and makes him expect that white men will regard him in such a light, then Christianity is a totally bad thing for him— it spoils the native, and the missionary is usually classed as a meddlesome fellow who makes it his business to interfere with things out of his province altogether, and with whom it is impossible to live in harmony.

There is also the method which refuses to regard anything save the interests of the native, which regards the trader as anathema, and encourages the natives to expect no justice or decent treatment from any others than their religious teachers. This may or may not be a successful missionary plan in certain lands—one can quite understand how it would tend to produce a very spurious sort of Christianity and a very objectionable type of native. It is difficult to estimate the real effect of Christianity upon the native without the evidences of one's own senses and experience. The mission is naturally prone to judge of it by the best types, and these will usually in a young mission be found in its own immediate vicinity—amongst its native teachers, pastors, or artisans; whilst those who come into the country for trade are very likely to come across the worst types at first, in men who, through connection with the mission, understand some

English, and get ready employment without any particular inquiries being made into their reason for leaving the mission. If these turn out unsatisfactory we should not wonder.

We quite understand that too much may be expected from the native Christian. A man who has the inheritance of Christian ancestry for six or eight centuries should not expect very much from Christians whose heredity in paganism is just as long, if with all the opportunity he has had of being influenced by Christianity he does not believe in missions in the name of Christ to any people or to all.

One will find all modes of dealing with natives between these two extremes, and the ideal method never quite realised in any. It is difficult to combine firmness with strict regard for abstract right, in dealing with what a native conscience has to be educated into believing to be crime. Scott's observations on native questions were begun in the Transvaal on his way out to Blantyre.

He arrived at Blantyre just when British Central Africa was being invaded by planters and traders, and at a time when the mission was placed in a peculiarly delicate situation. As in other lands, the missionary had here led the way; the trader followed; and the authority of the Queen came last of all. The missionary was really the judge and arbiter of all disputes among natives, and he had for a long time unquestioned authority. He was the " Father " of the people, and before civilised nations came to open up the country, questions of native rights as against those of white men hardly could arise. What prejudices he had against the native he had lost in the daily contact his mission-work gave with them. But circumstances changed when men came to work the country for their profit, and not with the immediate purpose of benefiting the natives. Probably to expect that the last should be treated with kindly consideration was to expect a moral impossibility, and at any rate Scott held the strongest views as to the difficulty of obtaining a fair attitude to black men on the part of whites. He was not one who thought that the white man should be subordinate to the black; but injustice he could not tolerate.

In one year there had been a very late season, and great difficulty was experienced in getting labourers for the work of the settlements. The difficulty was all the greater because of the scarcity of food, which weakened the natives and unfitted them for hard work. When the rains did come they set to work on their own gardens, which formed the source of their own food-supply and of that of the mission as well. The Government officer at Chilomo stopped for the time all dock-building operations there, because, he said, "the natives were and ought to be hoeing their own gardens just now." The difficulty of the settler was certainly very awkward, as his plantation required attention just as much as any native garden, and one instance occurred in which natives were forced by the strong hand away from their gardens to work on a plantation. Naturally they fell back on the mission for protection, and so, without seeking a quarrel, the missionaries were involved in one. Scott remarks on this subject:—

“There is no one in the country to speak out if we do not. Of course we know as well as any one that government of natives is not like government at home. One man, one vote, would never do here. I fully believe we have the right to decide what is best for the natives, and to tell them what they are to do, and they will obey. But the moment you appeal to such a paternal government, we ask, ‘Where is the *paternal feeling*, which is the only justification of paternal government ?’ Prejudice against the natives, which blinds the eye to all justice, is almost ineradicable. It is just the penalty we pay as a nation. We did the African long years of injustice. We have received the punishment that was meet—we cannot think justly or feel kindly towards them. That same prejudice is so strong and so widespread that it may be counted upon by those who wish to gain their own ends, and are not particular as to the means.

“ I know that people at home do not understand this. They ask, ‘Are you missionaries the only immaculate, the only just people ?’ I have only to say that every one of our nation has that prejudice born in him like original sin. Each one, missionary or otherwise, has to have it slain in him."

Any prejudices he had against the natives were certainly slain. His perfectly sane way of looking at every question prevented him from falling into the snare of spoiling them. When a boy would be the better of it he could administer a good " licking," and did so. He had, however, the " paternal pity " which justified his rule. Everywhere he won the unbounded love and confidence of the natives, and he saw quite well that they understood and appreciated thorough straightforward dealing. His physical powers of endurance were a constant marvel to them. He would arrive himself from a journey, and in an hour or so his carriers would begin to drop in one after another, limp and lame, completely unable to keep up with the Doctor. It was his opinion, and few men in British Central Africa had better grounds for forming an opinion, that " Africans are not spiritually set against good—at least few of them are." On his famous trudge after

Chikumbu on Mount Mlanje, of which we have already spoken, that chief's boy Sambo enlisted himself in the Doctor's service; "so now," he says—

> "'I have a little slave
> To labour in the sun,'

as the hymn says. He was the sharpest and most trusted boy Chikumbu had, but what he will turn out I cannot say."

The following shows the kindly, brotherly heart which won the affections of Africans, as perhaps few have done except Livingstone. It occurs in an account of his last pioneering tour in the Lomwe country:—

"We have been coming back till yesterday, and travelling faster than the Royal Mail (B.C.A.) We had therefore to divide our loads. I thought from the map that three days would take us to Namuli, so gave my word to the men that we should go ahead three days and no more. Nema, whom you know, was faint-hearted and would go back, so I let him. Michael, the Kola boy, also went back; but our wee Trojans stuck to us except wee Chibwana, but he is but a ' bairn.' I did not ask our ' weans ' to go, as I did not know what we might meet, but they came of their own accord,—Robin, Twere, and Salanko. Salanko is an awfu' nice wee chap, though they always would put some tins into the *mtanga* (basket) upside down, so that at night everything was either corn - floury, or jammy, or marrow-fatty, or condensed milky, or pears-in-syrupy, and then I had to scold them, although I told them I did not want to have to do it. They are only bairns of course."

In the second six months of his stay in Africa he was at Domasi, and there a fellow-missionary tells me he does not know how the Doctor slept at night. He had a folding-down chair, but his room was very small; there was no hospital at the station, and, as we have seen, his room was used to supply the want.

In every corner of his own wide parish on the Ndirande Hills he was well known, and the usual timidity at the approach of a white man was discarded when the Doctor came. The children

Salanko.

crowded about him, and it was with difficulty that he kept them from many an undue delay. When one remembers that the usual plan of a black mother to frighten her child into quiet or obedience is to say, "White man will come for you," just as children at home are often told "The black man will come for you," we have some idea of the extent to which the Doctor had won their confidence and love. He continually put himself to the trouble of discovering the nature and disposition of those with whom he had to deal, and managed the natives of Africa with the same tact, firmness, and love which made him the hero of the boys at Greenside.

When the Shiré Highlands were included in the Protectorate of British Central Africa, the position of the missionaries became increasingly difficult. With a civil government before which cases must go, it was a matter of course that their old position as arbiters of every situation should disappear, whilst the natives would naturally look to them still for redress or sympathy if they considered themselves hardly used. Indeed there could, in the nature of things, be no court of appeal except the sentiment of those who had been in the country before the administration was undertaken by the Crown. It says very much for Dr Scott that whilst he was one of the very strongest opponents of everything like oppression or injustice, he never once lost the respect and esteem of those officers whom he opposed. But he spared himself no trouble in bringing to light everything that could tell in favour of the natives when they were in trouble. One can easily at a distance understand the friction that constantly arises between missions and the officers of an Administration. They look at their duties from opposite standpoints. The Administration is there to develop the country, the missionary to develop the native. For the development of the country the native may or may not be necessary, but at any rate his interests will be subordinate to the general object pursued. It will be unfortunate if he should think that injustice is done to him by decisions given very likely by men who often do not understand, and sometimes do not care to understand, his genius ; but that is merely an accident of administration, and is not to be deplored if the development of the country goes on.

The missionary, in view of the development of men, regards everything that weakens the native's confidence in the absolute uprightness and justice of all whom he regards as Christians as really a force making against the object of his work. He would naturally palliate many things that an Administrator would punish. The "Jeddart justice," which secures that somebody is punished for a crime, may easily find illustration in the decisions given in new courts in new countries.

Robberies on the transit roads were uncomfortably common in his time in the Shiré Highlands, and on one occasion some Atonga carriers were attacked and robbed. The police apprehended some men belonging to Malunga's village—a part of Scott's Ndirande parish. He had been working amongst these people for a long time. Many converts had come in, and naturally he was anxious that everything should be done to put their case on the best footing. He got from the officer leave to take one of the police over the road on which they said the robbers had been tracked to a spot leading to Malunga's, and soon satisfied himself that they were unable to find any trace whatever. But in spite of all his efforts the decision was given that the robbery had been committed by Malunga's people, and the sentence pronounced that the whole village — Christians as well as others — should be removed, and Malunga imprisoned in a way something like "during her Majesty's pleasure" at home.

As the decision meant the destruction of one of the most promising parts of his own work, it was hardly to be expected that he would take it philosophically; but whilst he failed in getting their sentence reversed, his protests secured its delay until after the year's crops had been reaped. One would not have been surprised had this result brought about a breach in the relations between Scott and the Administration officers, but of all the testimonies to his worth we have received, none are kinder than those given by the men he opposed here most strongly.

CHAPTER XVI.

MARRIAGE—AFRICAN HOME LIFE—STATION IN ANGONILAND.

Dr Scott was married on Thursday, 10th November 1892, to Margaret Wilson, daughter of Dr J. Stewart Wilson, minister at New Abbey, Dumfries, and grand-daughter of Dr John Brown of Broughton Place U.P. Church, Edinburgh, and Professor of Exegetical Theology to the United Presbyterian Church. The occasion was an opportunity for a demonstration of the affection borne for him by the natives, a description of which is given in one of his wife's letters, which, full as they are of little details of African life and replete with interest from a missionary point of view, we hope may be given to a wider circle than the friends who have been privileged to read them :—

"On Thursday, after church, when Willie and I had come into the house, the whole of the twenty-one boys whose dormitories are attached to our house came in and shook hands solemnly with us to wish us welcome, and then one of them made a neat speech, which of course had to be interpreted to me by ·Willie. He said they all hoped we should be very happy, and that they were very glad to see a *donna* in the house again. There had been a doctor and his *donna* there before, and they liked them ; but the doctor had died and the *donna* had gone away and left them, so that they had been desolate and could never say 'Yes, ma'am,' unless they went to the *ma-ganga* (manse), and now they were very glad that they had a *donna* of their own that they could say 'Yes, ma'am,' to again, and to whom they could come with their troubles.

"It was a very neat speech, but you should have both heard and seen him during it. It was splendid. He was very eloquent, and gesticulated,

and made queer faces all the time. Every now
and then he turned round to the twenty behind
him, and they clapped hands tremendously, showing that these were their sentiments. Willie
made a speech in reply for me, and then they all
said 'Good-night,' and went off to bed. Wasn't
it nice of them ? and it was all their own idea."

His home now became the resort of all those
who required surgical or medical advice, and few
weeks passed without some sick European being
resident with them. He was anxious for a
hospital that never came, and till it should come
he constituted his own house the hospital, install-
ing his wife as his staff-nurse. When the patients
had a taste for music they were able to join in
the few musical evenings which he could afford,
and at all times they had the best medicine of a
light-hearted cheerful doctor whose address and
countenance always suggested recovery.

"We have had an invalid in the house again,
an engineer who was to put up the gunboats on
the lakes when they arrived there. He has had
a lot of fever since he came into the country, but

when he was on the Upper River he took it so badly that he was ordered home. Yesterday he arrived here on his way home, and will be here for a day or two before he can go on. One of our patients used to groan terribly when he was recovering. He said he was groaning with joy at the thought that he had nothing more to groan about!"

Kind as he was to all his fellow-countrymen, Scott's sense of the brotherhood of man made him not less kind to every native who had trouble. He truly entered into the fellowship of the sufferings of Christ. To Mrs Scott's letters we are indebted for all the details of his life at this time, and for a picture of him which would never have been preserved if it had depended on himself.

" A poor little child of seven died here to-day. Its mother and grandmother brought it to the surgery, and said it had been ill for four days. It was quite unconscious, poor wee thing! Willie got a hot bath and mustard for it. We put it in, and it seemed to do it good, and then we poured a little brandy down its throat. Its teeth were tightly clenched, but we managed to get it down. We rolled it up in blankets after its bath, and after a bit we gave it more brandy and then another bath, and Willie thought it would pull through. I beat up an egg with a few drops of brandy, and we tried to get it to swallow it, but we had just begun when the grandmother closed its eyes with her hand and said, ' Iai, Dotolo, iai ' (No, Doctor, no), and the wee thing just stopped breathing. It made no movement at all, poor wee thing ! They never said a word, but took off the blankets, gave them to Willie, swung it on the mother's back, tied it on with some calico just like a shawl, and carried it away without one word. It was most pathetic, and it was all done so quietly that we could hardly realise that the child was really dead. It looked such a pretty child, too. I thought how terrible it would be to have any of one's own people in such a dreadfully hopeless state, and to be struggling to keep it alive.

" The mother sat on the floor all the time with

her arms crossed in front, bowing her shoulders. She never took her eyes off us, but never said one word. Poor Willie was greatly distressed about it, for he thought he might have been able to pull her through, and says if they had only brought it sooner to him he thinks he could have saved its life."

The question of domestic servants assumes a different aspect in Africa from that which it has at home, and many a lady would cease her repinings for ever if she had a set of "scamps" like the Doctor's boys, backed by the encouragement of a husband who keenly enjoyed all their pranks. Robin, Bertie, and Kamanga were the chief boys in the house, and they could only be described as "broths of boys."

"Robin came in one day at lunch and told Willie that Tom needed medicine, so Willie asked 'What for?' Robin replied, 'Oh, it was only medicine.' Willie said again, 'What for?' whereupon the wretch said, 'Oh! for cheek,' and fled from the room."

Their house became known as the Calton Jail,

because one day Robin and Bertie for their mis-deeds had to be shut up in the bathroom, and afterwards this was found written on the wall in English, " This is the prison. Robin and Bertie are in it."

To keep the boys at their work was a her-culean task that made Mrs Scott quite limp by the end of the morning.

" They always want me to call them lazy boys, and then they say ' Very well, that is all right. Lazy boys never sweep or wash, but go and do nothing,' and then they pretend to go off. The other evening Willie was out and I was alone, when Robin, Bertie, and Tom came in and sat down, and began all kinds of nonsense. Then they asked me if I wouldn't give them some new calicoes to wear, as theirs were old, and we had a long discussion, as it was not long since I had given them calicoes. But I had to own that they were getting very bad, so at last I promised they would get them. Robin leapt up, made for the door, and went out, but returned immediately with a grand stride, went up to papa's photo, and began, with his arm out and an air as theatrical as Irving's, a long speech, telling papa how good the *donna* was to him to give him calico, and whenever he said, '*Donna*, I'm very hungry,' the *donna* always said to him, 'Go to the pantry to get green maize.' Then he went out, came in again, and speechified in the same way to mamma's photo. He says papa is his 'friend' and mamma is his 'dear.' They are all just as funny as can be, and as sharp as needles."

The African is in many ways only a child, and keeps his childish fancies longer than we are accustomed to see. Round the camp-fires on a *ulendo* roars of laughter proceeded from the vicinity of the Doctor. We can understand from this scene the popularity he enjoyed:—

"We have no dinner-bell yet, as the box in which it is packed has not come up; but Robin detected the Swiss cow-bell one day and asked me if he might ring that. I said 'Yes,' without really thinking. He was in high glee, and started off round the verandah with that awful thing, ringing it as if for dear life, and Bertie after him with a little table-bell that you strike with your finger. The row was awful. I thought the Manse people would think we were mad, so I went out and told Robin that that would do. However, Willie had heard the row and was highly delighted with it, so he got hold of it and did the same as Robin had done, only much worse, with that small imp at his heels. I got hold of it at last and hid it, but Robin slipped round by another way and saw where I had put it. It was to the fore again in a few minutes. I have given up trying to stop it now, except that I make a dive at Robin every now and then when the noise becomes too awful, and when he gets anywhere within reach. But it is no good. He always slips off somehow or other, so I let them ring as much as they please, and hope that they soon will get tired of it."

Scott's fun was only the relaxation of a few minutes in the midst of a constant press of work. He was doctor for all the Europeans, and his practice amongst the natives was tremendous. On one especially busy day he had no fewer than sixty-eight cases. At the same time he had his preaching work to do, and the nearest point of his parish work among the Ndirande hills was four miles off. *Machilas* he despised. He walked everywhere. Often, I am told by his friend, Mr James Reid, he was away long distances at nightfall, and came home long after everyone had retired. Ministers at home will probably think that their lines have fallen in pleasant places when they know what a missionary's Sunday is like.

In the morning he breakfasted at six o'clock, and very often walked off to Mandala, a mile distant, to see some patient, returning by seven o'clock for morning service, which he conducted on alternate Sundays. At 7.30 the surgery was opened and his patients came in crowds. At 8.30 the native service at the church was held, and at 10.30 the service for English residents. This last, which occupied an hour, he conducted in turn. His sermons were always full of solid matter, very frequently prepared at night when every other person was asleep. After dinner he set off at noon, walking with cricket-shoes and with a huge towel wrapped round his head, to the Ndirande Hill, in four villages of which he had Sunday services. He was hampered by orders from home that no building was to be done without permission, but no committee could forbid him to put up erections at his own expense. A meeting-house cost £15, and out of his own slender purse he built three of these in his own district. He returned by 5.45 to Blantyre for tea, and attended the evening service at 6.30. Not seldom a letter would be waiting him after service asking his attendance for some patient at the Zambesi Industrial Mission. This involved a trudge in the dark from ten to fourteen miles, but the hard work of the day never deterred him from starting at once and doing all he could for the agents of a mission which, in defiance of all laws of comity of Missions, had settled in his own district and taken away not a few converts from Blantyre. This work went on year after year.

Hard - worked ministers at home may console themselves with the reflection that their circumstances are not the worst possible.

Before he took up the Ndirande Hill few converts had been made, but during his time they came in thick and fast, and his wife's letters constantly tell of baptisms taking place. The native Christians, too, show that self - interest does not necessarily bulk largely in their minds. One boy has been offered large wages to leave the Mission, but he continues there as a teacher at the smaller wage rather than go.

In the intervals of his medical work he was to be found frequently in the joiner's shop helping to teach the natives, and superintending them if Mr M'Ilwain was absent. Indeed during the furlough of the latter he took entire charge of this branch of the work, and saved a substitute from home, who would otherwise have been necessary to keep the work from collapse, as it may probably take a generation or two to develop natives who can take the place of white men in positions of command.

Mlanje, too, occupied his attention, and one expedition was undertaken because, for want of the title-deeds, the Administration were refusing to recognise the purchase of land made by the mission from Chikumbu. Afterwards, however, these were recovered; but in the meantime Scott and his friend Mr Reid succeeded in finding some of the witnesses to the deed of sale, and in getting from them a certificate to that effect. On a later visit, caused by threatened war in the neighbourhood of the mission, his wonderful walking powers were shown. He left Blantyre at four in the morning and reached Mount Mlanje that night. After a short sleep he started again in the early morning and came straight on the next day, arriving just when evening service was proceeding. He walked right into church, took his place beside his wife, and joined in the hymn they were singing, the words being, " No, never part again." He had walked altogether over 80 miles, and been busy at Mount Mlanje as well.

His life from November 1892 till June 1894 seemed to have been spent here, there, and everywhere, in answer to calls for his medical skill. He was still the "jack - of - all - trades" of the mission, being sent whenever sound judgment and ready resource were required, sparing all men but himself, and working sometimes "like twelve men." Frequently he was worn out, and the tonic that restored him most quickly was one of those tremendous walks which would have invalided anybody else. At one time he has a patient in the Zambesi Industrial Mission which entails a walk of two hours every day. At another he is summoned to attend a doctor belonging to another mission, sets off, although from the reports received he thinks the patient cannot live till his arrival, hears on his way of the doctor's death, and returns in less time than any one had previously occupied in doing the distance.

Two events afforded him special satisfaction— the arrival of the mission steamer Henry Henderson, and the planting of a station in Angoniland. The steamer was named after the pioneer of the mission, and after numerous changes and repairs at Chinde, she came up the fastest boat

on the river except the gunboats. She was nicknamed the "pious paddler" and Scott looked forward with satisfaction to the river being wrought
at last by means of her, and to new facilities
for missionaries in their journey up from the
coast.

The station in Angoniland was taken up by two
ladies, Miss Bell and Miss Werner, and it fell to
Scott to choose the spot to build the house necessary. Then he accompanied the ladies to their
new destination and saw them begin work, satisfied
that at length the train was laid for future work
in a sphere he always looked upon as his own.
He left Pantumbi, the new station, allowing himself two days to reach Blantyre, in time to attend
a European lady who required his care, walked the
hundred miles, and arrived in good time and in
perfect condition. When he had seen his patient
out of danger he returned again to finish the
buildings on which he was engaged.

The arrival of a daughter, Marianne, on the 24th
March 1894, brought a new joy to Dr Scott; but
the needs of Angoniland took him away from home

immediately after, and he had scant time to cultivate the acquaintance of the little stranger, as in
June he thought it necessary to send her home
with her mother.   He accompanied them to Chinde
to see them off, and then returned to Blantyre,
hoping to follow them in the beginning of the next
year.   His furlough was already due, but the
mission needed him, as there was none to take his
place.   Like a soldier, he stuck to his post.

CHAPTER XVII.

IN THE "ONE-MAN-ONE-GUN COUNTRY."

BLANTYRE was visited in the end of May 1894 by a plague of locusts. As they came towards the station the air was quite full of them. All round about they had been a perfect scourge, and down by the river they had devoured every green blade. Their appearance was like a very heavy snowstorm, and they filled the air with a rushing sound. The people about the station turned out, firing guns and making all sorts of noises to drive them away; but the pest came in millions, and though the people set to work to sow and plant again after the plague had passed, the harvest was sure to be late, and the prospect of a "locust famine" next year became uncomfortably certain.

On his return from Chinde after seeing his wife and child off for home, it fell to him to get up a *ulendo* for the purchase of food. Combined with this was a prospecting tour in a totally new district—the Lomwe country, to the east of Shirwa. He was accompanied by Dr Henry E. Scott of Domasi for part of the way, as the latter wished to see the Lolo country, and by Mr James Reid. At starting the expedition consisted of a hundred native people—carriers all. They had with them the usual camp equipment, and scientific instruments necessary for an expedition over ground that had not been surveyed, besides the calico and beads which form the current coin amongst the natives. Moreover, it was imperative that a good many days' food should be taken with them.

They passed over familiar ground till, on 17th August 1894, they reached Ntemanyama's village, to the east of the southern extremity of Lake Shirwa, whose waters are salt. Here they found the chief rather afraid of the military authorities, whose men had been in his district endeavouring to trace a theft. Scott explained to him that there was no cause for fear if they themselves were friendly, and assured him of the aid of the mission in the event of any *mlandu* (case) arising with white men.   He had the satisfactory assur-

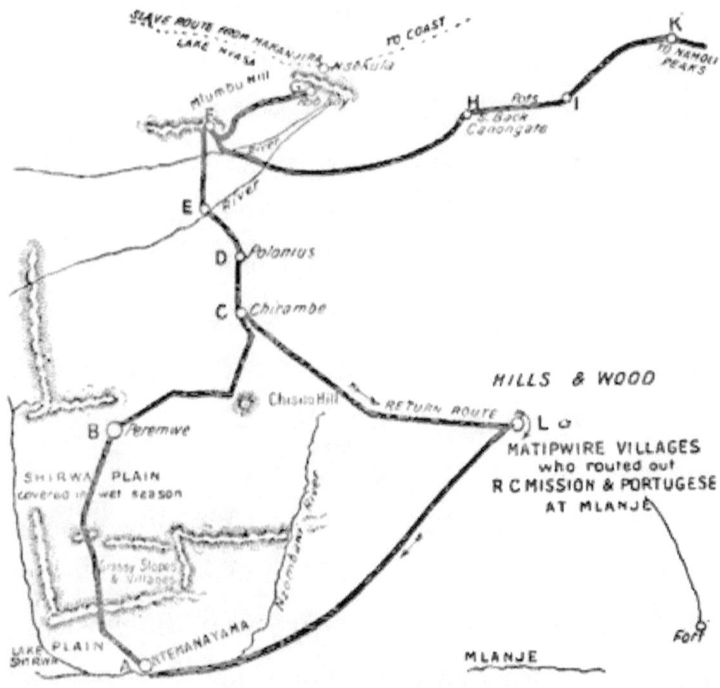

Sketch Route Map—Lomwe Journey.

ance that Ntemanyama was anxious to have a mission station in his territory.

From this point they struck northwards, passing numerous small villages on the way.

The surface bore evident marks of having at one time formed part of the bed of the lake. They found the earth impregnated with salt: the lake overflows much of the country in the wet season, and from the soil the natives extract, by a simple process, a coarse salt of a dirty grey colour. The number of salt-earth heaps at the side of the houses gives the villages a rather uncomfortable appearance. The day's journey took the travellers to Peremwe, a village without a chief. They were told that long previously the last chief had died of snake-bite, and no successor could be found because of the fear that the chieftainship was unlucky and might bring a violent death.

Their route led them next to Chirambe. They left Chisito hill on the right, and passed over a well-populated ridge to where they intended to make their headquarters for a time. They found the people there not over-dressed—indeed one letter describes them as "basking in smiles." The land was more densely populated than Angoniland. No wild beasts were to be found. Some of the natives had the old Lolo style of dressing the hair, like Patagonians. It was done up in curl-bark till it reached as far as to the shoulders. Altogether they seemed "frightfully ugly," an appearance increased by the filing of the teeth. The natives here seldom wash, but there is a good excuse for it in the scarcity of water. The travellers themselves used, for drinking and cooking, water which in ordinary circumstances they would have hesitated to walk through; and the allowance they had for their ablutions was three spongefuls apiece! At this point Dr H. E. Scott left the expedition for his own station. The mission boys proved themselves to be of very good mettle,—"Salanko has done well all the way—he is a capital wee chap; so have Chilwana, and Twere, and Robin, and that wee scamp Limweche as cheeky as ever."

There they succeeded in buying in two days 5000 lb. of rice.

The real difficulties of the expedition began after they left Chirambe. Their next halting-place was the village of a chief Namatema (i.e., "cut meat")—"an oldish man, a beautiful liar, a

sly old fox, and very, very like a whale."   Before
many hours were over he was dubbed Polonius.
He came to them, and with a roguish smile called
them his friends, but his friendship was of the
sort that manifested itself most prominently in
endless hindrances to their progress. They wished
to reach the Mlumbu Hills, thirty miles distant,
but he looked pathetically at them, and said, "Ah
no, you can't go there—no road, only wilderness
and wild beasts; and besides, did not the white
men come to buy rice, &c. The people are coming
to-morrow." Argument and expostulation are of
no avail. Guides to the next village he would
not furnish, as it was hostile, and his men would
be killed. Scott and Reid determined to go on
themselves, and before they had gone eight or nine
miles into Polonius's "wilderness" they came to
a large village. Scott walked right into it, but
found only some women and children, with whom
he sat down to talk before they could run away.
Leaving his companion, the Doctor returned for
his men, and found Polonius most willing to give
carriers when the road had been found.

Mlumbu Hill, from Kolomana's Village.

On the following morning they reached the
Mlumbu Hill, and found the people shy and
suspicious. They lunched under some trees in
the courtyard of the village under the wondering
gaze of the inhabitants, and were kept from *ennui*
by the presence of snakes in the branches above.
On the hill they rested overnight, and started in
the morning to reach a chief called Kolomana,
hoping that he would guide them to Nsikula, a
powerful slaving chief whose land is crossed by
the slave-route from Lake Nyasa to the coast.
Lest they should meet an unfriendly reception if
they approached Kolomana's *en masse*, two men
were sent on to announce their presence. Shortly
these returned to say that the people had fled.
The caravan advanced, but in a few minutes was
brought to a standstill by Scott being unpleasantly
confronted with the muzzles of half-a-dozen guns
at full cock. He at once threw up his hands to
show he was unarmed, and explained his purpose
through the interpreter. Another delay occurred
until the chief could be communicated with.
Permission to proceed was granted, and they

went on with one as guide, whom they called the "Dougal Cratur." Mr Reid's diary says of this worthy: "I really admire the fellow. He would, I am sure, have given the best-made Yao a stiff struggle for the first place in physique; his old flintlock was well ornamented with brass nails and native medicine; he had au ugly knife in his belt, and wore bits of hide for sandals. We had sent back for our men to come on. It was a funny sight. First went the Dougal Cratur, keeping his weather-eye on us; then the Doctor with his fantastic towel head - dress; then I followed. We were without guns, being led, goodness knows where, by this fine specimen of a lawless Highlander. Every dozen steps he stopped and looked round at us; our men had not come up, and I had half a thought of returning for them in case they should get into some mess. Our friend Dougal did not like it, for he kept looking round suspiciously, so I abandoned my intention, and we got into procession once more. We did not so much as talk to each other, as it might cause our guide to think we were concocting plans.

At last by a circuitous route we reached the village."

All along the path were the marks of slave-gangs, and whenever they sat down they saw slave-sticks hanging from the branches of the trees. One slave-gang had recently passed, and now another was expected. As the day wore on they sent a messenger to Nsikula. This chief is in close alliance with all the slave-traders in Nyasa-land, and is blood-brother to Kawinga, of whom we shall hear again. Nsikula curtly told the messenger he would have nothing to do with the white men. Long before, he had murdered the brother of a neighbouring chief, who threatened in reprisal to bring the white man with "his war," and he naturally supposed this was the fulfilment of the threat. There was then nothing possible except to return to Mlumbu hill, and to journey in another direction. At Mlumbu they were surprised by a visit from their old friend Polonius, who walked into the village with a *capitao*, bearing letters from Blantyre. Scott called him to account for his former statement that he was unfriendly

with the people on the hill.   "Oh, but," he replied,
"we were bringing letters to the white men and
nobody would dare to touch me!"

They next went eastward towards the Namuli
range of mountains.   The people made no secret
of their slaving propensities, and offered "black
ivory" for sale frequently.   At one point there
was considerable danger, and it seemed as if they
would never see another sun rise.   They were
passing a stream which wended through a deep
gully, when suddenly there rushed past them
a host of enraged natives yelling, "War! war!!
war!!!"   Every cry brought more men and more
guns.   The native boys of the caravan fixed cartridges into their guns, and were with difficulty
restrained from firing, although one shot would
have been followed by the massacre of the whole
party.   The missionaries marched steadily ahead
with their followers through the yelling crowd, and
at every clearing a file of seven or eight of their
would-be assailants stepped out with guns to the
shoulder.   The carriers would not walk across the
line of fire, and on each such occasion either the

Doctor or Mr Reid stood facing the guns whilst the caravan passed behind them. By quiet and fearless persistence they marched unscathed out of the most dangerous part of their journey.

They continued till they reached within a day or two's journey of the mountains, and then returned to Chirambe, and from that point by a new way to Ntemanayama.

Many of the incidents of this journey, as seen with the humorous eye of Dr Scott, we have left himself to tell in the account he gave the Blantyre people of this *ulendo* after his return from

"THE ONE–MAN–ONE–GUN COUNTRY.

"This is the kind of vote that sways the public away east towards the Namuli peaks, and the colour it gives to the country is most peculiar. It may be, one man, one gun, no powder, for all we saw, for we scarcely heard a gun all the way, but perhaps the powder is kept for greater occasions than a visit from two irresponsible white men.

"I think all the old Tower muskets must be

congregated in that country—'Tower' marked on them in plain English. What mines of taxes! if but the working were less hazardous. The people have no cloth—even bark-cloth is a luxury, the least possible quantity being counted sufficient. Yet every man, or semblance of a man, has a gun.

"The people on the confines of British territory have no guns: I mean we saw not one, and cloth is plentiful there. We noticed a tiara of shirt-buttons instead of beads at one place, I forget exactly where. I wonder what traveller has been paying Alolo carriers in shirt-buttons.

"One place we nicknamed the 'South Back Canongate, Edinburgh,' for it reminded us forcibly of home rowdyism.

"I never saw people who so enjoyed stealing as the people of that village did. If I were one of them, I should know how good a magpie feels when it has a gold brooch safe on the top of the Abbey, or Mr Morgan's tame baboon, when it gets Mr Elmslie's towel safe up the roof, or a company of screaming parrots when they have a native garden to themselves. We bought a fowl there, and soon heard its screams as it disappeared in the darkness. Our *capitaos* were quick, though, and came back out of the darkness, fowl and man attached. 'It was his brother who had run off with it, and he had gone to get it back!' We are all brothers, but we made a compact that we should not buy from our brethren that night, but in the morning by daylight; and furthermore, that we did not expect them to call for us that night, as we did not know what might happen. Then we put all our stuff into the 'band-stand,' and the carriers outside of it, and fires outside that, and took turns practising elevations with the sextant to pass the time. Our brethren kept themselves awake in the next house well into the night, but at last gave it up and turned in.

"The 'band-stand' is a useful feature of the villages in that quarter. It is a house, sometimes large, in the middle of the village, built without filling in the walls. It seems to belong to No One, and is used, I suppose, for hearing cases and village talk.

"We slept at the 'South Back' on our return journey, because the conditions of life were known. It was a well - understood bargain— 'We are very good friends, but anything lying about becomes our property.' We left a calico bag of precious oat - meal just ever so little beyond the firelight we were cooking by, and found when we were putting in the loads for the night that it had changed owners. The thought of no porridge for the rest of the journey was vexing; but we were relieved when one of our men, who chanced to go out during the night, found a native gourd at the door with all the oatmeal poured carefully into it. The calico bag was not to be seen, however. We were awakened in the morning by a cheery voice calling over the wall, 'Mvuka mlota' (rice for sale).

"The people were decidedly friendly, but we could not hold service with them, as that would give too many chances for our property to change hands.

Purchasing Rice in the Lomwe Country.

"There was the greatest difference in the character of the different villages, due, I daresay, to the one-man-one-gun tone allowing full scope for modern individualism. One village would be quiet and douce, with two old—very old men—the oldest men I have seen in Africa—talking at their ease in the open village court; the next just a collection of jumping rowdies, who treated us to a sham fight for some miles along the path. It looked too like a real fight at first, so like that our men were cheerily putting cartridges into their guns, and threatened seriously the peaceful missionary character of the expedition, but by a one-sided forbearance it at last became apparent that it was one man, one gun, no powder. So we sat down at the next village and talked matters over.

"Scarcely a man in that country seems able to go six miles from his own village without finding himself in an enemy's country, the fundamental rule being one man, one gun. We wrote down men to take loads many times, but after six or eight miles they always found that there were private reasons for preventing them going farther.

" We had to pay our ' South Back ' men off at the end of six miles, and found the corner of Mr Reid's towel showing below the calico that he had just paid one of them with. The thief would probably have found it if we had not. It made a very lame day's march, however, this stopping, so the next lot we wrote off to go the whole way without fail. At the next village, however (that of the old, old men), they remembered that there were difficulties ahead. We spent about an hour discussing the matter, and at last persuaded them to come on. It turned out afterwards that one of them had not come, and his load had been taken by one of our boys. The result was that during the sham fight that happened soon, one of his companions disappeared with his load.

" We had taken care not to give him anything of any value to him, but it meant the loss of a kitchen - pot to us. Never leave a *mlandu* unsettled behind you in a strange country. We traced our pot to where it had been taken on our way back, but could not get a *mlandu* spoken at all, and as only one of our men knew the

language, the difficulties of getting satisfaction
were increased. Likewise the neighbours dropped
in to hear, each one laying his gun down by
his side, till there were more people present
than the case required. We did not expect to
get back our pot, but we thought it would not
be right to let it go without telling the people
who knew about it how very wrong it was to
steal. But missionaries' protests are not always
respected. Some happy man is cooking his
porridge in a silicated iron 'goblet,' in a village
in a conspicuous position at the entrance to the
Namuli group of mountains. There is a very
large flat rock to mark the spot just beside it,
with some enormous boulders on it that look
as if they might slip off at any moment.

"If one wants to make a determined march
in a given time through a country, the only
way is to have a large, well-armed *ulendo* sufficient to take all one's loads, and walk through
with it.

"But for mission-work, a humble dependence
on the supply of the country, and a constitutional

waiting for introductions from one chief to another, though a slow way, is certainly better.

"Slow it certainly is. We left Blantyre along with one of the chiefs as his guests. He was very anxious—more anxious than we knew why—that we should not go east past him.

"'The chief on ahead would think we were bringing war.'

"'Why so? We shall tell him we are not.'

"'Our people never go there. We have no dealings with him.'

"'But they need not fear if they go with us.'

"We spent a good many days waiting for a guide to take us on. At last we got one to go a fair day's march as we thought, to a chief farther east. We found that he was only six miles away, and a close friend of the one we had left; and no chief at all. There we could not get guide or carrier on any account. 'There were no people that way,' 'there was no road,' 'was desert,' &c., &c. At last we had to go on our two selves, and leave the loads to be brought on.

"As we expected, there was a very fair path

eastwards. Whenever one sees a ticket up, 'No road this way,' one may be quite sure of a very good road that way. Then having found out the way, we had no lack of carriers volunteering.

"When we got within hail of the chief Nsikula we found out the reason of the objection to our going there. There had been some fighting between Nsikula's people and the people near where we had come from. Our friends had come to ask assistance from the Government, and Nsikula had got to know of it.

"Naturally he would suppose that when a party containing two white men came from that direction, this was the veritable 'English Man.' However, beyond refusing to have anything to do with us, he caused us no trouble. We had determined to have his own answer, and had therefore marched till we reached his back-door, where he kept his bulldogs—fine large-limbed Makua, who had their guns ready for any emergency.

"They would not believe our message when

we said we meant peace, so we had to leave our *ulendo* behind to go up to them without our guns to show that our intentions were genuine. Then we went with them to their village and were soon good friends. If there is no Arab influence, and no previous unsettled *mlandu* with white men, one is, I think, generally pretty safe to go anywhere. I hope no one comes to grief over our kitchen-pot—we did our best to settle it at any rate.

"From that place we got a message sent to Nsikula, but, as I said, he refused to see us, so that we had to take a detour to avoid him.

"We were not in any caravan-route all the way, as the one to Mozambique lay to the north of us, and the one to Quilimane to the south; the people we were amongst did not know much beyond their doors. Zomba was unknown to the people near Nsikula, and we could not get the name Namuli at all till we were within two days of it. We were delayed so much that we did not get to the peaks themselves, but the view we had of them gave promise of some ex-

traordinary country—as fine, if not finer than
Mlanje. We stopped at an old chief's. He is
a leper, but a refined and kindly old man. I
saw more little native places of worship at his
village than I have seen anywhere. No trace
of Arab influence in the district. Worship was
easier there than elsewhere, but of course ignorance of the language prevented us being intelligible
to them to any degree. The value of an *ulendo*
of this kind ought to be more apparent among
one's own carriers, as brotherly relations become
strongly cemented after a month's travelling
together.

"I never saw a man yet, worth calling a man,
who did not stick up for his own boys. The
Administration officers dote upon their Makua
and Zanzibaris, however hard they may be on
the Yaos; Mandala men say that the Atonga
are the boys for them, however little they may
think of the Machinga; our Domasi friends
used to put the Machinga on the pinnacle of
fame, and tried to feel as missionaries should
towards the Mang'anja; and Blantyre Mission—

' *Touch a deacon*, tread on the tail of my coat!' If a phlegmatic philosopher wanted to prove that black was white, or white black, he could put these various experiences in parallel columns. It would be a curious study in historical psychology to explain the state of mind here indicated, but we shall leave the problem, and give it out as 'a sum to be done at home.'"

It is interesting to know that shortly after Scott's death, the tribe by whom the pot was stolen sent to the mission saying that they had it in safe keeping, and would return it if only the missionaries would come back and live with them: and with the messengers they sent in gifts for the mourning. It may be that Scott had succeeded in sowing seed there which will yield a rich harvest after many days.

About himself and his future prospects he wrote in September of this year:—

"If Mr Hetherwick brings out a doctor, I shall be free to start work in Angoniland, or the Lomwe Country, or Cholo, and to work the river from there. If he does not bring out a doctor, I can see nothing for it but to stay in Blantyre till a doctor comes, and then see where to build our nest. I am in splendid health, and all right. I think I shall keep so, as far as any one can say."

CHAPTER XVIII.

WITH THE TROOPS ON THE CHIKALA EXPEDITION— ILLNESS—DEATH.

WE have now come almost to the end of our story. The last months of Scott's life were passed in the same ceaseless, unsparing devotion to his duty. His mind was ever occupied with thoughts of the new station at which he might build a house in view of the return of his wife and child. He was looking also for relief which never came. Medical authorities incline to the belief that four years is a sufficient length of time for a man to work in British Central Africa before furlough is taken. He had now been nearly six years there, and had crowded into that space of time as much as two ordinary men could have accomplished.

Appeals from home to return he disregarded, as his absence would have meant the collapse of a large portion of the medical work, seeing that Dr H. E. Scott of Domasi had gone home on furlough. His habitual cheerfulness never forsook him, and the few letters we have of this period show that he maintained his interest in every department of human affairs.

A letter to his wife, dated 4th January 1895, is full of the old schoolboy spirit, and of shrewd ideas about art :—

" I am writing with my own BLOOD, because the ink is done. I have not got any more of it, so rather than let you go without a letter I have done the deed. I hope it will last me my five pages.

" The ' Art Journals ' were very welcome with the Academy pictures. It is humiliating how few of the names of the painters I know. ' Punch Pictures ' are also delightful, but I have not had time to enjoy them yet. I mean, I spent too long time over the ' Art Journals,' and K. [K. stands for Conscience] would not allow me to look into them in peace, but kept nudging me all the time. When K.'s back is turned I shall have a squint at them.

"I was surprised no photograph of 'the mutual bundle' came by this mail, but I see you had not got to Edinburgh. I am not sure but one of your own doing would be as good as you will get. . . . Your photographs are at least not 'touched up' like the wretched photographer's productions. Don't let any photographer touch up my baby, or I'll touch him up. If she has a crooked nose, or a squint, or crow-feet at the corners of her pretty eyes, or premature wrinkles on her care-worn brow—I want them all.

"I am doing a picture from the side of the house here. I snatch time between bugle and church-time. It takes in the church in the middle, Soche in the right, and the Maganga at the extreme left. It seems a little better than usual, though I don't know. It is very patchy as yet, but I hope to get it knocked into shape. I should like to hope for a later development, not only in painting but all round, for both of us, so that we won't feel useless in this precious life that we have together. I should not wonder if I might be able to make some money for the mission by painting, especially if a late development comes. . . .

" Archdeacon Maples came across me one evening when I was painting, and wondered why I did not ' wash in ' the picture first. He used to paint, and had a brother a good artist. The Archdeacon is a very jolly man — tells no end of stories; and is a real good man with no lack of pluck and humour."

In the beginning of 1895 Kawinga, whom we mentioned in last chapter as blood-brother to Nsikula, began to cause trouble. His territory lay on Chikala hill to the north of Domasi. A few years before, he had been visited by Consul Buchanan and Dr H. E. Scott, and had signed a treaty making over his country to the English; but in a short time his slaving instincts reasserted themselves, and he attacked some of the others who were under British protection. He succeeded in defeating Major Maguire, who proceeded with a party of soldiers to punish him, and was by his success encouraged in his slave-trading and road-robberies. The Commissioner left him unmolested (as he occupied a very impregnable position on the hills) until there should be a sufficient military force in the country to make the storming of it a certainty. In January, however, he attacked the Domasi chief, Malemia, and carried off some of his people as slaves. Malemia promptly pursued the robber and defeated Kawinga's people at the foot of Chikala. The success was followed up by Mr Sharpe, the Acting Commissioner, who marched right up to the foot of the mountain, burned all the villages on the way, and built a fort at Malemia's for his protection. For a month everything was quiet, but in February, Kawinga suddenly burst from his stronghold with a force of some 1500 or 2000 warriors whom he had collected with the aid of Sarafi of Mangoche, and Matapwiri of Mlanje—two notorious slavers like himself.

He divided his forces into three bodies—one to attack Malemia's *boma*, a second to destroy Domasi mission-station, and the third to burn the plantation of Messrs Hynde & Stark. The last party was repelled before they reached the plantation; the second contingent was met and defeated by a body of Government troops who were out collecting firewood, and whose presence probably saved the lives of all in the mission. At the *boma* the enemy found only eight Sikh soldiers, one Englishman, and eight Makuas. They made the mistake of not "rushing" the *boma*, and endeavoured to overcome their opponents by shooting from whatever cover they could get. Kawinga had a reputation for a "medicine" which rendered his men bullet-proof, but the Sikhs picked them off with ease, shooting many of them through the forehead, on which the "medicine" had been painted. Firing began at 8 A.M. and was continued till noon, when the ammunition of the defenders became exhausted, and they threw open the door of the fort to make a sortie. Just at this point Messrs Hynde and Stark appeared with their workers armed with whatever weapons could be devised, having left their plantation to take care of itself whilst they might render needed aid to the *boma* or the mission. When they came upon the ground the enemy fled, leaving sixty of their number dead on the field.

It was now evident that if the country was to be secure, Kawinga must be expelled, and the Acting Commissioner decided to follow up this victory by an attack on the Chikala stronghold. He despatched a messenger for Captain Manning, who was with the Indian soldiers at Lake Nyasa, and another for Lieutenant Hamilton. Captain Gurney of the lake gunboats, who was at the Residency, volunteered to work the 7-pounder gun. The Rev. D. C. Scott, who was at Domasi, had written to Blantyre telling of the attack. He did not ask for assistance, but at once every available man left for the scene of war. Dr Scott had been ailing for some time, and had gone off with Mr M'Ilwain in search of some of the enormous timber which he was famed for discovering and bringing in to the station. The fever, however, he could not shake off with usual ease, and he was far from well when on his arrival on Saturday night he heard the news. He remained to do his Sunday work and then set out for Zomba, which he reached the next morning. He however broke down on the way, and had frequently to lie down by the roadside. He writes :—

"I had fever that night, but had no thermometer to test it. I have had a little every day since, and it is not away yet, though very nearly gone. We walked all night to get to the consulate on Monday morning in time for the expedition. I never was so 'done' in my life. Whenever I sat down I felt cold, so I had just to go on. It is no joke walking all night with fever on one."

At Zomba he felt so weak that he procured a *machila* to take him on to Domasi, and his arrival in such fashion sent a pang of fear through the heart of every friend. He lost no time in putting his services as a medical man at the disposal of the Commissioner, and found to his satisfaction that his arrival had anticipated a request from the authorities that he should accompany the expedition. During the week that elapsed before the expedition left he treated himself for the reduction of the fever, but rather unsuccessfully, and his friend Mr Reid begged to be allowed to go with him, as he was so poorly. Scott gratefully accepted the offer, and when they left for the front he seemed thoughtful and disinclined for conversation. They expected to meet with serious odds, but Kawinga's allies had been disheartened, and left him to fight his battle alone. The experience of being shelled across a valley was too novel for his warriors to bear philosophically, and the expedition, after surmounting difficulties innumerable, returned, leaving Kawinga's villages in ashes, and Chikala really, instead of nominally, in British hands.

On the return journey Scott found that some native volunteers had captured a woman, a boy, and a girl, and were making slaves of them. When he reported this to the Commissioner, they were at once handed over to him for the mission, and he took them into his own charge. When the expedition returned to Malemia's *boma*, Scott did not enter the fort, but proceeded to Domasi. In a few minutes he returned asking Mr Reid why he had sent for him. A native had brought him back with the story that he was wanted. The thought at once occurred that it was an invention to allow the original captors to possess themselves of their slaves, and this turned out to be the explanation. He never rested till he had them back again and the offenders severely punished. After some months the woman and the boy returned to Chikala, but the girl still remains at the mission in Domasi.

Of the real difficulties of the expedition we have the following graphic account which Scott penned on his deathbed:—

"THE CHIKALA EXPEDITION.

"Though so little was the actual effect of Kawinga's attack on the *boma* at Malemia, it would not be too much to say that it was an attempted invasion of Nyasaland. Almost every disaffected chief in or on the borders of Nyasaland was represented in it, and those who were not, were sitting, refusing carriers to any one, waiting to see the result. Five or six influential chiefs

T

probably were Kawinga's allies, though the number of his forces was a matter of guess. Perhaps 1500—just as likely more than that.

"The usual providential 'good luck' that attends the English in times of crisis did not fail in the present case. There happened to be the right kind of men, though few of them, in the *boma* at the time; Kawinga's forces fortunately thought it would be necessary to take the *boma* before going farther; the sortie from the *boma* when the ammunition was just about finished took place just as Messrs Stark and Hynde came up with their small party; and Bandawe and Atonga just came back from buying food at the right moment. And—Kawinga's people ran away—that is all.

"It is probable that as many as from 60 to 100 of them were killed. A large number of them, mostly Anguru, were shot round the *boma*. Kawinga had given them bullet-medicine largely, supposed to cause bullets to drop without wounding the man who possessed it. Most of them were shot through the medicine on their foreheads.

Anguru head-dress.

They crept up through the grass to get close to the *boma*, and when they put their heads up to take aim, were picked off by the Sikhs inside.

"From that time till Captain Manning's force arrived at Chikala (Kawinga's hill), there was absolute silence on Kawinga's part. The one piece of positive detailed information received by us, that the eastern approach by Mposa's village was defended by a strong stone *boma*, was found afterwards to be entirely false.

"It was in intention a bold and hazardous undertaking to attack Kawinga in his stronghold at that time, and it showed no small courage on the part of her Majesty's Acting Commissioner to face the necessity of it. The force was small. The Sikhs, who formed the nucleus, were little more than a handful. Their time is just up, and a term of service in Africa tells on them just as much as it does on Europeans. The undertaking would try them severely, as it required great physical endurance and activity; fever soon saps both of these. Counting Makua, Atonga, and

Yaos, the fighting force numbered about 200. That, with a 7-pounder gun, was what was available to storm Chikala.

"The physical difficulties in getting to Kawinga's are very great; with a determined force guarding it the place would be impregnable. It is a shelf containing from 2000 to 4000 acres standing out from the north side of Chikala mountain, with a stream flowing out of it towards the north-west, and it stands at least 2000 feet above the level of the plain at its base. It has a lip of rocks all round it, and from this lip there is a direct slope downwards as steep as it can be without being actually a precipice. The base forms a half-circle of perhaps eight miles, and is dotted all round with villages lying under the shelter of the great slope above. But the slope itself between them and Kawinga's plateau is too steep to be inhabited, and is therefore in its natural state of bush, boulders, thicket, and forest, in most places quite impracticable. Just at one or two places a ridge somewhat less encumbered runs up to the top of the rocks.

" Such is Kawinga's plateau from the north, but before an expedition coming from the south can get near it a very troublesome piece of country has to be got through.   There are two paths before it, one leading into Kawinga's at the east corner of the plateau by Mposa's, the other at the west, up the stream that flows out there.   Captain Maguire's party had to turn back from the path at Mposa's as being an impossible one, so the one at the west is the only one left.

" The difficulty there is that before one gets to the path at all one has to climb about 1200 feet, to cross a gully formed by a great spur from Chikala hill, and to descend just as far on the other side, all the road being commanded by hills on both sides occupied by Kawinga's villages.

" So that if all Kawinga's great hills and forests had been occupied by all Kawinga's great allies as well as his own great warriors, and if they all had shown great valour and determination to resist any invasion of their country, what a great deal of fighting there would have been !

" If any one wonders why we have given the

physical difficulties of the route so minutely, the reason is that they were practically the only ones encountered,—of fighting there was almost none. And to say so detracts nothing from, rather it enhances, the skill and courage with which the expedition was planned and carried out.

" It so happened that all Kawinga's allies had left him, and he seems to have had some trouble in settling his difficulties with them.   It was they who suffered most, and his bullet-medicine had turned out to be a terrible fraud.   He had been compelled to seize and give up as slaves a Mang'anja village of his own to satisfy them, and his own men were half-hearted.

" Other things helped the expedition.   The start was made at midnight from the *boma* at Malemia's, and the advance-guard was at least half-way up the pass mentioned before it was known that we were there at all.   The whole expedition reached the top of the pass by about eleven in the forenoon, and only a few straggling shots had been fired by the enemy.   No more could be done that day, so the expedition was withdrawn 1000 feet up the hill to the left, to a village in a good situation there. So far all was right.

"Then the 7-pounder told most powerfully—at least we suppose so. The people who had been turned out of their village were not remiss in firing from the rocks above; but after some shells had been dropped into a village across the valley away below us, the firing stopped, and there was no attack in the morning at all. Another thing that helped the expedition was the rain. It fell in torrents all the night we were on the hill, and all next day. It does not affect cartridges, but it must be very difficult to keep powder dry in an African downpour. And Africans themselves do not like rain, especially a cold driving rain with mist and wind in gusts. It is bad enough to be pelted with a driving rain with flannel on,—for flannel's flannel, wet or dry,—but it must be much worse with nothing on but a loin-cloth.

"So it happened that, except for some little firing from the bush by men who ran from their villages as the expedition passed, there was no opposition. Lieutenant Hamilton, who had the advance-guard, took the path which leads up the stream mentioned, and attacked Kawinga's village. Captain Manning, who took charge of all the baggage, marched round the hill till he found a fairly good ridge to get up by, and formed a junction with Lieutenant Hamilton on the top. The casualties on our side consisted of a scratch one of the carriers got on the forehead with a spent bullet. We are heartily glad there were no more, for we had started fully expecting very much worse. That expectation, indeed, was the reason of Mr Reid's and my own presence there.

"It would take a long chapter to show the importance of Chikala as a health station, as a check on the slave-trade, and as a geographical outlook. These will probably be dealt with elsewhere in full, and we shall only mention them here.

"We would like to thank the authorities for the honour showed us in asking us to accompany the expedition. To sleep 'heids and thraws,' round and round in a diminutive native hut, as the eight of us had to do, certainly promotes mutual forbearance and good-fellowship."

He returned to Blantyre in the end of February still stricken by fever, and was forced to take to bed, from which, however, he rose to attend to a patient at Mandala. He walked thither, but had to ask for a *machila* to take him home.

On the 15th of March he wrote to his wife his last letter home :—

" I am still where I was when I wrote a fortnight ago, in bed with this same old fever. It was almost away, and I was going to get up next day, when all of a sudden it came back again, with companions in the shape of pains like pleurisy stitches that would scarcely let me breathe. (I think more neuralgia due to fever than anything else.) A man has two sides, so they first did me on the one side and then on the other. I think I am through with them now. When due to malaria these things are not serious, but only painful at the time. Temperature was up to 104° on two nights only : last two nights it has been down to 100°. It has been a long dragging fever, and I shall be very glad when it departs, and lets me back to my work again.

"I eat well and sleep fairly, and have no sickness. Of course I am a little weak with such a long spell—that is nearly all about it. It is not a fever that is the least likely to turn into any other kind, and recovery is just a matter of time. Now you know all about it, and I think it is well to tell you. I know you will be vexed that you are not here, and I must say I would be mighty glad to see you, but there's the vast hiatus that comes in between the wish and the reality.

"I think the fever is going away really now, but one can't tell exactly. If it were to drag on too long I should start for home, but I do not think this will be necessary. I almost have to see where I am to bring you back to before we come out again, and if possible have a house and everything ready. I can see into that nicely this dry season, and be home, I should say, in the autumn. If the Committee don't send out a doctor to be here by the beginning of the dry season, I shall leave Blantyre without a doctor,

and go to do the business I have to do. I think
that's square.

"Lomwe country seems to be opening up
nicely. Chirambe has been himself to the 'South
Back Canongate,' and gave the chief there 'part of
the present we sent to him.' (That's too good to
be true.) Anyway, he has been there and made
friends. He brought back some hoes for sale.
He is coming in soon, so I shall see and talk with
him. He is very friendly himself, and very
anxious for us to build at his place. I hope to
get there with Mr Reid, and go right on to
Namuli to see the whole country. I shouldn't
wonder if we found it suitable to settle. At any
rate, I shall try to be home with something quite
definite. . . .

"All your news about baby's doings is delightful. We'll have a good time of it, the three of
us, when I get into the middle. I am very glad
she is turning out so little trouble, and is so good
always, and that she cheers up your father a bit.

"I suppose the little Free kirk stands the same
as ever at the entrance of the great wide avenue,

that's lined by walls built long ago by no one knows whom, and shadowed by those glorious limes.   Which is a sort of parable, for there is a glorious broad avenue, which makes every one who enters it beautiful with side-lights and reflected lights, and which leads upwards.   Up goes the bandbox, 'This is the way to the avenue, the only way to the avenue.'

"But I must not try high-falutin', or I'll be like ———'s sermon on 'Multitudes, multitudes in the valley of decision.'   Mother said she never made out at the time or since what he was driving at, and she rather thought he was not quite sure himself.   Queer how one remembers these things. . . .

"The whole Blantyre folk have conspired to fill me with jellies, puddings, and soups, far more than I could eat if I were well.   It is wonderful how kind one's neighbours are when one is ill."

On the same day he despatched a messenger for Dr Robertson, saying that there was a lot of sickness, and he felt too weak to attend to his patients.   When his colleague arrived he discussed his own case with him, and decided on the treatment which should be begun the next day. On that day (Sunday, the 17th March) he was seized with the pains which betokened severe congestion of the lungs, and he grew evidently weaker. He was nursed with unremitting care by his colleague and by Mr Reid, his companion in many a journey and danger, and the latter was struck in the last days by his gratefulness for the very slightest service. On Wednesday his temperature rose considerably, and for a little he lost heart; but in the afternoon he said, "Reid, this fever is not going away,—something must be done. I'll go home to-morrow by the steamer. Can't you leave your work and go to Durban with me?" Though his friend had a feeling that he could not recover, he began packing at once, and got carriers for the start next morning. About midnight, however, Scott called Dr Robertson's attention to his pulse, which had become weak, fast, and easily compressible. His brother, who had just arrived from Domasi on his way to Scotland with his dying wife, was at once summoned, and for two hours the unequal fight with death was maintained. On his narrow bed he lay panting, his features unnaturally sharp, and a wearied expression on his face. Yet he fought nobly for his life. A lamp cast its feeble yellow light on the room where the strong young man, separated by a soldier's sense of duty from wife and child, lay struggling with death, giving directions to his brother to watch his pulse and note the changes, and to his colleague regarding the injection of the drugs. The strain of deepest anxiety stamped the faces of the three, who watched hoping against hope that his wonderful vitality might yet assert itself. At a quarter to two he realised he was dying, and he looked pitifully at his brother and Mr Reid, and with the words, "Oh, I'm done!" he ceased his struggles, and in a few minutes passed away.

The shock to the community was indescribable. The Ndirande hill people—his own parishioners— were in Blantyre within an hour or two, mourning with all the grief of men who had lost their best friend. "We have no Doctor now!" was their general wail. At his funeral one of the oldest of the European residents said, "Why has he been taken? He was the best man who ever came to the Shiré Highlands." The officer who commanded the forces in the Chikala expedition had never met him except during the fortnight they were together there, but when he heard of the Doctor's death he burst into tears, which do him as much honour as his valour. The news of his death was carried one hundred miles into Angoniland within thirty-six hours.

Tributes of affection and sorrow were numerous. A member of the Administration wrote on hearing of his death : " It is not the mission alone, but the whole country, which is the poorer and the sadder for this calamity. It is perhaps some slight consolation to know that Dr Scott died bravely at his post, as truly a martyr as any of those of history, and that the whole of British Central Africa mourns the death and honours the memory of the Christian Hero."

The most intimate of his colleagues says of

him : " The influence his life has had on mine is known only to myself. He did not live in vain : never man worked more diligently and unselfishly in the cause of his Maker than he did. Every call to duty was to him a call from God— willingly obeyed. I thank God it was my privilege to know him. . . . His was a noble life, and we thank God for it. If you wished only to see and realise how he was esteemed of men, and—best of all, and what he himself lived for—the love of the natives for him, you had only to be in Blantyre last week to see what a pure, unselfish, and Christlike example his had been to all."

In reply to the writer's request, Mr Sharpe, H.M. Acting Commissioner in British Central Africa at the time of Scott's death, wrote as follows :—

" There could be only one answer to your letter. Dr Scott was a really *good* man, always ready to help others, regardless of any trouble or discomfort to himself in his desire to at once reach those who required his services. No one in British Central Africa, I think, has ever been more ready to go off at a moment's notice any distance to look after those who were ill. There is not a settler in British Central Africa, whatever his occupation, who would not tell you just what I have now said. We have all had to thank him.

"His last journey was with me to look after the possible injured in the Kawinga Campaign : he was himself constantly suffering from fever during the whole of that expedition, and I fear it hastened his death ; but during the whole time he never complained, marched with the others, and was always ready to help.

"He was known to all natives throughout the Shiré Highlands, and farther, and to them was the essence of kindness. As you well know, his loss was deeply felt by all of us."

Most touching of all, perhaps, was the voice given to the sorrow of the natives in a letter written to Mrs Scott by an African girl who was one of their servants :—

"DEAR POOREST MAMMA,—I am writing this

letter to you now with much sorrow.   My *donna*, at Chinde you said to me, ' Abbey, farewell ! you will stay at Blantyre, and be a good girl; and I shall come back to you.'   And, indeed, I have kept in mind that my *donna* said she would come back, and I have remembered it every day. But now I know that she will not come to me, and that my eyes will never see her again.

" Dr Scott told me every day, ' Abbey, I shall go and bring the *donna*,' and my heart was glad; but now I am a poor girl—for my master is dead.

" Indeed all here at Blantyre are sorrowing because he, your husband, is dead.   Also in the mission they lament for you and for your little child. Every Sunday I shall take flowers and lay them on my master's grave.   I shall go and plant some there, and kneel down and cry because there is great sorrow in my heart for Dr Scott and for myself in my misery.—I am, your very sad girl,

" ABBEY-NDENDERMERE."

On the day following his death this notice

was sent out by two members of the Administration :—

"BLANTYRE, 22*d* *March* 1895.

"It has been suggested that a subscription be raised in British Central Africa for the purpose of erecting a suitable monument in Blantyre to the late Dr W. A. Scott, whose sudden death is deeply deplored by the community at large. With this view we venture to send you this notice, and shall be glad to receive any subscription you may think fit to give for this purpose. Any amount in excess will be put at the disposal of Mrs W. A. Scott.

(Signed)   J. E. MACMASTER.
T. H. LLOYD."

A sum of over £300 was collected. Part of the money was spent in putting a memorial window into the church at Blantyre, and the balance sent to Mrs Scott.

The Young Men's Guild sent a memorial brass tablet to be put in the church.

Over his grave there is placed a cross of white marble, with the inscription :—

"Where I am, there ye may be also."

WILLIAM AFFLECK SCOTT, M.B., C.M.

BORN MARCH 11TH, 1862.

DIED MARCH 21ST, 1895.

"*Mwai u-li ni a-ku-yera-m'mtima: chifukwa iwo a-dza-ona Mulungu.*"

("Blessed are the pure in heart: for they shall see God.")

Since his death native hands have placed fresh flowers every Sunday morning on his grave.

He died at the age of thirty-three, beloved by all, hardly known to his Church, which scarcely yet recognises what a gift from God she had in him—a true son of Livingstone, and one who truly proved himself to be

A HERO OF THE DARK CONTINENT.

INDEX.

Catalogue

of

Messrs Blackwood & Sons' Publications

PHILOSOPHICAL CLASSICS FOR ENGLISH READERS.

Edited by WILLIAM KNIGHT, LL.D.,

Professor of Moral Philosophy in the University of St Andrews.

In crown 8vo Volumes, with Portraits, price 3s. 6d.

Contents of the Series.

DESCARTES, by Professor Mahaffy, Dublin.—BUTLER, by Rev. W. Lucas Collins, M.A.—BERKELEY, by Professor Campbell Fraser.—FICHTE, by Professor Adamson, Glasgow. — KANT, by Professor Wallace, Oxford.—HAMILTON, by Professor Veitch, Glasgow.—HEGEL, by the Master of Balliol. —LEIBNIZ, by J. Theodore Merz. — VICO, by Professor Flint, Edinburgh.—HOBBES, by Professor Croom Robertson. — HUME, by the Editor. — SPINOZA, by the Very Rev. Principal Caird, Glasgow.—BACON: Part I. The Life, by Professor Nichol.— BACON: Part II. Philosophy, by the same Author.—LOCKE, by Professor Campbell Fraser.

FOREIGN CLASSICS FOR ENGLISH READERS.

Edited by Mrs OLIPHANT.

In crown 8vo, 2s. 6d.

Contents of the Series.

DANTE, by the Editor. — VOLTAIRE, by General Sir E. B. Hamley, K.C.B. —PASCAL, by Principal Tulloch. — PETRARCH, by Henry Reeve, C.B.—GOETHE, by A. Hayward, Q.C.—MOLIÈRE, by the Editor and F. Tarver, M.A.—MONTAIGNE, by Rev. W. L. Collins, M.A.—RABELAIS, by Sir Walter Besant. — CALDERON, by E. J. Hasell.—SAINT SIMON, by Clifton W. Collins, M.A. — CERVANTES, by the Editor. — CORNEILLE AND RACINE, by Henry M. Trollope. — MADAME DE SÉVIGNÉ, by Miss Thackeray.—LA FONTAINE, AND OTHER FRENCH FABULISTS, by Rev. W. Lucas Collins, M.A.—SCHILLER, by James Sime, M.A., Author of 'Lessing, his Life and Writings.'—TASSO, by E. J. Hasell. — ROUSSEAU, by Henry Grey Graham. — ALFRED DE MUSSET, by C. F. Oliphant.

ANCIENT CLASSICS FOR ENGLISH READERS.

Edited by the Rev. W. LUCAS COLLINS, M.A.

Complete in 28 Vols. crown 8vo, cloth, price 2s. 6d. each.   And may also be had in 14 Volumes, strongly and neatly bound, with calf or vellum back, £3, 10s.

Contents of the Series.

HOMER: THE ILIAD, by the Editor.— HOMER: THE ODYSSEY, by the Editor.— HERODOTUS, by George C. Swayne, M.A.— XENOPHON, by Sir Alexander Grant, Bart., LL.D. — EURIPIDES, by W. B. Donne.— ARISTOPHANES, by the Editor.—PLATO, by Clifton W. Collins, M.A.—LUCIAN, by the Editor. — ÆSCHYLUS, by the Right Rev. the Bishop of Colombo. — SOPHOCLES, by Clifton W. Collins, M.A. — HESIOD AND THEOGNIS, by the Rev. J. Davies, M.A.— GREEK ANTHOLOGY, by Lord Neaves. — VIRGIL, by the Editor.—HORACE, by Sir Theodore Martin, K.C.B. — JUVENAL, by Edward Walford, M.A. — PLAUTUS AND TERENCE, by the Editor. — THE COMMENTARIES OF CÆSAR, by Anthony Trollope. —TACITUS, by W. B. Donne.—CICERO, by the Editor. — PLINY'S LETTERS, by the Rev. Alfred Church, M.A., and the Rev. W. J. Brodribb, M.A. — LIVY, by the Editor.—OVID, by the Rev. A. Church, M.A. — CATULLUS, TIBULLUS, AND PROPERTIUS, by the Rev. Jas. Davies, M.A. — DEMOSTHENES, by the Rev. W. J. Brodribb, M.A.—ARISTOTLE, by Sir Alexander Grant, Bart., LL.D.—THUCYDIDES, by the Editor. — LUCRETIUS, by W. H. Mallock, M.A.—PINDAR, by the Rev. F. D. Morice, M.A.

Saturday Review.—"It is difficult to estimate too highly the value of such a series as this in giving 'English readers' an insight, exact as far as it goes, into those olden times which are so remote, and yet to many of us so close."

CATALOGUE

OF

MESSRS BLACKWOOD & SONS'

PUBLICATIONS.

ALISON.

History of Europe. By Sir ARCHIBALD ALISON, Bart., D.C.L.

1. From the Commencement of the French Revolution to the Battle of Waterloo.
   LIBRARY EDITION, 14 vols., with Portraits. Demy 8vo, £10, 10s.
   ANOTHER EDITION, in 20 vols. crown 8vo, £6.
   PEOPLE'S EDITION, 13 vols. crown 8vo, £2, 11s.

2. Continuation to the Accession of Louis Napoleon.
   LIBRARY EDITION, 8 vols. 8vo, £6, 7s. 6d.
   PEOPLE'S EDITION, 8 vols. crown 8vo, 34s.

Epitome of Alison's History of Europe. Thirtieth Thousand, 7s. 6d.

Atlas to Alison's History of Europe. By A. Keith Johnston.
   LIBRARY EDITION, demy 4to, £3, 3s.
   PEOPLE'S EDITION, 31s. 6d.

Life of John Duke of Marlborough. With some Account of his Contemporaries, and of the War of the Succession. Third Edition. 2 vols. 8vo. Portraits and Maps, 30s.

Essays : Historical, Political, and Miscellaneous. 3 vols. demy 8vo, 45s.

ACROSS FRANCE IN A CARAVAN : BEING SOME ACCOUNT OF A JOURNEY FROM BORDEAUX TO GENOA IN THE "ESCARGOT," taken in the Winter 1889-90. By the Author of 'A Day of my Life at Eton.' With fifty Illustrations by John Wallace, after Sketches by the Author, and a Map. Cheap Edition, demy 8vo, 7s. 6d.

ACTA SANCTORUM HIBERNIÆ ; Ex Codice Salmanticensi. Nunc primum integre edita opera CAROLI DE SMEDT et JOSEPHI DE BACKER, e Soc. Jesu, Hagiographorum Bollandianorum ; Auctore et Sumptus Largiente JOANNE PATRICIO MARCHIONE BOTHAE. In One handsome 4to Volume, bound in half roxburghe, £2, 2s.; in paper cover, 31s. 6d.

ADOLPHUS. Some Memories of Paris. By F. ADOLPHUS. Crown 8vo, 6s.

AIKMAN.

Manures and the Principles of Manuring. By C. M. AIKMAN, D.Sc., F.R.S.E., &c., Professor of Chemistry, Glasgow Veterinary College; Examiner in Chemistry, University of Glasgow, &c. Crown 8vo, 6s. 6d.

Farmyard Manure : Its Nature, Composition, and Treatment. Crown 8vo, 1s. 6d.

AIRD. Poetical Works of Thomas Aird. Fifth Edition, with Memoir of the Author by the Rev. JARDINE WALLACE, and Portrait. Crown 8vo, 7s. 6d.

ALLARDYCE.
The City of Sunshine. By ALEXANDER ALLARDYCE, Author of 'Earlscourt,' &c. New Edition. Crown 8vo, 6s.
Balmoral: A Romance of the Queen's Country. New Edition. Crown 8vo, 6s.

ALMOND. Sermons by a Lay Head-master. By HELY HUTCH-INSON ALMOND, M.A. Oxon., Head-Master of Loretto School. Crown 8vo, 5s.

ANCIENT CLASSICS FOR ENGLISH READERS. Edited by Rev. W. LUCAS COLLINS, M.A. Price 2s. 6d. each. *For List of Vols., see p. 2.*

ANDERSON. Daniel in the Critics' Den. A Reply to Dean Farrar's 'Book of Daniel.' By ROBERT ANDERSON, LL.D., Barrister-at-Law, Assistant Commissioner of Police of the Metropolis; Author of 'The Coming Prince,' 'Human Destiny,' &c. Post 8vo, 4s. 6d.

AYTOUN.
Lays of the Scottish Cavaliers, and other Poems. By W. EDMONDSTOUNE AYTOUN, D.C.L., Professor of Rhetoric and Belles-Lettres in the University of Edinburgh. New Edition. Fcap. 8vo, 3s. 6d.
ANOTHER EDITION. Fcap. 8vo, 7s. 6d.
CHEAP EDITION. 1s. Cloth, 1s. 3d.
An Illustrated Edition of the Lays of the Scottish Cavaliers. From designs by Sir NOEL PATON. Cheaper Edition. Small 4to, 10s. 6d.
Bothwell: a Poem. Third Edition. Fcap., 7s. 6d.
Poems and Ballads of Goethe. Translated by Professor AYTOUN and Sir THEODORE MARTIN, K.C.B. Third Edition. Fcap., 6s.
The Ballads of Scotland. Edited by Professor AYTOUN. Fourth Edition. 2 vols. fcap. 8vo, 12s.
Memoir of William E. Aytoun, D.C.L. By Sir THEODORE MARTIN, K.C.B. With Portrait. Post 8vo, 12s.

BACH.
On Musical Education and Vocal Culture. By ALBERT B. BACH. Fourth Edition. 8vo, 7s. 6d.
The Principles of Singing. A Practical Guide for Vocalists and Teachers. With Course of Vocal Exercises. Second Edition. With Portrait of the Author. Crown 8vo, 6s.
The Art Ballad: Loewe and Schubert. With Musical Illus-trations. With a Portrait of LOEWE. Third Edition. Small 4to, 5s.

BEDFORD & COLLINS. Annals of the Free Foresters, from 1856 to the Present Day. By W. K. R. BEDFORD, W. E. W. COLLINS, and other Contributors. With 55 Portraits and 59 other Illustrations. Demy 8vo, 21s. *net.*

BELLAIRS. Gossips with Girls and Maidens, Betrothed and Free. By LADY BELLAIRS. New Edition. Crown 8vo, 3s. 6d. Cloth, extra gilt edges, 5s.

BELLESHEIM. History of the Catholic Church of Scotland. From the Introduction of Christianity to the Present Day. By ALPHONS BEL-LESHEIM, D.D., Canon of Aix-la-Chapelle. Translated, with Notes and Additions, by D. OSWALD HUNTER BLAIR, O.S.B., Monk of Fort Augustus. Cheap Edition. Complete in 4 vols. demy 8vo, with Maps. Price 21s. net.

BENTINCK. Racing Life of Lord George Cavendish Bentinck, M.P., and other Reminiscences. By JOHN KENT, Private Trainer to the Good-wood Stable. Edited by the Hon. FRANCIS LAWLEY. With Twenty-three full-page Plates, and Facsimile Letter. Third Edition. Demy 8vo, 25s.

BEVERIDGE.

Culross and Tulliallan ; or, Perthshire on Forth. Its History
and Antiquities. With Elucidations of Scottish Life and Character from the
Burgh and Kirk-Session Records of that District. By DAVID BEVERIDGE. 2 vols.
8vo, with Illustrations, 42s.

Between the Ochils and the Forth ; or, From Stirling Bridge
to Aberdour. Crown 8vo, 6s.

BICKERDYKE. A Banished Beauty. By JOHN BICKERDYKE,
Author of 'Days in Thule, with Rod, Gun, and Camera,' 'The Book of the All-
Round Angler,' 'Curiosities of Ale and Beer,' &c. With Illustrations. Crown
8vo, 6s.

BIRCH.

Examples of Stables, Hunting-Boxes, Kennels, Racing Estab-
lishments, &c. By JOHN BIRCH, Architect, Author of 'Country Architecture,'
&c. With 30 Plates. Royal 8vo, 7s.

Examples of Labourers' Cottages, &c. With Plans for Im-
proving the Dwellings of the Poor in Large Towns. With 34 Plates. Royal 8vo, 7s.

Picturesque Lodges. A Series of Designs for Gate Lodges,
Park Entrances, Keepers', Gardeners', Bailiffs', Grooms', Upper and Under Servants' Lodges, and other Rural Residences. With 16 Plates. 4to, 12s. 6d.

BLACK. Heligoland and the Islands of the North Sea. By
WILLIAM GEORGE BLACK. Crown 8vo, 4s.

BLACKIE.

Lays and Legends of Ancient Greece. By JOHN STUART
BLACKIE, Emeritus Professor of Greek in the University of Edinburgh. Second
Edition. Fcap. 8vo, 5s.

The Wisdom of Goethe. Fcap. 8vo. Cloth, extra gilt, 6s.

Scottish Song : Its Wealth, Wisdom, and Social Significance.
Crown 8vo. With Music. 7s. 6d.

A Song of Heroes. Crown 8vo, 6s.

John Stuart Blackie : A Biography. By ANNA M. STODDART.
With 3 Plates. Third Edition. 2 vols. demy 8vo, 21s.
POPULAR EDITION. With Portrait. Crown 8vo, 6s.

BLACKMORE. The Maid of Sker. By R. D. BLACKMORE,
Author of 'Lorna Doone,' &c. New Edition. Crown 8vo, 6s. Cheaper Edition. Crown 8vo, 3s. 6d.

BLACKWOOD.

Blackwood's Magazine, from Commencement in 1817 to December 1896. Nos. 1 to 974, forming 160 Volumes.

Index to Blackwood's Magazine. Vols. 1 to 50. 8vo, 15s.

Tales from Blackwood. First Series. Price One Shilling each,
in Paper Cover. Sold separately at all Railway Bookstalls.
They may also be had bound in 12 vols., cloth, 18s. Half calf, richly gilt, 30s.
Or the 12 vols. in 6, roxburghe, 21s. Half red morocco, 28s.

Tales from Blackwood. Second Series. Complete in Twenty-
four Shilling Parts. Handsomely bound in 12 vols., cloth, 30s. In leather back,
roxburghe style, 37s. 6d. Half calf, gilt, 52s. 6d. Half morocco, 55s.

Tales from Blackwood. Third Series. Complete in Twelve
Shilling Parts. Handsomely bound in 6 vols., cloth, 15s.; and in 12 vols., cloth,
18s. The 6 vols. in roxburghe, 21s. Half calf, 25s. Half morocco, 28s.

Travel, Adventure, and Sport. From 'Blackwood's Magazine.'
Uniform with 'Tales from Blackwood.' In Twelve Parts, each price 1s. Handsomely bound in 6 vols., cloth, 15s. And in half calf, 25s.

BLACKWOOD.

New Educational Series. *See separate Catalogue.*
New Uniform Series of Novels (Copyright).
Crown 8vo, cloth. Price 3s. 6d. each. Now ready:—

THE MAID OF SKER. By R. D. Blackmore.
WENDERHOLME. By P. G. Hamerton.
THE STORY OF MARGRÉDEL. By D. Storrar Meldrum.
MISS MARJORIBANKS. By Mrs Oliphant.
THE PERPETUAL CURATE, and THE RECTOR. By the Same.
SALEM CHAPEL, and THE DOCTOR'S FAMILY. By the Same.
A SENSITIVE PLANT. By E. D. Gerard.
LADY LEE'S WIDOWHOOD. By General Sir E. B. Hamley.
KATIE STEWART, and other Stories. By Mrs Oliphant.
VALENTINE AND HIS BROTHER. By the Same.
SONS AND DAUGHTERS. By the Same.
MARMORNE. By P. G. Hamerton.

REATA. By E. D. Gerard.
BEGGAR MY NEIGHBOUR. By the Same.
THE WATERS OF HERCULES. By the Same.
FAIR TO SEE. By L. W. M. Lockhart.
MINE IS THINE. By the Same.
DOUBLES AND QUITS. By the Same.
ALTIORA PETO. By Laurence Oliphant.
PICCADILLY. By the Same. With Illustrations.
LADY BABY. By D. Gerard.
THE BLACKSMITH OF VOE. By Paul Cushing.
THE DILEMMA. By the Author of 'The Battle of Dorking.'
MY TRIVIAL LIFE AND MISFORTUNE. By A Plain Woman.
POOR NELLIE. By the Same.

Standard Novels. Uniform in size and binding. Each complete in one Volume.

FLORIN SERIES, Illustrated Boards. Bound in Cloth, 2s. 6d.

TOM CRINGLE'S LOG. By Michael Scott.
THE CRUISE OF THE MIDGE. By the Same.
CYRIL THORNTON. By Captain Hamilton.
ANNALS OF THE PARISH. By John Galt.
THE PROVOST, &c. By the Same.
SIR ANDREW WYLIE. By the Same.
THE ENTAIL. By the Same.
MISS MOLLY. By Beatrice May Butt.
REGINALD DALTON. By J. G. Lockhart.

PEN OWEN. By Dean Hook.
ADAM BLAIR. By J. G. Lockhart.
LADY LEE'S WIDOWHOOD. By General Sir E. B. Hamley.
SALEM CHAPEL. By Mrs Oliphant.
THE PERPETUAL CURATE. By the Same.
MISS MARJORIBANKS. By the Same.
JOHN: A Love Story. By the Same.

SHILLING SERIES, Illustrated Cover. Bound in Cloth, 1s. 6d.

THE RECTOR, and THE DOCTOR'S FAMILY. By Mrs Oliphant.
THE LIFE OF MANSIE WAUCH. By D. M. Moir.
PENINSULAR SCENES AND SKETCHES. By F. Hardman.

SIR FRIZZLE PUMPKIN, NIGHTS AT MESS, &c.
THE SUBALTERN.
LIFE IN THE FAR WEST. By G. F. Ruxton.
VALERIUS: A Roman Story. By J. G. Lockhart.

BON GAULTIER'S BOOK OF BALLADS. Fifteenth Edition. With Illustrations by Doyle, Leech, and Crowquill. Fcap. 8vo, 5s.

BRADDON. Thirty Years of Shikar. By Sir EDWARD BRADDON, K.C.M.G. With Illustrations by G. D. Giles, and Map of Oudh Forest Tracts and Nepal Terai. Demy 8vo, 18s.

BROUGHAM. Memoirs of the Life and Times of Henry Lord Brougham. Written by HIMSELF. 3 vols. 8vo, £2, 8s. The Volumes are sold separately, price 16s. each.

BROWN. The Forester: A Practical Treatise on the Planting and Tending of Forest-trees and the General Management of Woodlands. By JAMES BROWN, LL.D. Sixth Edition, Enlarged. Edited by JOHN NISBET, D.Œc., Author of 'British Forest Trees,' &c. In 2 vols. royal 8vo, with 350 Illustrations, 42s. net.

BROWN. Stray Sport. By J. MORAY BROWN, Author of 'Shikar Sketches,' 'Powder, Spur, and Spear,' 'The Days when we went Hog-Hunting.' 2 vols. post 8vo, with Fifty Illustrations, 21s.

BROWN. A Manual of Botany, Anatomical and Physiological. For the Use of Students. By ROBERT BROWN, M.A., Ph.D. Crown 8vo, with numerous Illustrations, 12s. 6d

BRUCE.

In Clover and Heather. Poems by WALLACE BRUCE. New and Enlarged Edition. Crown 8vo, 3s. 6d.
A limited number of Copies of the First Edition, on large hand-made paper, 12s. 6d.
Here's a Hand. Addresses and Poems. Crown 8vo, 5s. Large Paper Edition, limited to 100 copies, price 21s.

BUCHAN. Introductory Text-Book of Meteorology. By ALEXANDER BUCHAN, LL.D., F.R.S.E., Secretary of the Scottish Meteorological Society, &c. New Edition. Crown 8vo, with Coloured Charts and Engravings.
[In preparation.

BURBIDGE.

Domestic Floriculture, Window Gardening, and Floral Decorations. Being Practical Directions for the Propagation, Culture, and Arrangement of Plants and Flowers as Domestic Ornaments. By F. W. BURBIDGE. Second Edition. Crown 8vo, with numerous Illustrations, 7s. 6d.
Cultivated Plants: Their Propagation and Improvement. Including Natural and Artificial Hybridisation, Raising from Seed, Cuttings, and Layers, Grafting and Budding, as applied to the Families and Genera in Cultivation. Crown 8vo, with numerous Illustrations, 12s. 6d.

BURGESS. The Viking Path: A Tale of the White Christ. By J. J. HALDANE BURGESS, Author of 'Rasmie's Büddie,' 'Shetland Sketches,' &c. Crown 8vo, 6s.

BURKE. The Flowering of the Almond Tree, and other Poems. By CHRISTIAN BURKE. Pott 4to, 5s.

BURROWS.

Commentaries on the History of England, from the Earliest Times to 1865. By MONTAGU BURROWS, Chichele Professor of Modern History in the University of Oxford; Captain R.N.; F.S.A., &c.; "Officier de l'Instruction Publique," France. Crown 8vo, 7s. 6d.
The History of the Foreign Policy of Great Britain. Demy 8vo, 12s.

BURTON.

The History of Scotland: From Agricola's Invasion to the Extinction of the last Jacobite Insurrection. By JOHN HILL BURTON, D.C.L., Historiographer-Royal for Scotland. New and Enlarged Edition, 8 vols., and Index. Crown 8vo, £3, 3s.
History of the British Empire during the Reign of Queen Anne. In 3 vols. 8vo. 36s.
The Scot Abroad. Third Edition. Crown 8vo, 10s. 6d.
The Book-Hunter. New Edition. With Portrait. Crown 8vo, 7s. 6d.

BUTCHER. Armenosa of Egypt. A Romance of the Arab Conquest. By the Very Rev. Dean BUTCHER, D.D., F.S.A., Chaplain at Cairo. Crown 8vo, 6s.

BUTE. The Altus of St Columba. With a Prose Paraphrase and Notes. In paper cover, 2s. 6d.

BUTT.

Theatricals: An Interlude. By BEATRICE MAY BUTT. Crown 8vo, 6s.
Miss Molly. Cheap Edition, 2s.
Eugenie. Crown 8vo, 6s. 6d.
Elizabeth, and other Sketches. Crown 8vo, 6s.
Delicia. New Edition. Crown 8vo, 2s. 6d.

CAIRD. Sermons. By JOHN CAIRD, D.D., Principal of the University of Glasgow. Seventeenth Thousand. Fcap. 8vo, 5s.

CALDWELL. Schopenhauer's System in its Philosophical Significance (the Shaw Fellowship Lectures, 1893). By WILLIAM CALDWELL, M.A., D.Sc., Professor of Moral and Social Philosophy, Northwestern University, U.S.A.; formerly Assistant to the Professor of Logic and Metaphysics, Edin., and Examiner in Philosophy in the University of St Andrews. Demy 8vo, 10s. 6d. net.

CALLWELL. The Effect of Maritime Command on Land Campaigns since Waterloo. By Major C. E. CALLWELL, R.A. With Plans. Post 8vo, 6s. net.

CAMPBELL. Sermons Preached before the Queen at Balmoral. By the Rev. A. A. CAMPBELL, Minister of Crathie. Published by Command of Her Majesty. Crown 8vo, 4s. 6d.

CAMPBELL. Records of Argyll. Legends, Traditions, and Recollections of Argyllshire Highlanders, collected chiefly from the Gaelic. With Notes on the Antiquity of the Dress, Clan Colours, or Tartans of the Highlanders. By Lord ARCHIBALD CAMPBELL. Illustrated with Nineteen full-page Etchings. 4to, printed on hand-made paper, £3, 3s.

CANTON. A Lost Epic, and other Poems. By WILLIAM CANTON. Crown 8vo, 5s.

CARSTAIRS.
Human Nature in Rural India. By R. CARSTAIRS. Crown 8vo, 6s.
British Work in India. Crown 8vo, 6s.

CAUVIN. A Treasury of the English and German Languages. Compiled from the best Authors and Lexicographers in both Languages. By JOSEPH CAUVIN, LL.D. and Ph.D., of the University of Göttingen, &c. Crown 8vo, 7s. 6d.

CHARTERIS. Canonicity; or, Early Testimonies to the Existence and Use of the Books of the New Testament. Based on Kirchhoffer's 'Quellensammlung.' Edited by A. H. CHARTERIS, D.D., Professor of Biblical Criticism in the University of Edinburgh. 8vo, 18s.

CHENNELLS. Recollections of an Egyptian Princess. By her English Governess (Miss E. CHENNELLS). Being a Record of Five Years' Residence at the Court of Ismael Pasha Khédive. Second Edition. With Three Portraits. Post 8vo, 7s. 6d.

CHESNEY. The Dilemma. By General Sir GEORGE CHESNEY, K.C.B., M.P., Author of 'The Battle of Dorking,' &c. New Edition. Crown 8vo, 3s. 6d.

CHRISTISON. Life of Sir Robert Christison, Bart., M.D., D.C.L. Oxon., Professor of Medical Jurisprudence in the University of Edinburgh. Edited by his SONS. In 2 vols. 8vo. Vol. I.—Autobiography. 16s. Vol. II.—Memoirs. 16s.

CHURCH. Chapters in an Adventurous Life. Sir Richard Church in Italy and Greece. By E. M. CHURCH. With Photogravure Portrait. Demy 8vo, 10s. 6d.

CHURCH SERVICE SOCIETY.
A Book of Common Order: being Forms of Worship issued by the Church Service Society. Seventh Edition, carefully revised. In 1 vol. crown 8vo, cloth, 3s. 6d.; French morocco, 5s. Also in 2 vols. crown 8vo, cloth, 4s.; French morocco, 6s. 6d.
Daily Offices for Morning and Evening Prayer throughout the Week. Crown 8vo, 3s. 6d.
Order of Divine Service for Children. Issued by the Church Service Society. With Scottish Hymnal. Cloth, 3d.

CLOUSTON. Popular Tales and Fictions: their Migrations and Transformations. By W. A. CLOUSTON, Editor of 'Arabian Poetry for English Readers,' &c. 2 vols. post 8vo, roxburghe binding, 25s.

COCHRAN. A Handy Text-Book of Military Law. Compiled chiefly to assist Officers preparing for Examination; also for all Officers of the Regular and Auxiliary Forces. Comprising also a Synopsis of part of the Army Act. By Major F. COCHRAN, Hampshire Regiment Garrison Instructor, North British District. Crown 8vo, 7s. 6d.

COLQUHOUN. The Moor and the Loch. Containing Minute Instructions in all Highland Sports, with Wanderings over Crag and Corrie, Flood and Fell. By JOHN COLQUHOUN. Cheap Edition. With Illustrations. Demy 8vo, 10s. 6d.

COLVILE. Round the Black Man's Garden. By Lady Z. COLVILE, F.R.G.S. With 2 Maps and 50 Illustrations from Drawings by the Author and from Photographs. Demy 8vo, 16s.

CONDER. The Bible and the East. By Lieut.-Col. C. R. CONDER, R.E., LL.D., D.C.L., M.R.A.S., Author of 'Tent Work in Palestine,' &c. With Illustrations and a Map. Crown 8vo, 5s.

CONSTITUTION AND LAW OF THE CHURCH OF SCOTLAND. With an Introductory Note by the late Principal Tulloch. New Edition, Revised and Enlarged. Crown 8vo, 3s. 6d.

COTTERILL. Suggested Reforms in Public Schools. By C. C. COTTERILL, M.A. Crown 8vo, 3s. 6d.

COUNTY HISTORIES OF SCOTLAND. In demy 8vo volumes of about 350 pp. each. With 2 Maps. Price 7s. 6d. net.

    Fife and Kinross. By ÆNEAS J. G. MACKAY, LL.D., Sheriff of these Counties.

    Dumfries and Galloway. By Sir HERBERT MAXWELL, Bart., M.P. *[Others in preparation.*

CRANSTOUN.

    The Elegies of Albius Tibullus. Translated into English Verse, with Life of the Poet, and Illustrative Notes. By JAMES CRANSTOUN, LL.D., Author of a Translation of 'Catullus.' Crown 8vo, 6s. 6d.

    The Elegies of Sextus Propertius. Translated into English Verse, with Life of the Poet, and Illustrative Notes. Crown 8vo, 7s. 6d.

CRAWFORD. Saracinesca. By F. MARION CRAWFORD, Author of 'Mr Isaacs,' &c., &c. Eighth Edition. Crown 8vo, 6s.

CRAWFORD.

    The Doctrine of Holy Scripture respecting the Atonement. By the late THOMAS J. CRAWFORD, D.D., Professor of Divinity in the University of Edinburgh. Fifth Edition. 8vo, 12s.

    The Fatherhood of God, Considered in its General and Special Aspects. Third Edition, Revised and Enlarged. 8vo, 9s.

    The Preaching of the Cross, and other Sermons. 8vo, 7s. 6d.

    The Mysteries of Christianity. Crown 8vo, 7s. 6d.

CROSS. Impressions of Dante, and of the New World; with a Few Words on Bimetallism. By J. W. CROSS, Editor of 'George Eliot's Life, as related in her Letters and Journals.' Post 8vo, 6s.

CUMBERLAND. Sport on the Pamirs and Turkistan Steppes. By Major C. S. CUMBERLAND. With Map and Frontispiece. Demy 8vo, 10s. 6d.

CURSE OF INTELLECT. Third Edition. Fcap. 8vo, 2s. 6d. net.

CUSHING. The Blacksmith of Voe. By PAUL CUSHING, Author of 'The Bull i' th' Thorn,' 'Cut with his own Diamond.' Cheap Edition. Crown 8vo, 3s. 6d.

DAVIES.

Norfolk Broads and Rivers; or, The Waterways, Lagoons, and Decoys of East Anglia. By G. Christopher Davies. Illustrated with Seven full-page Plates. New and Cheaper Edition. Crown 8vo, 6s.

Our Home in Aveyron. Sketches of Peasant Life in Aveyron and the Lot. By G. Christopher Davies and Mrs Broughall. Illustrated with full-page Illustrations. 8vo, 15s. Cheap Edition, 7s. 6d.

DE LA WARR. An Eastern Cruise in the 'Edeline.' By the Countess De La Warr. In Illustrated Cover. 2s.

DESCARTES. The Method, Meditations, and Principles of Philosophy of Descartes. Translated from the Original French and Latin. With a New Introductory Essay, Historical and Critical, on the Cartesian Philosophy. By Professor Veitch, LL.D., Glasgow University. Eleventh Edition. 6s. 6d.

DOGS, OUR DOMESTICATED: Their Treatment in reference to Food, Diseases, Habits, Punishment, Accomplishments. By 'Magenta.' Crown 8vo, 2s. 6d.

DOUGLAS.

The Ethics of John Stuart Mill. By Charles Douglas, M.A., D.Sc., Lecturer in Moral Philosophy, and Assistant to the Professor of Moral Philosophy in the University of Edinburgh. In 1 vol. post 8vo.

[In the press.

John Stuart Mill: A Study of his Philosophy. Crown 8vo, 4s. 6d. net.

DOUGLAS. Chinese Stories. By Robert K. Douglas. With numerous Illustrations by Parkinson, Forestier, and others. New and Cheaper Edition. Small demy 8vo, 5s.

DOUGLAS. Iras: A Mystery. By Theo. Douglas, Author of 'A Bride Elect.' Crown 8vo, 3s. 6d.

DU CANE. The Odyssey of Homer, Books I.-XII. Translated into English Verse. By Sir Charles Du Cane, K.C.M.G. 8vo, 10s. 6d.

DUDGEON. History of the Edinburgh or Queen's Regiment Light Infantry Militia, now 3rd Battalion The Royal Scots; with an Account of the Origin and Progress of the Militia, and a Brief Sketch of the Old Royal Scots. By Major R. C. Dudgeon, Adjutant 3rd Battalion the Royal Scots. Post 8vo, with Illustrations, 10s. 6d.

DUNSMORE. Manual of the Law of Scotland as to the Relations between Agricultural Tenants and the Landlords, Servants, Merchants, and Bowers. By W. Dunsmore. 8vo, 7s. 6d.

ELIOT.

George Eliot's Life, Related in Her Letters and Journals. Arranged and Edited by her husband, J. W. Cross. With Portrait and other Illustrations. Third Edition. 3 vols. post 8vo, 42s.

George Eliot's Life. With Portrait and other Illustrations. New Edition, in one volume. Crown 8vo, 7s. 6d.

Works of George Eliot (Standard Edition). 21 volumes, crown 8vo. In buckram cloth, gilt top, 2s. 6d. per vol.; or in roxburghe binding, 3s. 6d. per vol.

    Adam Bede. 2 vols.—The Mill on the Floss. 2 vols.—Felix Holt, the Radical. 2 vols.—Romola. 2 vols.—Scenes of Clerical Life. 2 vols.—Middlemarch. 3 vols.—Daniel Deronda. 3 vols.—Silas Marner. 1 vol.—Jubal. 1 vol.—The Spanish Gipsy. 1 vol.—Essays. 1 vol.—Theophrastus Such. 1 vol.

Life and Works of George Eliot (Cabinet Edition). 24 volumes, crown 8vo, price £6. Also to be had handsomely bound in half and full calf. The Volumes are sold separately, bound in cloth, price 5s. each.

ELIOT.

Novels by George Eliot. Cheap Edition.
Adam Bede. Illustrated. 3s. 6d., cloth.—The Mill on the Floss. Illustrated. 3s. 6d., cloth.—Scenes of Clerical Life. Illustrated. 3s., cloth.—Silas Marner: the Weaver of Raveloe. Illustrated. 2s. 6d., cloth.—Felix Holt, the Radical. Illustrated. 3s. 6d., cloth.—Romola. With Vignette. 3s. 6d., cloth.

Middlemarch. Crown 8vo, 7s. 6d.

Daniel Deronda. Crown 8vo, 7s. 6d.

Essays. New Edition. Crown 8vo, 5s.

Impressions of Theophrastus Such. New Edition. Crown 8vo, 5s.

The Spanish Gypsy. New Edition. Crown 8vo, 5s.

The Legend of Jubal, and other Poems, Old and New. New Edition. Crown 8vo, 5s.

Wise, Witty, and Tender Sayings, in Prose and Verse. Selected from the Works of GEORGE ELIOT. New Edition. Fcap. 8vo, 3s. 6d.

ESSAYS ON SOCIAL SUBJECTS. Originally published in the 'Saturday Review.' New Edition. First and Second Series. 2 vols. crown 8vo, 6s. each.

FAITHS OF THE WORLD, The. A Concise History of the Great Religious Systems of the World. By various Authors. Crown 8vo, 5s.

FALKNER. The Lost Stradivarius. By J. MEADE FALKNER. Second Edition. Crown 8vo, 6s.

FERGUSON. Sir Samuel Ferguson in the Ireland of his Day. By LADY FERGUSON, Author of 'The Irish before the Conquest,' 'Life of William Reeves, D.D., Lord Bishop of Down, Connor, and Dromore,' &c., &c. With Two Portraits. 2 vols. post 8vo, 21s.

FERRIER.

Philosophical Works of the late James F. Ferrier, B.A. Oxon., Professor of Moral Philosophy and Political Economy, St Andrews. New Edition. Edited by Sir ALEXANDER GRANT, Bart., D.C.L., and Professor LUSHINGTON. 3 vols. crown 8vo, 34s. 6d.

Institutes of Metaphysic. Third Edition. 10s. 6d.

Lectures on the Early Greek Philosophy. 4th Edition. 10s. 6d.

Philosophical Remains, including the Lectures on Early Greek Philosophy. New Edition. 2 vols. 24s.

FLINT.

Historical Philosophy in France and French Belgium and Switzerland. By ROBERT FLINT, Corresponding Member of the Institute of France, Hon. Member of the Royal Society of Palermo, Professor in the University of Edinburgh, &c. 8vo, 21s.

Agnosticism. Being the Croall Lecture for 1887-88.
[In the press.

Theism. Being the Baird Lecture for 1876. Ninth Edition, Revised. Crown 8vo, 7s. 6d

Anti-Theistic Theories. Being the Baird Lecture for 1877. Fifth Edition. Crown 8vo, 10s. 6d.

FOREIGN CLASSICS FOR ENGLISH READERS. Edited by Mrs OLIPHANT. Price 2s. 6d. *For List of Volumes, see page 2.*

FOSTER. The Fallen City, and other Poems. By WILL FOSTER. Crown 8vo, 6s.

FRANCILLON. Gods and Heroes ; or, The Kingdom of Jupiter.
By R. E. FRANCILLON. With 8 Illustrations. Crown 8vo, 5s.

FRANCIS. Among the Untrodden Ways. By M. E. FRANCIS
(Mrs Francis Blundell), Author of 'In a North Country Village,' 'A Daughter of
the Soil,' 'Frieze and Fustian,' &c. Crown 8vo, 3s. 6d.

FRASER.

Philosophy of Theism. Being the Gifford Lectures delivered
before the University of Edinburgh in 1894-95. First Series. By ALEXANDER
CAMPBELL FRASER, D.C.L. Oxford ; Emeritus Professor of Logic and Metaphysics in the University of Edinburgh. Post 8vo, 7s. 6d. net.

Philosophy of Theism. Being the Gifford Lectures delivered
before the University of Edinburgh in 1895-96. Second Series. Post 8vo,
7s. 6d. net.

FRASER. St Mary's of Old Montrose : A History of the Parish
of Maryton. By the Rev. WILLIAM RUXTON FRASER, M.A., F.S.A. Scot.,
Emeritus Minister of Maryton ; Author of 'History of the Parish and Burgh of
Laurencekirk.' Crown 8vo, 3s. 6d.

FULLARTON.

Merlin : A Dramatic Poem. By RALPH MACLEOD FULLAR-
TON. Crown 8vo, 5s.

Tanhäuser. Crown 8vo, 6s.

Lallan Sangs and German Lyrics. Crown 8vo, 5s.

GALT.

Novels by JOHN GALT. With General Introduction and
Prefatory Notes by S. R. CROCKETT. The Text Revised and Edited by D.
STORRAR MELDRUM, Author of 'The Story of Margrédel.' With Photogravure
Illustrations from Drawings by John Wallace. Fcap. 8vo, 3s. net each vol.

ANNALS OF THE PARISH, and THE AYRSHIRE LEGATEES. 2 vols.—SIR ANDREW
WYLIE. 2 vols.—THE ENTAIL ; or, The Lairds of Grippy. 2 vols.—THE PRO-
VOST, and THE LAST OF THE LAIRDS. 2 vols.

See also STANDARD NOVELS, *p. 6.*

GENERAL ASSEMBLY OF THE CHURCH OF SCOTLAND.

Scottish Hymnal, With Appendix Incorporated. Published
for use in Churches by Authority of the General Assembly. 1. Large type,
cloth, red edges, 2s. 6d.; French morocco, 4s. 2. Bourgeois type, limp cloth, 1s.;
French morocco, 2s. 3. Nonpareil type, cloth, red edges, 6d.; French morocco,
1s. 4d. 4. Paper covers, 3d. 5. Sunday-School Edition, paper covers, 1d.,
cloth, 2d. No. 1, bound with the Psalms and Paraphrases, French morocco, 8s.
No. 2, bound with the Psalms and Paraphrases, cloth, 2s.; French morocco, 3s.

Prayers for Social and Family Worship. Prepared by a
Special Committee of the General Assembly of the Church of Scotland. Entirely
New Edition, Revised and Enlarged. Fcap. 8vo, red edges, 2s.

Prayers for Family Worship. A Selection of Four Weeks'
Prayers. New Edition. Authorised by the General Assembly of the Church of
Scotland. Fcap. 8vo, red edges, 1s. 6d.

One Hundred Prayers. Prepared by the Committee on Aids
to Devotion. 16mo, cloth limp, 6d.

Morning and Evening Prayers for Affixing to Bibles. Prepared
by the Committee on Aids to Devotion. 1d. for 6, or 1s. per 100.

GERARD.

Reata : What's in a Name. By E. D. GERARD. Cheap
Edition. Crown 8vo, 3s. 6d.

Beggar my Neighbour. Cheap Edition. Crown 8vo, 3s. 6d.

The Waters of Hercules. Cheap Edition. Crown 8vo, 3s. 6d.

A Sensitive Plant. Crown 8vo, 3s. 6d.

GERARD.

A Foreigner. An Anglo-German Study. By E. GERARD. Crown 8vo, 6s.

The Land beyond the Forest. Facts, Figures, and Fancies from Transylvania. With Maps and Illustrations. 2 vols. post 8vo, 25s.

Bis: Some Tales Retold. Crown 8vo, 6s.

A Secret Mission. 2 vols. crown 8vo, 17s.

GERARD.

The Wrong Man. By DOROTHEA GERARD. Second Edition. Crown 8vo, 6s.

Lady Baby. Cheap Edition. Crown 8vo, 3s. 6d.

Recha. Second Edition. Crown 8vo, 6s.

The Rich Miss Riddell. Second Edition. Crown 8vo, 6s.

GERARD. Stonyhurst Latin Grammar. By Rev. JOHN GERARD. Second Edition. Fcap. 8vo, 3s.

GILL.

Free Trade: an Inquiry into the Nature of its Operation. By RICHARD GILL. Crown 8vo, 7s. 6d.

Free Trade under Protection. Crown 8vo, 7s. 6d.

GORDON CUMMING.

At Home in Fiji. By C. F. GORDON CUMMING. Fourth Edition, post 8vo. With Illustrations and Map. 7s. 6d.

A Lady's Cruise in a French Man-of-War. New and Cheaper Edition. 8vo. With Illustrations and Map. 12s. 6d.

Fire-Fountains. The Kingdom of Hawaii: Its Volcanoes, and the History of its Missions. With Map and Illustrations. 2 vols. 8vo, 25s.

Wanderings in China. New and Cheaper Edition. 8vo, with Illustrations, 10s.

Granite Crags: The Yō-semité Region of California. Illustrated with 8 Engravings. New and Cheaper Edition. 8vo, 8s. 6d.

GRAHAM. Manual of the Elections (Scot.) (Corrupt and Illegal Practices) Act, 1890. With Analysis, Relative Act of Sederunt, Appendix containing the Corrupt Practices Acts of 1883 and 1885, and Copious Index. By J. EDWARD GRAHAM, Advocate. 8vo, 4s. 6d.

GRAND.

A Domestic Experiment. By SARAH GRAND, Author of 'The Heavenly Twins,' 'Ideala: A Study from Life.' Crown 8vo, 6s.

Singularly Deluded. Crown 8vo, 6s.

GRANT. Bush-Life in Queensland. By A. C. GRANT. New Edition. Crown 8vo, 6s.

GRANT. Life of Sir Hope Grant. With Selections from his Correspondence. Edited by HENRY KNOLLYS, Colonel (H.P.) Royal Artillery, his former A.D.C., Editor of 'Incidents in the Sepoy War;' Author of 'Sketches of Life in Japan,' &c. With Portraits of Sir Hope Grant and other Illustrations. Maps and Plans. 2 vols. demy 8vo, 21s.

GRIER.

In Furthest Ind. The Narrative of Mr EDWARD CARLYON of Ellswether, in the County of Northampton, and late of the Honourable East India Company's Service, Gentleman. Wrote by his own hand in the year of grace 1697. Edited, with a few Explanatory Notes, by SYDNEY C. GRIER. Post 8vo, 6s.

His Excellency's English Governess. Crown 8vo, 6s.

An Uncrowned King: A Romance of High Politics. Crown 8vo, 6s.

GUTHRIE-SMITH. Crispus: A Drama. By H. GUTHRIE-SMITH. Fcap. 4to, 5s.

HAGGARD. Under Crescent and Star. By Lieut.-Col. ANDREW HAGGARD, D.S.O., Author of 'Dodo and I,' 'Tempest Torn,' &c. With a Portrait. Second Edition. Crown 8vo, 6s.

HALDANE. Subtropical Cultivations and Climates. A Handy Book for Planters, Colonists, and Settlers. By R. C. HALDANE. Post 8vo, 9s.

HAMERTON.

Wenderholme: A Story of Lancashire and Yorkshire Life. By P. G. HAMERTON, Author of 'A Painter's Camp.' New Edition. Crown 8vo, 3s. 6d.

Marmorne. New Edition. Crown 8vo, 3s. 6d.

HAMILTON.

Lectures on Metaphysics. By Sir WILLIAM HAMILTON, Bart., Professor of Logic and Metaphysics in the University of Edinburgh. Edited by the Rev. H. L. MANSEL, B.D., LL.D., Dean of St Paul's; and JOHN VEITCH, M.A., LL.D., Professor of Logic and Rhetoric, Glasgow. Seventh Edition. 2 vols. 8vo, 24s.

Lectures on Logic. Edited by the SAME. Third Edition, Revised. 2 vols., 24s.

Discussions on Philosophy and Literature, Education and University Reform. Third Edition. 8vo, 21s.

Memoir of Sir William Hamilton, Bart., Professor of Logic and Metaphysics in the University of Edinburgh. By Professor VEITCH, of the University of Glasgow. 8vo, with Portrait, 18s.

Sir William Hamilton: The Man and his Philosophy. Two Lectures delivered before the Edinburgh Philosophical Institution, January and February 1883. By Professor VEITCH. Crown 8vo, 2s.

HAMLEY.

The Operations of War Explained and Illustrated. By General Sir EDWARD BRUCE HAMLEY, K.C.B., K.C.M.G. Fifth Edition, Revised throughout. 4to, with numerous Illustrations, 30s.

National Defence; Articles and Speeches. Post 8vo, 6s.

Shakespeare's Funeral, and other Papers. Post 8vo, 7s. 6d.

Thomas Carlyle: An Essay. Second Edition. Crown 8vo, 2s. 6d.

On Outposts. Second Edition. 8vo, 2s.

Wellington's Career; A Military and Political Summary. Crown 8vo, 2s.

Lady Lee's Widowhood. New Edition. Crown 8vo, 3s. 6d. Cheaper Edition, 2s. 6d.

Our Poor Relations. A Philozoic Essay. With Illustrations, chiefly by Ernest Griset. Crown 8vo, cloth gilt, 3s. 6d.

The Life of General Sir Edward Bruce Hamley, K.C.B., K.C.M.G. By ALEXANDER INNES SHAND. With two Photogravure Portraits and other Illustrations. Cheaper Edition. With a Statement by Mr EDWARD HAMLEY. 2 vols. demy 8vo, 10s. 6d.

HARE. Down the Village Street: Scenes in a West Country Hamlet. By CHRISTOPHER HARE. Second Edition. Crown 8vo, 6s.

HARRADEN. In Varying Moods: Short Stories. By BEATRICE HARRADEN, Author of 'Ships that Pass in the Night.' Twelfth Edition. Crown 8vo, 3s. 6d.

HARRIS.

From Batum to Baghdad, *via* Tiflis, Tabriz, and Persian Kurdistan. By WALTER B. HARRIS, F.R.G.S., Author of 'The Land of an African Sultan; Travels in Morocco,' &c. With numerous Illustrations and 2 Maps. Demy 8vo, 12s.

HARRIS.

Tafilet. The Narrative of a Journey of Exploration to the Atlas Mountains and the Oases of the North-West Sahara. With Illustrations by Maurice Romberg from Sketches and Photographs by the Author, and Two Maps. Demy 8vo, 12s.

A Journey through the Yemen, and some General Remarks upon that Country. With 3 Maps and numerous Illustrations by Forestier and Wallace from Sketches and Photographs taken by the Author. Demy 8vo, 16s.

Danovitch, and other Stories. Crown 8vo, 6s.

HAWKER. The Prose Works of Rev. R. S. HAWKER, Vicar of Morwenstow. Including 'Footprints of Former Men in Far Cornwall.' Re-edited, with Sketches never before published. With a Frontispiece. Crown 8vo, 3s. 6d.

HAY. The Works of the Right Rev. Dr George Hay, Bishop of Edinburgh. Edited under the Supervision of the Right Rev. Bishop STRAIN. With Memoir and Portrait of the Author. 5 vols. crown 8vo, bound in extra cloth, £1, 1s. The following Volumes may be had separately—viz.:
The Devout Christian Instructed in the Law of Christ from the Written Word. 2 vols., 8s.—The Pious Christian Instructed in the Nature and Practice of the Principal Exercises of Piety. 1 vol., 3s.

HEATLEY.

The Horse-Owner's Safeguard. A Handy Medical Guide for every Man who owns a Horse. By G. S. HEATLEY, M.R.C.V.S. Crown 8vo, 5s.

The Stock-Owner's Guide. A Handy Medical Treatise for every Man who owns an Ox or a Cow. Crown 8vo, 4s. 6d.

HEDDERWICK. Lays of Middle Age; and other Poems. By JAMES HEDDERWICK, LL.D., Author of 'Backward Glances.' Price 3s. 6d.

HEMANS.

The Poetical Works of Mrs Hemans. Copyright Editions. Royal 8vo, 5s. The Same with Engravings, cloth, gilt edges, 7s. 6d.

Select Poems of Mrs Hemans. Fcap., cloth, gilt edges, 3s.

HERKLESS. Cardinal Beaton: Priest and Politician. By JOHN HERKLESS, Professor of Church History, St Andrews. With a Portrait. Post 8vo, 7s. 6d.

HEWISON. The Isle of Bute in the Olden Time. With Illustrations, Maps, and Plans. By JAMES KING HEWISON, M.A., F.S.A. (Scot.), Minister of Rothesay. Vol. I., Celtic Saints and Heroes. Crown 4to, 15s. net. Vol. II., The Royal Stewards and the Brandanes. Crown 4to, 15s. net.

HIBBEN. Inductive Logic. By JOHN GRIER HIBBEN, Ph.D., Assistant Professor of Logic in Princeton University, U.S.A. Crown 8vo, 3s. 6d. net.

HOME PRAYERS. By Ministers of the Church of Scotland and Members of the Church Service Society. Second Edition. Fcap. 8vo, 3s.

HORNBY. Admiral of the Fleet Sir Geoffrey Phipps Hornby, G.C.B. A Biography. By Mrs FRED. EGERTON. With Three Portraits. Demy 8vo, 16s.

HUTCHINSON. Hints on the Game of Golf. By HORACE G. HUTCHINSON. Ninth Edition, Enlarged. Fcap. 8vo, cloth, 1s.

HYSLOP. The Elements of Ethics. By JAMES H. HYSLOP, Ph.D., Instructor in Ethics, Columbia College, New York, Author of 'The Elements of Logic.' Post 8vo, 7s. 6d. net.

IDDESLEIGH.

Lectures and Essays. By the late EARL of IDDESLEIGH, G.C.B., D.C.L., &c. 8vo, 16s.

Life, Letters, and Diaries of Sir Stafford Northcote, First Earl of Iddesleigh. By ANDREW LANG. With Three Portraits and a View of Pynes. Third Edition. 2 vols. post 8vo, 31s. 6d.
POPULAR EDITION. With Portrait and View of Pynes. Post 8vo, 7s. 6d.

IGNOTUS. The Supremacy and Sufficiency of Jesus Christ, as set forth in the Epistle to the Hebrews. By IGNOTUS. Crown 8vo, 3s. 6d.

INDEX GEOGRAPHICUS: Being a List, alphabetically arranged, of the Principal Places on the Globe, with the Countries and Subdivisions of the Countries in which they are situated, and their Latitudes and Longitudes. Imperial 8vo, pp. 676, 21s.

JEAN JAMBON. Our Trip to Blunderland; or, Grand Excursion to Blundertown and Back. By JEAN JAMBON. With Sixty Illustrations designed by CHARLES DOYLE, engraved by DALZIEL. Fourth Thousand. Cloth, gilt edges, 6s. 6d. Cheap Edition, cloth, 3s. 6d. Boards, 2s. 6d.

JEBB. A Strange Career. The Life and Adventures of JOHN GLADWYN JEBB. By his Widow. With an Introduction by H. RIDER HAGGARD, and an Electrogravure Portrait of Mr Jebb. Third Edition. Demy 8vo, 10s. 6d. CHEAP EDITION. With Illustrations by John Wallace. Crown 8vo, 3s. 6d.

 Some Unconventional People. By Mrs GLADWYN JEBB, Author of 'Life and Adventures of J. G. Jebb.' With Illustrations. Crown 8vo, 3s. 6d.

JENNINGS. Mr Gladstone: A Study. By LOUIS J. JENNINGS, M.P., Author of 'Republican Government in the United States,' 'The Croker Memoirs,' &c. Popular Edition. Crown 8vo, 1s.

JERNINGHAM.

 Reminiscences of an Attaché. By HUBERT E. H. JERNINGHAM. Second Edition. Crown 8vo, 5s.

 Diane de Breteuille. A Love Story. Crown 8vo, 2s. 6d.

JOHNSTON.

 The Chemistry of Common Life. By Professor J. F. W. JOHNSTON. New Edition, Revised. By ARTHUR HERBERT CHURCH, M.A. Oxon.; Author of 'Food: its Sources, Constituents, and Uses,' &c. With Maps and 102 Engravings. Crown 8vo, 7s. 6d.

 Elements of Agricultural Chemistry. An entirely New Edition from the Edition by Sir CHARLES A. CAMERON, M.D., F.R.C.S.I., &c. Revised and brought down to date by C. M. AIKMAN, M.A., B.Sc., F.R.S.E., Professor of Chemistry, Glasgow Veterinary College. 17th Edition. Crown 8vo, 6s. 6d.

 Catechism of Agricultural Chemistry. An entirely New Edition from the Edition by Sir CHARLES A. CAMERON. Revised and Enlarged by C. M. AIKMAN, M.A., &c. 95th Thousand. With numerous Illustrations. Crown 8vo, 1s.

JOHNSTON. Agricultural Holdings (Scotland) Acts, 1883 and 1889; and the Ground Game Act, 1880. With Notes, and Summary of Procedure, &c. By CHRISTOPHER N. JOHNSTON, M.A., Advocate. Demy 8vo, 5s.

JOKAI. Timar's Two Worlds. By MAURUS JOKAI. Authorised Translation by Mrs HEGAN KENNARD. Cheap Edition. Crown 8vo, 6s.

KEBBEL. The Old and the New: English Country Life. By T. E. KEBBEL, M.A., Author of 'The Agricultural Labourers,' 'Essays in History and Politics,' 'Life of Lord Beaconsfield.' Crown 8vo, 5s.

KERR. St Andrews in 1645-46. By D. R. KERR. Crown 8vo, 2s. 6d.

KINGLAKE.

 History of the Invasion of the Crimea. By A. W. KINGLAKE. Cabinet Edition, Revised. With an Index to the Complete Work. Illustrated with Maps and Plans. Complete in 9 vols., crown 8vo, at 6s. each.

 History of the Invasion of the Crimea. Demy 8vo. Vol. VI. Winter Troubles. With a Map, 16s. Vols. VII. and VIII. From the Morrow of Inkerman to the Death of Lord Raglan. With an Index to the Whole Work. With Maps and Plans. 28s.

KINGLAKE.

Eothen. A New Edition, uniform with the Cabinet Edition of the 'History of the Invasion of the Crimea.' 6s.
CHEAPER EDITION. With Portrait and Biographical Sketch of the Author. Crown 8vo, 3s. 6d.

KIRBY. In Haunts of Wild Game: A Hunter-Naturalist's Wanderings from Kahlamba to Libombo. By FREDERICK VAUGHAN KIRBY, F.Z.S. (Maqaqamba). With numerous Illustrations by Charles Whymper, and a Map. Large demy 8vo, 25s.

KLEIN. Among the Gods. Scenes of India, with Legends by the Way. By AUGUSTA KLEIN. With 22 Full-page Illustrations. Demy 8vo, 15s.

KNEIPP. My Water-Cure. As Tested through more than Thirty Years, and Described for the Healing of Diseases and the Preservation of Health. By SEBASTIAN KNEIPP, Parish Priest of Wörishofen (Bavaria). With a Portrait and other Illustrations. Authorised English Translation from the Thirtieth German Edition, by A. de F. Cheap Edition. With an Appendix, containing the Latest Developments of Pfarrer Kneipp's System, and a Preface by E. Gerard. Crown 8vo, 3s. 6d.

KNOLLYS. The Elements of Field-Artillery. Designed for the Use of Infantry and Cavalry Officers. By HENRY KNOLLYS, Colonel Royal Artillery; Author of 'From Sedan to Saarbrück,' Editor of 'Incidents in the Sepoy War,' &c. With Engravings. Crown 8vo, 7s. 6d.

LANG. Life, Letters, and Diaries of Sir Stafford Northcote, First Earl of Iddesleigh. By ANDREW LANG. With Three Portraits and a View of Pynes. Third Edition. 2 vols. post 8vo, 31s. 6d.
POPULAR EDITION. With Portrait and View of Pynes. Post 8vo, 7s. 6d.

LEES. A Handbook of the Sheriff and Justice of Peace Small Debt Courts. With Notes, References, and Forms. By J. M. LEES, Advocate, Sheriff of Stirling, Dumbarton, and Clackmannan. 8vo, 7s. 6d.

LINDSAY.

Recent Advances in Theistic Philosophy of Religion. By Rev. JAMES LINDSAY, M.A., B.D., B.Sc., F.R.S.E., F.G.S., Minister of the Parish of St Andrew's, Kilmarnock. Demy 8vo, 12s. 6d. net.

The Significance of the Old Testament for Modern Theology. Crown 8vo, 1s. net.

The Progressiveness of Modern Christian Thought. Crown 8vo, 6s.

Essays, Literary and Philosophical. Crown 8vo, 3s. 6d.

LOCKHART.

Doubles and Quits. By LAURENCE W. M. LOCKHART. New Edition. Crown 8vo, 3s. 6d.

Fair to See. New Edition. Crown 8vo, 3s. 6d.

Mine is Thine. New Edition. Crown 8vo, 3s. 6d.

LOCKHART.

The Church of Scotland in the Thirteenth Century. The Life and Times of David de Bernham of St Andrews (Bishop), A.D. 1239 to 1253. With List of Churches dedicated by him, and Dates. By WILLIAM LOCKHART, A.M., D.D., F.S.A. Scot., Minister of Colinton Parish. 2d Edition. 8vo, 6s.

Dies Tristes: Sermons for Seasons of Sorrow. Crown 8vo, 6s.

LORIMER.

The Institutes of Law: A Treatise of the Principles of Jurisprudence as determined by Nature. By the late JAMES LORIMER, Professor of Public Law and of the Law of Nature and Nations in the University of Edinburgh. New Edition, Revised and much Enlarged. 8vo, 18s.

The Institutes of the Law of Nations. A Treatise of the Jural Relation of Separate Political Communities. In 2 vols. 8vo. Volume I., price 16s. Volume II., price 20s.

LUGARD. The Rise of our East African Empire : Early Efforts in Uganda and Nyasaland. By F. D. LUGARD, Captain Norfolk Regiment. With 130 Illustrations from Drawings and Photographs under the personal superintendence of the Author, and 14 specially prepared Maps. In 2 vols. large demy 8vo, 42s.

M'CHESNEY.
Miriam Cromwell, Royalist : A Romance of the Great Rebellion. By DORA GREENWELL M'CHESNEY Crown 8vo, 6s.
Kathleen Clare : Her Book, 1637-41. With Frontispiece, and five full-page Illustrations by James A. Shearman. Crown 8vo, 6s.

M'COMBIE. Cattle and Cattle-Breeders. By WILLIAM M'COMBIE, Tillyfour. New Edition, Enlarged, with Memoir of the Author by JAMES MACDONALD, F.R.S.E., Secretary Highland and Agricultural Society of Scotland. Crown 8vo, 3s. 6d.

M'CRIE.
Works of the Rev. Thomas M'Crie, D.D. Uniform Edition. 4 vols. crown 8vo, 24s.
Life of John Knox. Crown 8vo, 6s. Another Edition, 3s. 6d.
Life of Andrew Melville. Crown 8vo, 6s.
History of the Progress and Suppression of the Reformation in Italy in the Sixteenth Century. Crown 8vo, 4s.
History of the Progress and Suppression of the Reformation in Spain in the Sixteenth Century. Crown 8vo, 3s. 6d.

M'CRIE. The Public Worship of Presbyterian Scotland. Historically treated. With copious Notes, Appendices, and Index. The Fourteenth Series of the Cunningham Lectures. By the Rev. CHARLES G. M'CRIE, D.D. Demy 8vo, 10s. 6d.

MACDONALD. A Manual of the Criminal Law (Scotland) Procedure Act, 1887. By NORMAN DORAN MACDONALD. Revised by the LORD JUSTICE-CLERK. 8vo, 10s. 6d.

MACDONALD AND SINCLAIR. History of Polled Aberdeen and Angus Cattle. Giving an Account of the Origin, Improvement, and Characteristics of the Breed. By JAMES MACDONALD and JAMES SINCLAIR. Illustrated with numerous Animal Portraits. Post 8vo, 12s. 6d.

MACDOUGALL AND DODDS. A Manual of the Local Government (Scotland) Act, 1894. With Introduction, Explanatory Notes, and Copious Index. By J. PATTEN MACDOUGALL, Legal Secretary to the Lord Advocate, and J. M. DODDS. Tenth Thousand, Revised. Crown 8vo, 2s. 6d. net.

MACINTYRE. Hindu-Koh : Wanderings and Wild Sports on and beyond the Himalayas. By Major-General DONALD MACINTYRE, V.C., late Prince of Wales' Own Goorkhas, F.R.G.S. *Dedicated to H.R.H. The Prince of Wales.* New and Cheaper Edition, Revised, with numerous Illustrations. Post 8vo, 3s. 6d.

MACKAY.
A Manual of Modern Geography ; Mathematical, Physical, and Political. By the Rev. ALEXANDER MACKAY, LL.D., F.R.G.S. 11th Thousand, Revised to the present time. Crown 8vo, pp. 688, 7s. 6d.
Elements of Modern Geography. 55th Thousand, Revised to the present time. Crown 8vo, pp. 300, 3s.
The Intermediate Geography. Intended as an Intermediate Book between the Author's 'Outlines of Geography' and 'Elements of Geography.' Eighteenth Edition, Revised. Fcap. 8vo, pp. 238, 2s.
Outlines of Modern Geography. 191st Thousand, Revised to the present time. Fcap. 8vo, pp. 128, 1s.
Elements of Physiography. New Edition. Rewritten and Enlarged. With numerous Illustrations. Crown 8vo. [*In the press.*

MACKENZIE. Studies in Roman Law. With Comparative Views of the Laws of France, England, and Scotland. By Lord MACKENZIE, one of the Judges of the Court of Session in Scotland. Sixth Edition, Edited by JOHN KIRKPATRICK, M.A., LL.B., Advocate, Professor of History in the University of Edinburgh. 8vo, 12s.

MACPHERSON. Glimpses of Church and Social Life in the Highlands in Olden Times. By ALEXANDER MACPHERSON, F.S.A. Scot. With 6 Photogravure Portraits and other full-page Illustrations. Small 4to, 25s.

M'PHERSON. Golf and Golfers. Past and Present. By J. GORDON M'PHERSON, Ph.D., F.R.S.E. With an Introduction by the Right Hon. A. J. BALFOUR, and a Portrait of the Author. Fcap. 8vo, 1s. 6d.

MACRAE. A Handbook of Deer-Stalking. By ALEXANDER MACRAE, late Forester to Lord Henry Bentinck. With Introduction by Horatio Ross, Esq. Fcap. 8vo, with 2 Photographs from Life. 3s. 6d.

MAIN. Three Hundred English Sonnets. Chosen and Edited by DAVID M. MAIN. New Edition. Fcap. 8vo, 3s. 6d.

MAIR. A Digest of Laws and Decisions, Ecclesiastical and Civil, relating to the Constitution, Practice, and Affairs of the Church of Scotland. With Notes and Forms of Procedure. By the Rev. WILLIAM MAIR, D.D., Minister of the Parish of Earlston. New Edition, Revised. Crown 8vo, 9s. net.

MARCHMONT AND THE HUMES OF POLWARTH. By One of their Descendants. With numerous Portraits and other Illustrations. Crown 4to, 21s. net.

MARSHMAN. History of India. From the Earliest Period to the present time. By JOHN CLARK MARSHMAN, C.S.I. Third and Cheaper Edition. Post 8vo, with Map, 6s.

MARTIN.

The Æneid of Virgil. Books I.-VI. Translated by Sir THEODORE MARTIN, K.C.B. Post 8vo, 7s. 6d.

Goethe's Faust. Part I. Translated into English Verse. Second Edition, crown 8vo, 6s. Ninth Edition, fcap. 8vo, 3s. 6d.

Goethe's Faust. Part II. Translated into English Verse. Second Edition, Revised. Fcap. 8vo, 6s.

The Works of Horace. Translated into English Verse, with Life and Notes. 2 vols. New Edition. Crown 8vo, 21s.

Poems and Ballads of Heinrich Heine. Done into English Verse. Third Edition. Small crown 8vo, 5s.

The Song of the Bell, and other Translations from Schiller, Goethe, Uhland, and Others. Crown 8vo, 7s. 6d.

Madonna Pia: A Tragedy; and Three Other Dramas. Crown 8vo, 7s. 6d.

Catullus. With Life and Notes. Second Edition, Revised and Corrected. Post 8vo, 7s. 6d.

The 'Vita Nuova' of Dante. Translated, with an Introduction and Notes. Third Edition. Small crown 8vo, 5s.

Aladdin: A Dramatic Poem. By ADAM OEHLENSCHLAEGER. Fcap. 8vo, 5s.

Correggio: A Tragedy. By OEHLENSCHLAEGER. With Notes. Fcap. 8vo, 3s.

MARTIN. On some of Shakespeare's Female Characters. By HELENA FAUCIT, Lady MARTIN. Dedicated by permission to Her Most Gracious Majesty the Queen. Fifth Edition. With a Portrait by Lehmann. Demy 8vo, 7s. 6d.

MARWICK. Observations on the Law and Practice in regard to Municipal Elections and the Conduct of the Business of Town Councils and Commissioners of Police in Scotland. By Sir JAMES D. MARWICK, LL.D., Town-Clerk of Glasgow. Royal 8vo, 30s.

MATHESON.

Can the Old Faith Live with the New? or, The Problem of Evolution and Revelation. By the Rev. GEORGE MATHESON, D.D. Third Edition. Crown 8vo, 7s. 6d.

The Psalmist and the Scientist; or, Modern Value of the Religious Sentiment. Third Edition. Crown 8vo, 5s.

Spiritual Development of St Paul. Third Edition. Cr. 8vo, 5s.

The Distinctive Messages of the Old Religions. Second Edition. Crown 8vo, 5s.

Sacred Songs. New and Cheaper Edition. Crown 8vo, 2s. 6d.

MAURICE. The Balance of Military Power in Europe. An Examination of the War Resources of Great Britain and the Continental States. By Colonel MAURICE, R.A., Professor of Military Art and History at the Royal Staff College. Crown 8vo, with a Map, 6s.

MAXWELL.

A Duke of Britain. A Romance of the Fourth Century. By Sir HERBERT MAXWELL, Bart., M.P., F.S.A., &c., Author of 'Passages in the Life of Sir Lucian Elphin.' Fourth Edition. Crown 8vo, 6s.

Life and Times of the Rt. Hon. William Henry Smith, M.P. With Portraits and numerous Illustrations by Herbert Railton, G. L. Seymour, and Others. 2 vols. demy 8vo, 25s.

POPULAR EDITION. With a Portrait and other Illustrations. Crown 8vo, 3s. 6d.

Scottish Land-Names: Their Origin and Meaning. Being the Rhind Lectures in Archæology for 1893. Post 8vo, 6s.

Meridiana: Noontide Essays. Post 8vo, 7s. 6d.

Post Meridiana: Afternoon Essays. Post 8vo, 6s.

Dumfries and Galloway. Being one of the Volumes of the County Histories of Scotland. With Four Maps. Demy 8vo, 7s. 6d. net.

MELDRUM.

The Story of Margrédel: Being a Fireside History of a Fifeshire Family. By D. STORRAR MELDRUM. Cheap Edition. Crown 8vo, 3s. 6d.

Grey Mantle and Gold Fringe. Crown 8vo, 6s.

MERZ. A History of European Thought in the Nineteenth Century. By JOHN THEODORE MERZ. Vol. I., post 8vo, 10s. 6d. net.

MICHEL. A Critical Inquiry into the Scottish Language. With the view of Illustrating the Rise and Progress of Civilisation in Scotland. By FRANCISQUE-MICHEL, F.S.A. Lond. and Scot., Correspondant de l'Institut de France, &c. 4to, printed on hand-made paper, and bound in roxburghe, 66s.

MICHIE.

The Larch: Being a Practical Treatise on its Culture and General Management. By CHRISTOPHER Y. MICHIE, Forester, Cullen House. Crown 8vo, with Illustrations. New and Cheaper Edition, Enlarged, 5s.

The Practice of Forestry. Crown 8vo, with Illustrations. 6s.

MIDDLETON. The Story of Alastair Bhan Comyn; or, The Tragedy of Dunphail. A Tale of Tradition and Romance. By the Lady MIDDLETON. Square 8vo, 10s. Cheaper Edition, 5s.

MILLER. The Dream of Mr H——, the Herbalist. By HUGH MILLER, F.R.S.E., late H.M. Geological Survey, Author of 'Landscape Geology.' With a Photogravure Frontispiece. Crown 8vo, 2s. 6d.

MINTO.

A Manual of English Prose Literature, Biographical and Critical: designed mainly to show Characteristics of Style. By W. MINTO, M.A., Hon. LL.D. of St Andrews; Professor of Logic in the University of Aberdeen. Third Edition, Revised. Crown 8vo, 7s. 6d.

Characteristics of English Poets, from Chaucer to Shirley. New Edition, Revised. Crown 8vo, 7s. 6d.

Plain Principles of Prose Composition. Crown 8vo, 1s. 6d.

MINTO.
The Literature of the Georgian Era. Edited, with a Biographical Introduction, by Professor KNIGHT, St Andrews. Post 8vo, 6s.

MOIR. Life of Mansie Wauch, Tailor in Dalkeith. By D. M. Moir. With CRUIKSHANK's Illustrations. Cheaper Edition. Crown 8vo, 2s. 6d. Another Edition, without Illustrations, fcap. 8vo, 1s. 6d.

MOLE. For the Sake of a Slandered Woman. By MARION Mole. Fcap. 8vo, 2s. 6d. net.

MOMERIE.
Defects of Modern Christianity, and other Sermons. By Rev. ALFRED WILLIAMS MOMERIE, M.A., D.Sc., LL.D. Fifth Edition. Crown 8vo, 5s.

The Basis of Religion. Being an Examination of Natural Religion. Third Edition. Crown 8vo, 2s. 6d.

The Origin of Evil, and other Sermons. Eighth Edition, Enlarged. Crown 8vo, 5s.

Personality. The Beginning and End of Metaphysics, and a Necessary Assumption in all Positive Philosophy. Fifth Edition, Revised. Crown 8vo, 3s.

Agnosticism. Fourth Edition, Revised. Crown 8vo, 5s.

Preaching and Hearing ; and other Sermons. Fourth Edition, Enlarged. Crown 8vo, 5s.

Belief in God. Third Edition. Crown 8vo, 3s.

Inspiration ; and other Sermons. Second Edition, Enlarged. Crown 8vo, 5s.

Church and Creed. Third Edition. Crown 8vo, 4s. 6d.

The Future of Religion, and other Essays. Second Edition. Crown 8vo, 3s. 6d.

The English Church and the Romish Schism. Second Edition. Crown 8vo, 2s. 6d.

MONCREIFF.
The Provost-Marshal. A Romance of the Middle Shires. By the Hon. FREDERICK MONCREIFF. Crown 8vo, 6s.

The X Jewel. A Romance of the Days of James VI. Crown 8vo, 6s.

MONTAGUE. Military Topography. Illustrated by Practical Examples of a Practical Subject. By Major-General W. E. MONTAGUE, C.B., P.S.C., late Garrison Instructor Intelligence Department, Author of 'Campaigning in South Africa.' With Forty-one Diagrams. Crown 8vo, 5s.

MONTALEMBERT. Memoir of Count de Montalembert. A Chapter of Recent French History. By Mrs OLIPHANT, Author of the 'Life of Edward Irving,' &c. 2 vols. crown 8vo, £1, 4s.

MORISON.
Doorside Ditties. By JEANIE MORISON. With a Frontispiece. Crown 8vo, 3s. 6d.

Æolus. A Romance in Lyrics. Crown 8vo, 3s.

There as Here. Crown 8vo, 3s.
. A limited impression on hand-made paper, bound in vellum, 7s. 6d.

Selections from Poems. Crown 8vo, 4s. 6d.

Sordello. An Outline Analysis of Mr Browning's Poem. Crown 8vo, 3s.

Of "Fifine at the Fair," "Christmas Eve and Easter Day," and other of Mr Browning's Poems. Crown 8vo, 3s.

The Purpose of the Ages. Crown 8vo, 9s.

Gordon : An Our-day Idyll. Crown 8vo, 3s.

Saint Isadora, and other Poems. Crown 8vo, 1s. 6d.

Snatches of Song. Paper, 1s. 6d. ; cloth, 3s.

MORISON.
Pontius Pilate. Paper, 1s. 6d. ; cloth, 3s.
Mill o' Forres. Crown 8vo, 1s.
Ane Booke of Ballades. Fcap. 4to, 1s.

MOZLEY. Essays from 'Blackwood.' By the late ANNE Mozley, Author of 'Essays on Social Subjects'; Editor of 'The Letters and Correspondence of Cardinal Newman,' 'Letters of the Rev. J. B. Mozley,' &c. With a Memoir by her Sister, FANNY MOZLEY. Post 8vo, 7s. 6d.

MUNRO. The Lost Pibroch, and other Sheiling Stories. By NEIL MUNRO. Crown 8vo, 6s.

MUNRO. Rambles and Studies in Bosnia - Herzegovina and Dalmatia. With an Account of the Proceedings of the Congress of Archæologists and Anthropologists held at Sarajevo in 1894. By ROBERT MUNRO, M.A., M.D., F.R.S.E., Author of 'The Lake-Dwellings of Europe,' &c. With numerous Illustrations. Demy 8vo, 12s. 6d. net.

MUNRO. On Valuation of Property. By WILLIAM MUNRO, M.A., Her Majesty's Assessor of Railways and Canals for Scotland. Second Edition, Revised and Enlarged. 8vo, 3s. 6d.

MURDOCH. Manual of the Law of Insolvency and Bankruptcy: Comprehending a Summary of the Law of Insolvency, Notour Bankruptcy, Composition - Contracts, Trust - Deeds, Cessios, and Sequestrations; and the Winding-up of Joint-Stock Companies in Scotland; with Annotations on the various Insolvency and Bankruptcy Statutes; and with Forms of Procedure applicable to these Subjects. By JAMES MURDOCH, Member of the Faculty of Procurators in Glasgow. Fifth Edition, Revised and Enlarged. 8vo, 12s. net.

MY TRIVIAL LIFE AND MISFORTUNE: A Gossip with no Plot in Particular. By A PLAIN WOMAN. Cheap Edition. Crown 8vo, 3s. 6d.
By the SAME AUTHOR.
POOR NELLIE. Cheap Edition. Crown 8vo, 3s. 6d.

MY WEATHER - WISE COMPANION. Presented by B. T. Fcap. 8vo, 1s. net.

NAPIER. The Construction of the Wonderful Canon of Logarithms. By JOHN NAPIER of Merchiston. Translated, with Notes, and a Catalogue of Napier's Works, by WILLIAM RAE MACDONALD. Small 4to, 15s. *A few large-paper copies on Whatman paper,* 30s.

NEAVES. Songs and Verses, Social and Scientific. By An Old Contributor to 'Maga.' By the Hon. Lord NEAVES. Fifth Edition. Fcap. 8vo, 4s.

NICHOLSON.
A Manual of Zoology, for the Use of Students. With a General Introduction on the Principles of Zoology. By HENRY ALLEYNE NICHOLSON, M.D., D.Sc., F.L.S., F.G.S., Regius Professor of Natural History in the University of Aberdeen. Seventh Edition, Rewritten and Enlarged. Post 8vo, pp. 956, with 555 Engravings on Wood, 18s.

Text-Book of Zoology, for Junior Students. Fifth Edition, Rewritten and Enlarged. Crown 8vo, with 358 Engravings on Wood, 10s. 6d.

Introductory Text-Book of Zoology, for the Use of Junior Classes. Sixth Edition, Revised and Enlarged, with 166 Engravings, 3s.

Outlines of Natural History, for Beginners : being Descriptions of a Progressive Series of Zoological Types. Third Edition, with Engravings, 1s. 6d.

A Manual of Palæontology, for the Use of Students. With a General Introduction on the Principles of Palæontology. By Professor H. ALLEYNE NICHOLSON and RICHARD LYDEKKER, B.A. Third Edition, entirely Rewritten and greatly Enlarged. 2 vols. 8vo, £3, 3s.

The Ancient Life-History of the Earth. An Outline of the Principles and Leading Facts of Palæontological Science. Crown 8vo, with 276 Engravings, 10s. 6d.

NICHOLSON.

On the "Tabulate Corals" of the Palæozoic Period, with
Critical Descriptions of Illustrative Species. Illustrated with 15 Lithographed
Plates and numerous Engravings. Super-royal 8vo, 21s.

Synopsis of the Classification of the Animal Kingdom. 8vo,
with 106 Illustrations, 6s.

On the Structure and Affinities of the Genus Monticulipora
and its Sub-Genera, with Critical Descriptions of Illustrative Species. Illustrated
with numerous Engravings on Wood and Lithographed Plates. Super-royal
8vo, 18s.

NICHOLSON.

Thoth. A Romance. By Joseph Shield Nicholson, M.A.,
D.Sc., Professor of Commercial and Political Economy and Mercantile Law in
the University of Edinburgh. Third Edition. Crown 8vo, 4s. 6d.

A Dreamer of Dreams. A Modern Romance. Second Edition. Crown 8vo, 6s.

NICOLSON AND MURE. A Handbook to the Local Govern-
ment (Scotland) Act, 1889. With Introduction, Explanatory Notes, and Index.
By J. Badenach Nicolson, Advocate, Counsel to the Scotch Education
Department, and W. J. Mure, Advocate, Legal Secretary to the Lord Advocate
for Scotland. Ninth Reprint. 8vo, 5s.

OLIPHANT.

Masollam: A Problem of the Period. A Novel. By Laurence
Oliphant. 3 vols. post 8vo, 25s. 6d.

Scientific Religion; or, Higher Possibilities of Life and
Practice through the Operation of Natural Forces. Second Edition. 8vo, 16s.

Altiora Peto. Cheap Edition. Crown 8vo, boards, 2s. 6d.;
cloth, 3s. 6d. Illustrated Edition. Crown 8vo, cloth, 6s.

Piccadilly. With Illustrations by Richard Doyle. New Edition, 3s. 6d. Cheap Edition, boards, 2s. 6d.

Traits and Travesties; Social and Political. Post 8vo, 10s. 6d.

Episodes in a Life of Adventure; or, Moss from a Rolling
Stone. Cheaper Edition. Post 8vo, 3s. 6d.

Haifa: Life in Modern Palestine. Second Edition. 8vo, 7s. 6d.

The Land of Gilead. With Excursions in the Lebanon.
With Illustrations and Maps. Demy 8vo, 21s.

Memoir of the Life of Laurence Oliphant, and of Alice
Oliphant, his Wife. By Mrs M. O. W. Oliphant. Seventh Edition. 2 vols.
post 8vo, with Portraits. 21s.
Popular Edition. With a New Preface. Post 8vo, with Portraits. 7s. 6d.

OLIPHANT.

Who was Lost and is Found. By Mrs Oliphant. Second
Edition. Crown 8vo, 6s.

Miss Marjoribanks. New Edition. Crown 8vo, 3s. 6d.

The Perpetual Curate, and The Rector. New Edition. Crown
8vo, 3s. 6d.

Salem Chapel, and The Doctor's Family. New Edition.
Crown 8vo, 3s. 6d.

Katie Stewart, and other Stories. New Edition. Crown 8vo,
cloth, 3s. 6d.

Katie Stewart. Illustrated boards, 2s. 6d.

Valentine and his Brother. New Edition. Crown 8vo, 3s. 6d.

Sons and Daughters. Crown 8vo, 3s. 6d.

Two Stories of the Seen and the Unseen. The Open Door
—Old Lady Mary. Paper covers, 1s.

OLIPHANT. Notes of a Pilgrimage to Jerusalem and the Holy Land. By F. R. OLIPHANT. Crown 8vo, 3s. 6d.

OSWALD. By Fell and Fjord; or, Scenes and Studies in Iceland. By E. J. OSWALD. Post 8vo, with Illustrations. 7s. 6d.

PAGE.

Introductory Text-Book of Geology. By DAVID PAGE, LL.D., Professor of Geology in the Durham University of Physical Science, Newcastle. With Engravings and Glossarial Index. New Edition. Revised by Professor LAPWORTH of Mason Science College, Birmingham.   [*In preparation.*

Advanced Text-Book of Geology, Descriptive and Industrial. With Engravings, and Glossary of Scientific Terms. New Edition. Revised by Professor LAPWORTH.   [*In preparation.*

Introductory Text-Book of Physical Geography. With Sketch-Maps and Illustrations. Edited by Professor LAPWORTH, LL.D., F.G.S., &c., Mason Science College, Birmingham. Thirteenth Edition, Revised and Enlarged. 2s. 6d.

Advanced Text-Book of Physical Geography. Third Edition. Revised and Enlarged by Professor LAPWORTH. With Engravings. 5s.

PATON.

Spindrift. By Sir J. NOEL PATON. Fcap., cloth, 5s.

Poems by a Painter. Fcap., cloth, 5s.

PATON. Body and Soul. A Romance in Transcendental Pathology. By FREDERICK NOEL PATON. Third Edition. Crown 8vo, 1s.

PATRICK. The Apology of Origen in Reply to Celsus. A Chapter in the History of Apologetics. By the Rev. J. PATRICK, D.D. Post 8vo, 7s. 6d.

PAUL. History of the Royal Company of Archers, the Queen's Body-Guard for Scotland. By JAMES BALFOUR PAUL, Advocate of the Scottish Bar. Crown 4to, with Portraits and other Illustrations. £2, 2s.

PEILE. Lawn Tennis as a Game of Skill. By Lieut.-Col. S. C. F. PEILE, B.S.C. Revised Edition, with new Scoring Rules. Fcap. 8vo, cloth, 1s.

PETTIGREW. The Handy Book of Bees, and their Profitable Management. By A. PETTIGREW. Fifth Edition, Enlarged, with Engravings. Crown 8vo, 3s. 6d.

PFLEIDERER. Philosophy and Development of Religion. Being the Edinburgh Gifford Lectures for 1894. By OTTO PFLEIDERER, D.D. Professor of Theology at Berlin University. In 2 vols. post 8vo, 15s. net.

PHILOSOPHICAL CLASSICS FOR ENGLISH READERS. Edited by WILLIAM KNIGHT, LL.D., Professor of Moral Philosophy, University of St Andrews. In crown 8vo volumes, with Portraits, price 3s. 6d.

[*For List of Volumes, see page 2.*

POLLARD. A Study in Municipal Government: The Corporation of Berlin. By JAMES POLLARD, C.A., Chairman of the Edinburgh Public Health Committee, and Secretary of the Edinburgh Chamber of Commerce. Second Edition, Revised. Crown 8vo, 3s. 6d.

POLLOK. The Course of Time: A Poem. By ROBERT POLLOK, A.M. Cottage Edition, 32mo, 8d. The Same, cloth, gilt edges, 1s. 6d. Another Edition, with Illustrations by Birket Foster and others, fcap., cloth, 3s. 6d., or with edges gilt, 4s.

PORT ROYAL LOGIC. Translated from the French; with Introduction, Notes, and Appendix. By THOMAS SPENCER BAYNES, LL.D., Professor in the University of St Andrews. Tenth Edition, 12mo, 4s.

POTTS AND DARNELL.

Aditus Faciliores: An Easy Latin Construing Book, with Complete Vocabulary. By A. W. POTTS, M.A., LL.D., and the Rev. C. DARNELL, M.A., Head-Master of Cargilfield Preparatory School Edinburgh. Tenth Edition, fcap. 8vo, 3s. 6d.

POTTS AND **DARNELL.**

Aditus Faciliores Graeci. An Easy Greek Construing Book, with Complete Vocabulary. Fifth Edition, Revised. Fcap. 8vo, 3s.

POTTS. School Sermons. By the late ALEXANDER WM. POTTS, LL.D., First Head-Master of Fettes College. With a Memoir and Portrait. Crown 8vo, 7s. 6d.

PRINGLE. The Live Stock of the Farm. By ROBERT O. PRINGLE. Third Edition. Revised and Edited by JAMES MACDONALD. Crown 8vo, 7s. 6d.

PRYDE. Pleasant Memories of a Busy Life. By DAVID PRYDE, M.A., LL.D., Author of 'Highways of Literature,' 'Great Men in European History,' 'Biographical Outlines of English Literature,' &c. With a Mezzotint Portrait. Post 8vo, 6s.

PUBLIC GENERAL STATUTES AFFECTING SCOTLAND from 1707 to 1847, with Chronological Table and Index. 3 vols. large 8vo, £3, 3s.

PUBLIC GENERAL STATUTES AFFECTING SCOTLAND, COLLECTION OF. Published Annually, with General Index.

RAE. The Syrian Church in India. By GEORGE MILNE RAE, M.A., D.D., Fellow of the University of Madras; late Professor in the Madras Christian College. With 6 full-page Illustrations. Post 8vo, 10s. 6d.

RAMSAY. Scotland and Scotsmen in the Eighteenth Century. Edited from the MSS. of JOHN RAMSAY, Esq. of Ochtertyre, by ALEXANDER ALLARDYCE, Author of 'Memoir of Admiral Lord Keith, K.B.,' &c. 2 vols. 8vo, 31s. 6d.

RANKIN.

A Handbook of the Church of Scotland. By JAMES RANKIN, D.D., Minister of Muthill; Author of 'Character Studies in the Old Testament,' &c. An entirely New and much Enlarged Edition. Crown 8vo, with 2 Maps, 7s. 6d.

The First Saints. Post 8vo, 7s. 6d.

The Creed in Scotland. An Exposition of the Apostles Creed. With Extracts from Archbishop Hamilton's Catechism of 1552, John Calvin's Catechism of 1556, and a Catena of Ancient Latin and other Hymns. Post 8vo, 7s. 6d.

The Worthy Communicant. A Guide to the Devout Observance of the Lord's Supper. Limp cloth, 1s. 3d.

The Young Churchman. Lessons on the Creed, the Commandments, the Means of Grace, and the Church. Limp cloth, 1s. 3d.

First Communion Lessons. 25th Edition. Paper Cover, 2d.

RANKINE. A Hero of the Dark Continent. Memoir of Rev. Wm. Affleck Scott, M.A., M.B., C.M., Church of Scotland Missionary at Blantyre, British Central Africa. By W. HENRY RANKINE, B.D., Minister at St Boswells. With a Portrait and other Illustrations. Crown 8vo, 5s.

RECORDS OF THE TERCENTENARY FESTIVAL OF THE UNIVERSITY OF EDINBURGH. Celebrated in April 1884. Published under the Sanction of the Senatus Academicus. Large 4to, £2, 12s. 6d.

ROBERTSON. The Early Religion of Israel. As set forth by Biblical Writers and Modern Critical Historians. Being the Baird Lecture for 1888-89. By JAMES ROBERTSON, D.D., Professor of Oriental Languages in the University of Glasgow. Fourth Edition. Crown 8vo, 10s. 6d.

ROBERTSON.

Orellana, and other Poems. By J. LOGIE ROBERTSON, M.A. Fcap. 8vo. Printed on hand-made paper. 6s.

A History of English Literature. For Secondary Schools. With an Introduction by Professor MASSON, Edinburgh University. Cr. 8vo, 3s.

ROBERTSON.
English Verse for Junior Classes. In Two Parts. Part I.—Chaucer to Coleridge. Part II.—Nineteenth Century Poets. Crown 8vo, each 1s. 6d. net.

ROBERTSON. Our Holiday among the Hills. By JAMES and JANET LOGIE ROBERTSON. Fcap. 8vo, 3s. 6d.

ROBERTSON. Essays and Sermons. By the late W. ROBERTSON, B.D., Minister of the Parish of Sprouston. With a Memoir and Portrait. Crown 8vo, 5s. 6d.

RODGER. Aberdeen Doctors at Home and Abroad. The Story of a Medical School. By ELLA HILL BURTON RODGER. Demy 8vo, 10s. 6d.

ROSCOE. Rambles with a Fishing-Rod. By E. S. ROSCOE. Crown 8vo, 4s. 6d.

ROSS AND SOMERVILLE. Beggars on Horseback: A Riding Tour in North Wales. By MARTIN ROSS and E. Œ. SOMERVILLE. With Illustrations by E. Œ. SOMERVILLE. Crown 8vo, 3s. 6d.

RUTLAND.
Notes of an Irish Tour in 1846. By the DUKE OF RUTLAND, G.C.B. (Lord JOHN MANNERS). New Edition. Crown 8vo, 2s. 6d.
Correspondence between the Right Honble. William Pitt and Charles Duke of Rutland, Lord-Lieutenant of Ireland, 1781-1787. With Introductory Note by JOHN DUKE OF RUTLAND. 8vo, 7s. 6d.

RUTLAND.
Gems of German Poetry. Translated by the DUCHESS OF RUTLAND (Lady JOHN MANNERS). [*New Edition in preparation.*
Impressions of Bad-Homburg. Comprising a Short Account of the Women's Associations of Germany under the Red Cross. Crown 8vo, 1s. 6d.
Some Personal Recollections of the Later Years of the Earl of Beaconsfield, K.G. Sixth Edition. 6d.
Employment of Women in the Public Service. 6d.
Some of the Advantages of Easily Accessible Reading and Recreation Rooms and Free Libraries. With Remarks on Starting and Maintaining them. Second Edition. Crown 8vo, 1s.
A Sequel to Rich Men's Dwellings, and other Occasional Papers. Crown 8vo, 2s. 6d.
Encouraging Experiences of Reading and Recreation Rooms, Aims of Guilds, Nottingham Social Guide, Existing Institutions, &c., &c. Crown 8vo, 1s.

SAINTSBURY. The Flourishing of Romance and the Rise of Allegory (12th and 13th Centuries). By GEORGE SAINTSBURY, M.A., Professor of Rhetoric and English Literature in Edinburgh University. Being the first volume issued of "PERIODS OF EUROPEAN LITERATURE." Edited by Professor SAINTSBURY. Crown 8vo, 5s. net.

SALMON. Songs of a Heart's Surrender, and other Verse. By ARTHUR L. SALMON. Fcap. 8vo, 2s.

SCHEFFEL. The Trumpeter. A Romance of the Rhine. By JOSEPH VICTOR VON SCHEFFEL. Translated from the Two Hundredth German Edition by JESSIE BECK and LOUISA LORIMER. With an Introduction by Sir THEODORE MARTIN, K.C.B. Long 8vo, 3s. 6d.

SCHILLER. Wallenstein. A Dramatic Poem. By FRIEDRICH VON SCHILLER. Translated by C. G. N. LOCKHART. Fcap. 8vo, 7s. 6d.

SCOTT. Tom Cringle's Log. By MICHAEL SCOTT. New Edition. With 19 Full-page Illustrations. Crown 8vo, 3s. 6d.

SCOUGAL. Prisons and their Inmates; or, Scenes from a Silent World. By FRANCIS SCOUGAL. Crown 8vo, boards, 2s.

SELKIRK. Poems. By J. B. SELKIRK, Author of 'Ethics and Æsthetics of Modern Poetry,' 'Bible Truths with Shakespearian Parallels,' &c. New and Enlarged Edition. Crown 8vo, printed on antique paper, 6s.

SELLAR'S Manual of the Acts relating to Education in Scotland. By J. EDWARD GRAHAM, B.A. Oxon., Advocate. Ninth Edition. Demy 8vo, 12s. 6d.

SETH.

Scottish Philosophy. A Comparison of the Scottish and German Answers to Hume. Balfour Philosophical Lectures, University of Edinburgh. By ANDREW SETH, LL.D., Professor of Logic and Metaphysics in Edinburgh University. Second Edition. Crown 8vo, 5s.

Hegelianism and Personality. Balfour Philosophical Lectures. Second Series. Second Edition. Crown 8vo, 5s.

SETH. A Study of Ethical Principles. By JAMES SETH, M.A., Professor of Philosophy in Cornell University, U.S.A. Second Edition, Revised. Post 8vo, 10s. 6d. net.

SHADWELL. The Life of Colin Campbell, Lord Clyde. Illustrated by Extracts from his Diary and Correspondence. By Lieutenant-General SHADWELL, C.B. With Portrait, Maps, and Plans. 2 vols. 8vo, 36s.

SHAND.

The Life of General Sir Edward Bruce Hamley, K.C.B., K.C.M.G. By ALEX. INNES SHAND, Author of 'Kilcarra,' 'Against Time,' &c. With two Photogravure Portraits and other Illustrations. Cheaper Edition, with a Statement by Mr Edward Hamley. 2 vols. demy 8vo, 10s. 6d.

Half a Century; or, Changes in Men and Manners. Second Edition. 8vo, 12s. 6d.

Letters from the West of Ireland. Reprinted from the 'Times.' Crown 8vo, 5s.

SHARPE. Letters from and to Charles Kirkpatrick Sharpe. Edited by ALEXANDER ALLARDYCE, Author of 'Memoir of Admiral Lord Keith, K.B.,' &c. With a Memoir by the Rev. W. K. R. BEDFORD. In 2 vols. 8vo. Illustrated with Etchings and other Engravings. £2, 12s. 6d.

SIM. Margaret Sim's Cookery. With an Introduction by L. B. WALFORD, Author of 'Mr Smith: A Part of his Life,' &c. Crown 8vo, 5s.

SIMPSON. The Wild Rabbit in a New Aspect; or, Rabbit-Warrens that Pay. A book for Landowners, Sportsmen, Land Agents, Farmers, Gamekeepers, and Allotment Holders. A Record of Recent Experiments conducted on the Estate of the Right Hon. the Earl of Wharncliffe at Wortley Hall. By J. SIMPSON. Second Edition, Enlarged. Small crown 8vo, 5s.

SKELTON.

The Table-Talk of Shirley. By JOHN SKELTON, Advocate, C.B., LL.D., Author of 'The Essays of Shirley.' With a Frontispiece. Sixth Edition, Revised and Enlarged. Post 8vo, 7s. 6d.

The Table-Talk of Shirley. Second Series. Summers and Winters at Balmawhapple. With Illustrations. Two Volumes. Second Edition. Post 8vo, 10s. net.

Maitland of Lethington; and the Scotland of Mary Stuart. A History. Limited Edition, with Portraits. Demy 8vo, 2 vols., 28s. net.

The Handbook of Public Health. A Complete Edition of the Public Health and other Sanitary Acts relating to Scotland. Annotated, and with the Rules, Instructions, and Decisions of the Board of Supervision brought up to date with relative forms. Second Edition. With Introduction, containing the Administration of the Public Health Act in Counties. 8vo, 8s. 6d.

The Local Government (Scotland) Act in Relation to Public Health. A Handy Guide for County and District Councillors, Medical Officers, Sanitary Inspectors, and Members of Parochial Boards. Second Edition. With a new Preface on appointment of Sanitary Officers. Crown 8vo, 2s.

SKRINE. Columba: A Drama. By JOHN HUNTLEY SKRINE, Warden of Glenalmond ; Author of 'A Memory of Edward Thring.' Fcap. 4to, 6s.

SMITH.

Thorndale ; or, The Conflict of Opinions. By WILLIAM SMITH, Author of 'A Discourse on Ethics,' &c. New Edition. Crown 8vo, 10s. 6d.

Gravenhurst ; or, Thoughts on Good and Evil. Second Edition. With Memoir and Portrait of the Author. Crown 8vo, 8s.

The Story of William and Lucy Smith. Edited by GEORGE MERRIAM. Large post 8vo, 12s. 6d.

SMITH. Memoir of the Families of M'Combie and Thoms, originally M'Intosh and M'Thomas. Compiled from History and Tradition. By WILLIAM M'COMBIE SMITH. With Illustrations. 8vo, 7s. 6d.

SMITH. Greek Testament Lessons for Colleges, Schools, and Private Students, consisting chiefly of the Sermon on the Mount and the Parables of our Lord. With Notes and Essays. By the Rev. J. HUNTER SMITH, M.A., King Edward's School, Birmingham. Crown 8vo, 6s.

SMITH. The Secretary for Scotland. Being a Statement of the Powers and Duties of the new Scottish Office. With a Short Historical Introduction, and numerous references to important Administrative Documents. By W. C. SMITH, LL.B., Advocate. 8vo, 6s.

"SON OF THE MARSHES, A."

From Spring to Fall ; or, When Life Stirs. By "A SON OF THE MARSHES." Cheap Uniform Edition. Crown 8vo, 3s. 6d.

Within an Hour of London Town : Among Wild Birds and their Haunts. Edited by J. A. OWEN. Cheap Uniform Edition. Crown 8vo, 3s. 6d.

With the Woodlanders and by the Tide. Cheap Uniform Edition. Crown 8vo, 3s. 6d.

On Surrey Hills. Cheap Uniform Edition. Crown 8vo, 3s. 6d.

Annals of a Fishing Village. Cheap Uniform Edition. Crown 8vo, 3s. 6d.

SORLEY. The Ethics of Naturalism. Being the Shaw Fellowship Lectures, 1884. By W. R. SORLEY, M.A., Fellow of Trinity College, Cambridge, Professor of Moral Philosophy in the University of Aberdeen. Crown 8vo, 6s.

SPEEDY. Sport in the Highlands and Lowlands of Scotland with Rod and Gun. By TOM SPEEDY. Second Edition, Revised and Enlarged. With Illustrations by Lieut.-General Hope Crealocke, C.B., C.M.G., and others. 8vo, 15s.

SPROTT. The Worship and Offices of the Church of Scotland. By GEORGE W. SPROTT, D.D., Minister of North Berwick. Crown 8vo, 6s.

STATISTICAL ACCOUNT OF SCOTLAND. Complete, with Index. 15 vols. 8vo, £16, 16s.

STEPHENS.

The Book of the Farm ; detailing the Labours of the Farmer, Farm-Steward, Ploughman, Shepherd, Hedger, Farm-Labourer, Field-Worker, and Cattle-man. Illustrated with numerous Portraits of Animals and Engravings of Implements, and Plans of Farm Buildings. Fourth Edition. Revised, and in great part Rewritten by JAMES MACDONALD, F.R.S.E., Secretary Highland and Agricultural Society of Scotland. Complete in Six Divisional Volumes, bound in cloth, each 10s. 6d., or handsomely bound, in 3 volumes, with leather back and gilt top, £3, 3s.

Catechism of Practical Agriculture. 22d Thousand. Revised by JAMES MACDONALD, F.R.S.E. With numerous Illustrations. Crown 8vo, 1s.

The Book of Farm Implements and Machines. By J. SLIGHT and R. SCOTT BURN, Engineers. Edited by HENRY STEPHENS. Large 8vo, £2, 2s.

STEVENSON. British Fungi. (Hymenomycetes.) By Rev.
JOHN STEVENSON, Author of 'Mycologia Scotica,' Hon. Sec. Cryptogamic Society
of Scotland. Vols. I. and II., post 8vo, with Illustrations, price 12s. 6d. net each.

STEWART. Advice to Purchasers of Horses. By JOHN
STEWART, V.S. New Edition. 2s. 6d.

STEWART. Boethius: An Essay. By HUGH FRASER STEWART,
M.A., Trinity College, Cambridge. Crown 8vo, 7s. 6d.

STODDART. Angling Songs. By THOMAS TOD STODDART.
New Edition, with a Memoir by ANNA M. STODDART. Crown 8vo, 7s. 6d.

STODDART.

John Stuart Blackie: A Biography. By ANNA M. STODDART.
With 3 Plates. Third Edition. 2 vols. demy 8vo, 21s.
POPULAR EDITION, with Portrait. Crown 8vo, 6s.

Sir Philip Sidney: Servant of God. Illustrated by MARGARET
L. HUGGINS. With a New Portrait of Sir Philip Sidney. Small 4to, with a
specially designed Cover. 5s.

STORMONTH.

Dictionary of the English Language, Pronouncing, Etymological, and Explanatory. By the Rev. JAMES STORMONTH. Revised by the
Rev. P. H. PHELP. Library Edition. New and Cheaper Edition, with Supplement. Imperial 8vo, handsomely bound in half morocco, 18s. net.

Etymological and Pronouncing Dictionary of the English
Language. Including a very Copious Selection of Scientific Terms. For use in
Schools and Colleges, and as a Book of General Reference. The Pronunciation
carefully revised by the Rev. P. H. PHELP, M.A. Cantab. Thirteenth Edition,
with Supplement. Crown 8vo, pp. 800. 7s. 6d.

The School Etymological Dictionary and Word-Book. New
Edition, Revised   [In preparation.

STORY.

Nero; A Historical Play. By W. W. STORY, Author of
'Roba di Roma.' Fcap. 8vo, 6s.

Vallombrosa. Post 8vo, 5s.

Poems. 2 vols., 7s. 6d.

Fiammetta. A Summer Idyl. Crown 8vo, 7s. 6d.

Conversations in a Studio. 2 vols. crown 8vo, 12s. 6d.

Excursions in Art and Letters. Crown 8vo, 7s. 6d.

A Poet's Portfolio: Later Readings. 18mo, 3s. 6d.

STRACHEY. Talk at a Country House. Fact and Fiction.
By Sir EDWARD STRACHEY, Bart. With a Portrait of the Author. Crown 8vo,
4s. 6d. net.

STURGIS. Little Comedies, Old and New. By JULIAN STURGIS.
Crown 8vo, 7s. 6d.

SUTHERLAND. Handbook of Hardy Herbaceous and Alpine
Flowers, for General Garden Decoration. Containing Descriptions of upwards
of 1000 Species of Ornamental Hardy Perennial and Alpine Plants; along with
Concise and Plain Instructions for their Propagation and Culture. By WILLIAM
SUTHERLAND, Landscape Gardener; formerly Manager of the Herbaceous Depart-
ment at Kew. Crown 8vo, 7s. 6d.

TAYLOR. The Story of my Life. By the late Colonel
MEADOWS TAYLOR, Author of 'The Confessions of a Thug,' &c., &c. Edited by
his Daughter. New and Cheaper Edition, being the Fourth. Crown 8vo, 6s.

THOMSON.

The Diversions of a Prime Minister. By Basil Thomson. With a Map, numerous Illustrations by J. W. Cawston and others, and Reproductions of Rare Plates from Early Voyages of Sixteenth and Seventeenth Centuries. Small demy 8vo, 15s.

South Sea Yarns. With 10 Full-page Illustrations. Cheaper Edition. Crown 8vo, 3s. 6d.

THOMSON.

Handy Book of the Flower-Garden: Being Practical Directions for the Propagation, Culture, and Arrangement of Plants in Flower-Gardens all the year round. With Engraved Plans. By DAVID THOMSON, Gardener to his Grace the Duke of Buccleuch, K.T., at Drumlanrig. Fourth and Cheaper Edition. Crown 8vo, 5s.

The Handy Book of Fruit-Culture under Glass: Being a series of Elaborate Practical Treatises on the Cultivation and Forcing of Pines, Vines, Peaches, Figs, Melons, Strawberries, and Cucumbers. With Engravings of Hothouses, &c. Second Edition, Revised and Enlarged. Crown 8vo, 7s. 6d.

THOMSON. A Practical Treatise on the Cultivation of the Grape Vine. By WILLIAM THOMSON, Tweed Vineyards. Tenth Edition. 8vo, 5s.

THOMSON. Cookery for the Sick and Convalescent. With Directions for the Preparation of Poultices, Fomentations, &c. By BARBARA THOMSON. Fcap. 8vo, 1s. 6d.

THORBURN. Asiatic Neighbours. By S. S. THORBURN, Bengal Civil Service, Author of 'Bannú; or, Our Afghan Frontier,' 'David Leslie: A Story of the Afghan Frontier,' 'Musalmans and Money-Lenders in the Panjab.' With Two Maps. Demy 8vo, 10s. 6d. net.

THORNTON. Opposites. A Series of Essays on the Unpopular Sides of Popular Questions. By LEWIS THORNTON. 8vo, 12s. 6d.

TRANSACTIONS OF THE HIGHLAND AND AGRICULTURAL SOCIETY OF SCOTLAND. Published annually, price 5s.

TRAVERS.

Mona Maclean, Medical Student. A Novel. By GRAHAM TRAVERS. Twelfth Edition. Crown 8vo, 6s.

Fellow Travellers. Third Edition. Crown 8vo, 6s.

TRYON. Life of Admiral Sir George Tryon. By Rear-Admiral C. C. PENROSE FITZGERALD. With Portrait and numerous Illustrations. In one vol. demy 8vo. *[In the press.*

TULLOCH.

Rational Theology and Christian Philosophy in England in the Seventeenth Century. By JOHN TULLOCH, D.D., Principal of St Mary's College in the University of St Andrews, and one of her Majesty's Chaplains in Ordinary in Scotland. Second Edition. 2 vols. 8vo, 16s.

Modern Theories in Philosophy and Religion. 8vo, 15s.

Luther, and other Leaders of the Reformation. Third Edition, Enlarged. Crown 8vo, 3s. 6d.

Memoir of Principal Tulloch, D.D., LL.D. By Mrs OLIPHANT, Author of 'Life of Edward Irving.' Third and Cheaper Edition. 8vo, with Portrait, 7s. 6d.

TWEEDIE. The Arabian Horse: His Country and People. By Major-General W. TWEEDIE, C.S.I., Bengal Staff Corps; for many years H.B.M.'s Consul-General, Baghdad, and Political Resident for the Government of India in Turkish Arabia. In one vol. royal 4to, with Seven Coloured Plates and other Illustrations, and a Map of the Country. Price £3, 3s. net.

TYLER. **The Whence and the Whither of Man.** A Brief History of his Origin and Development through Conformity to Environment. The Morse Lectures of 1895. By JOHN M. TYLER, Professor of Biology, Amherst College, U.S.A. Post 8vo, 6s. net.

VEITCH.

Memoir of John Veitch, LL.D., Professor of Logic and Rhetoric, University of Glasgow. By MARY R. L. BRYCE. With Portrait and 3 Photogravure Plates. Demy 8vo, 7s. 6d.

Border Essays. By JOHN VEITCH, LL.D., Professor of Logic and Rhetoric, University of Glasgow. Crown 8vo, 4s. 6d. net.

The History and Poetry of the Scottish Border : their Main Features and Relations. New and Enlarged Edition. 2 vols. demy 8vo, 16s.

Institutes of Logic. Post 8vo, 12s. 6d.

The Feeling for Nature in Scottish Poetry. From the Earliest Times to the Present Day. 2 vols. fcap. 8vo, in roxburghe binding, 15s.

Merlin and other Poems. Fcap. 8vo, 4s. 6d.

Knowing and Being. Essays in Philosophy. First Series. Crown 8vo, 5s.

Dualism and Monism ; and other Essays. Essays in Philosophy. Second Series. With an Introduction by R. M. Wenley. Crown 8vo, 4s. 6d. net.

VIRGIL. **The Æneid of Virgil.** Translated in English Blank Verse by G. K. RICKARDS, M.A., and Lord RAVENSWORTH. 2 vols. fcap. 8vo, 10s.

WACE. **Christianity and Agnosticism.** Reviews of some Recent Attacks on the Christian Faith. By HENRY WACE, D.D., Principal of King's College, London ; Preacher of Lincoln's Inn ; Chaplain to the Queen. Second Edition. Post 8vo, 10s. 6d. net.

WADDELL. **An Old Kirk Chronicle : Being a History of Auld-** hame, Tyninghame, and Whitekirk, in East Lothian. From Session Records, 1615 to 1850. By Rev. P. HATELY WADDELL, B.D., Minister of the United Parish. Small Paper Edition, 200 Copies. Price £1. Large Paper Edition, 50 Copies. Price £1, 10s.

WALDO. **The Ban of the Gubbe.** By CEDRIC DANE WALDO. Crown 8vo, 2s. 6d.

WALFORD. **Four Biographies from ' Blackwood ' : Jane Taylor,** Hannah More, Elizabeth Fry, Mary Somerville. By L. B. WALFORD. Crown 8vo, 5s.

WARREN'S (SAMUEL) WORKS :—

Diary of a Late Physician. Cloth, 2s. 6d. ; boards, 2s.

Ten Thousand A-Year. Cloth, 3s. 6d. ; boards, 2s. 6d.

Now and Then. The Lily and the Bee. Intellectual and Moral Development of the Present Age. 4s. 6d.

Essays : Critical, Imaginative, and Juridical. 5s.

WENLEY.

Socrates and Christ : A Study in the Philosophy of Religion. By R. M. WENLEY, M.A., D.Sc., D.Phil., Professor of Philosophy in the University of Michigan, U.S.A. Crown 8vo, 6s.

Aspects of Pessimism. Crown 8vo, 6s.

WHITE.

The Eighteen Christian Centuries. By the Rev. JAMES WHITE. Seventh Edition. Post 8vo, with Index, 6s.

History of France, from the Earliest Times. Sixth Thousand. Post 8vo, with Index, 6s.

WHITE.
Archæological Sketches in Scotland—Kintyre and Knapdale.
By Colonel T. P. WHITE, R.E., of the Ordnance Survey. With numerous Illustrations. 2 vols. folio, £4, 4s. Vol. 1., Kintyre, sold separately, £2, 2s.
The Ordnance Survey of the United Kingdom. A Popular Account. Crown 8vo, 5s.

WILLIAMSON. The Horticultural Handbook and Exhibitor's Guide. A Treatise on Cultivating, Exhibiting, and Judging Plants, Flowers, Fruits, and Vegetables. By W. WILLIAMSON, Gardener. Revised by MALCOLM DUNN, Gardener to his Grace the Duke of Buccleuch and Queensberry, Dalkeith Park. New and Cheaper Edition, enlarged. Crown 8vo, paper cover, 2s.; cloth, 2s. 6d.

WILLIAMSON. Poems of Nature and Life. By DAVID R. WILLIAMSON, Minister of Kirkmaiden. Fcap. 8vo, 3s.

WILLS. Behind an Eastern Veil. A Plain Tale of Events occurring in the Experience of a Lady who had a unique opportunity of observing the Inner Life of Ladies of the Upper Class in Persia. By C. J. WILLS, Author of 'In the Land of the Lion and Sun,' 'Persia as it is,' &c., &c. Cheaper Edition. Demy 8vo, 5s.

WILSON.
Works of Professor Wilson. Edited by his Son-in-Law, Professor FERRIER. 12 vols. crown 8vo, £2, 8s.
Christopher in his Sporting-Jacket. 2 vols., 8s.
Isle of Palms, City of the Plague, and other Poems. 4s.
Lights and Shadows of Scottish Life, and other Tales. 4s.
Essays, Critical and Imaginative. 4 vols., 16s.
The Noctes Ambrosianæ. 4 vols., 16s.
Homer and his Translators, and the Greek Drama. Crown 8vo, 4s.

WORSLEY.
Poems and Translations. By PHILIP STANHOPE WORSLEY, M.A. Edited by EDWARD WORSLEY. Second Edition, Enlarged. Fcap. 8vo, 6s.
Homer's Odyssey. Translated into English Verse in the Spenserian Stanza. By P. S. Worsley. New and Cheaper Edition. Post 8vo, 7s. 6d. net.
Homer's Iliad. Translated by P. S. Worsley and Prof. Conington. 2 vols. crown 8vo, 21s.

YATE. England and Russia Face to Face in Asia. A Record of Travel with the Afghan Boundary Commission. By Captain A. C. YATE, Bombay Staff Corps. 8vo, with Maps and Illustrations, 21s.

YATE. Northern Afghanistan; or, Letters from the Afghan Boundary Commission. By Major C. E. YATE, C.S.I., C.M.G., Bombay Staff Corps, F.R.G.S. 8vo, with Maps, 18s.

YULE. Fortification: For the use of Officers in the Army, and Readers of Military History. By Colonel YULE, Bengal Engineers. 8vo, with Numerous Illustrations, 10s.

www.ingramcontent.com/pod-product-compliance
Lightning Source LLC
Chambersburg PA
CBHW021719110726
47902CB00005B/1256